My Life As A Sperm

One Man's Quest to Save the World

My Life As A Sperm

One Man's Quest to Save the World

WILLIAM DARRAH WHITAKER

QAV Media

Las Vegas

This is a work of fiction. Names, characters, places and incidents, or characters interacting with real persons is either a product of the author's imagination or amazingly coincidental (but still not meant to be a factual representation). Repeat after me - none of this really happened.

My Life As A Sperm

Copyright © 2015 William Darrah Whitaker

All rights reserved.

Editor: Cate Hogan
Cover Graphic: Thorsten Schmitt
Cover Design: Pradeep (FiverrCreator)

Contact Info:
www.wdarrahwhitaker.com   darrah@wdarrahwhitaker.com
www.buddyprice-agent.com   buddy@buddyprice-agent.com

ISBN: 978-0-986-26810-6
Library of Congress Catalog#: 2015931958

PRINTED IN THE UNITED STATES OF AMERICA

FOR

Cassie and Troy

Chapter One

"My name is Buddy Price, and I died twice yesterday."

The nurse didn't react; instead, she focused on switching my IV bag.

"How's that for a first line? Gotta hook 'em or you're toast."

She tossed the old bag into a nearby trash can. "Mmm hmmm."

I couldn't wait until Stacey showed. At least, she'd pay attention.

"The first time I died, I was gone for over two minutes."

The nurse hung my new IV, wiped her hands on her uniform and peered down at me over her granny glasses. "You need to take it easy, Mr. Price. You're just lucky to be alive."

"I told you I saw God."

"Yes, you did." She patted my shoulder. "Now get some rest."

I tried again. "He sent me back because I have a job to do."

"That's what you keep saying." Her rubber-soled clogs made an annoying squeak with each step toward the door. "I'll check back in a little while."

"Not the least bit curious?"

Apparently, she wasn't. She left me to ponder my continued existence in this antiseptic-white hospital room, devoid of all sensory stimulation except for a bedside table, two bare wood chairs and a TV tucked in the corner near the ceiling. I switched it on with the remote, tried a few channels, looking for something entertaining and finally gave up. You'd think with the prices they charged, you'd get more than basic cable.

Fortunately, a few minutes later, Stacey arrived.

"Oh my god, you look awful."

That was the first thing out of her mouth, not that it wasn't true. I'm sure I looked like shit. Who doesn't after getting rammed by a Tahoe going fifty?

"I got dressed up just for you." I shifted my leg, trying to reduce its dull throb.

"Come on. You're not dressed up at all."

Stacey's a loyal assistant and has been with me the past five years, but she's not necessarily the sharpest tool in the shed. Yeah, cliché, but when it fits, it fits. Anyway, she tolerates me which says a lot for her patience. I gotta like that about her.

"Ready?" I said.

She hung her oversized handbag on the back of one of the chairs. "Are you sure you're feeling okay for this?"

"I'm breathing, aren't I?"

"Mr. Zimmerman told me to let you rest," she said, pulling out her notepad and pen. "So you can't tell anyone."

I winked. "It'll be our little secret."

She maneuvered the chair closer and sat. "Okay. Ready."

"My name is Buddy Price, and I died twice yesterday. The first time I died, it was for over two min—"

"Hold on." She scribbled on her notepad. "I need another pen."

"Yeah, go ahead." I shifted my leg again. "You know, Stace, thirteen years I've worked in the Industry and, in that time, I've gotten a bit of a reputation."

My leg hadn't been broken in the accident, but I received a helluva charley horse. Walking, well, limping around earlier this morning had helped, so I pulled myself out of bed to try again while she fished inside her purse.

She looked up from her search. "Are you sure you're okay doing that?"

"Yeah, I'm fine," I said, dragging the IV stand with me toward the window. "It's funny what you think about when you're lying in the back of an ambulance." I steadied myself with my free hand on the window sill and turned. "Like the fact that no one gives a shit."

"No." She popped in a stick of gum. "That's not true. A lot of people care."

"See any flowers in the room?"

"It's early. No one knows what happened."

"Sure they do." I pointed toward *The Enquirer* sitting on the edge of my bed. "But we can talk about that later. Let's get back on track."

"I'm ready." She presented a new pen and blew a nice, pink bubble in celebration.

"I got T-boned in the intersection of Robertson and Santa Monica. I think somebody–"

"I already know what happened. You told me this morning when you called."

"Come on, Stace. This is for posterity."

"Never heard of him."

I held my tongue and reminded myself she was brilliant when it came to picking winner scripts. "Just write it down. I'll introduce you two later."

"Okay. Go on."

"I think someone famous was eating lunch at the Robertson Deli because the paparazzi swarmed. Some of them must have figured they were gonna get their very own Princess Di photo."

"I bet I know who those would be," she said with a quick smile.

"What's that supposed to mean?"

"Well, when you need them, you're nice, but, otherwise… I don't think Hollywood Bob likes you very much. Or Jim Dandy. Or Zoom Lindsay. Or Spiderman."

"Okay, I get it. I get it." I waved her off. "Let's get back to my story."

She nodded.

"So I remember lying half out of the car with all these guys shouting at me, 'Over here. Over here.' I'm glad I wasn't in one of those eco matchbox jobs or I'd have really been messed up."

"You want me to write down which car you were driving?"

"No, that's not important." I rubbed the left side of my head, my fingers running along a patch of unfamiliar smoothness where hair used to be. "Where was I?"

"They were taking your picture."

"Right." I sank into the other chair. "When I revived the first time, one asshole was standing right over the paramedic's shoulder snapping away.

He's the one who took that picture." The front page of the tabloid showed my eyes bugging out from the defibrillator. "I should get a commission."

She picked up *The Enquirer* to get a better look. "Well, at least, he got your good side."

"Stace, there's no good side when you're dead."

"Yeah, I guess so," she said, tossing the paper down.

"To tell you the truth, I was pretty upset when I died."

"How can you be upset if you're dead?"

I didn't feel like getting into it with her. "You know what, you're right."

She gave me a big, red-lipped smile.

"Let's say, I was *disappointed*." My leg signaled it was time to move again. I struggled to my feet and set the door as my next destination. "There was no white light for me, no tunnel with relatives cheering me to the finish line. I've read where people say they got all warm and fuzzy. Not me. All I got was darkness."

"That's not good."

"Tell me about it."

"Were you scared?"

"I wasn't there long enough." I reached the door and turned. "They brought me back. Hurt like a motherfucker, too."

"One time I stuck my fingernail file in an electrical socket and that hurt sooo much." She squinted as she seemed to relive the experience.

"Why in the world did you – never mind. Can I finish?"

She readied her pen. "I'm waiting."

"Geez, where was I? These drugs are doing a number on me."

"You were in a car accident."

"Great." I grimaced, but not because of the pain. "Thanks for that."

"No problem," she said, wiggling a little in her chair.

I remembered where I was as I limped back toward the window. "So, I'm driving along talking on my cell with Ethel Silvers. You know, that actress I'm trying to sign from…from…"

"*I was a Teenage Vampire.*"

"Yeah, we were talking about changing her name. No one's going to make it in this business with a name like Ethel."

"Ethel Merman."

"What?"

"Or Ethel Barrymore? Wasn't she somebody, too?"

I glanced over my shoulder. "Stacey!"

"Sorry." She waggled her hand at me and suppressed a smile. "Mind?"

I grappled with the back of my hospital gown. Failing to close the gap, I turned to face her. "You're not going to make it in this town with an old lady name, no matter how gorgeous you are. I was telling her that people don't see sexy with a name like Ethel, and that's when I got hit. You know who the other driver was?"

Stacey shook her head.

I raised my right hand. "Marty Schwartz."

"Marty? You're kidding."

"Small world, isn't it?"

Marty was a guy at ICA who I had butted heads with over some projects. A world-class dick.

"He went through his windshield and landed in the crosswalk right in front of Keanu Reeves. He handed Keanu his card and then died. I have it from a very reliable source he was coked out of his mind." The throbbing in my leg moved up to my head so I sidestepped toward the bed.

"How would you know he did all that? Well, okay, maybe you already knew about the coke, but how would you know what he did on the crosswalk?"

"You'll understand as soon as I get there."

She tapped her pen against her notepad. "I don't know about that."

I climbed back into bed. "I'm lost again."

"Keanu Reeves."

"Let's pick it up at the hospital. Okay, the next thing I know I'm in the ER getting patched up. The doctor tells me my left leg might be broken, some ribs were probably cracked and I had a little swelling on the brain which they would have to drill…" I pointed at my newly acquired bald patch, "…to relieve the pressure. While he's talking, I look over at this nurse who's there and I'm thinking, yeah, Doc, I'm lucky to be alive. I wouldn't want to miss out on a sight like that. You should have seen the casabas on her."

"I hope you don't get mad, but I'm dying for a cigarette. Are we going to take a break soon?"

"Hang on. I'm just getting to the good stuff."

"Because you're just being gross now."

"What can I say?" I said. "I'm a sucker for a pretty face."

"What's new?"

"Okay, back to me. They wrapped my leg, which wasn't broken after all, pumped me with painkillers, and I go and die again. Everything just goes dark. I'm thinking, shit, this is ridiculous. But then I start feeling this intense pressure, and I'm shot through this tunnel toward a white light. I'm feeling all warm and fuzzy so I'm okay with it. I don't see anybody waving me on like you're supposed to, but I'm thinking at least if I'm dead, I'm not going to be in the dark for the rest of my life."

"That's funny."

"What's funny?"

"You said for the rest of your life." She pointed her pen at me. "It's funny because you're dead."

"Okay, okay, figure of speech. Change that if it makes you happy. Anyway, I'm moving right along thinking I'm going to God, and that's a stretch for me. I'll be the first to admit I'm not the most religious guy. I don't think I've gone to church except when somebody died or got married. What's the difference, you know? But along the way, I feel like it's getting harder to move along. I know I need to get to the light, but there just isn't anything left in the tank."

"Well, you aren't in the best shape."

I couldn't resist a quick appraisal in the mirror across the room. "Yeah, I know. I know." I smoothed out my bed hair, what was left of it. "But that doesn't have anything to do with anything. Come on, Stace. Let me get this out."

"I'm just saying. You ought to take better care of yourself."

"I'm concentrating on this white light when I look over and see I'm not the only one there. A bunch of other guys are swimming along with me."

"You were swimming?"

"Yeah, swimming. And, listen to this, one of the guys next to me is none other than Marty Schwartz. He looks over and says, 'Sorry about hitting you, Buddy.' Can you believe the nerve of that guy? He just killed me and all I get is that."

"Yeah, well, what else could he say?"

"And, he goes on about how God's got this warped sense of humor because the one time he gets a chance to chat up Keanu Reeves, he ends up dead. See, that's how I know about Keanu."

"You could have read it somewhere."

"No, I'm telling you. This happened."

"Sure, Buddy."

"There's something else. I'm not in my body anymore."

"Well, that makes sense because you're dead."

"Yeah, but get this. I'm a sperm."

"A what?"

"A sperm. A bona fide, Grade-A sperm."

"A sperm?" Her frown confirmed she didn't believe a word.

"As God is my witness, and I can say that because God *was* my witness."

"This is all sounding crazy."

"I'm a sperm and I see that Marty and I and this other kid are the only ones left, and we're doing all that we can to get to that white light. That light, it turns out it's God, and he's holding this little egg in his hand. Well, it was big compared to me, but in God's hand, it was small. God's got some height."

"You were a sperm?" Stacey's frown only grew deeper.

"Go with it."

"Yeah, I'll go with it," she said, shaking her head and blowing another bubble.

"Anyway, he looks down at the three of us and says, 'Who of you are worthy of another chance?' Marty, of course, pipes up and says that he's the guy for the job. Just like Marty. How many clients has he tried to steal from us?"

"Lots."

"So Marty starts in with God, asking him about his robe, where he got it, that his sandals are looking very chic. He tells Him how he's repping some kid who did *Jesus Christ Superstar* in community theater and now he's making him millions. Like that means something."

"I didn't know sperm could talk."

"But I keep my mouth shut, because it's God and I'm still freaking out a little. Well, the guy to my right is this kid from Cleveland. Don't ask me how I know, but I just know."

"How *did* you know?"

"Are you listening to me? I said I knew."

"Okay, Buddy. You don't have to bite my head off."

"Yeah, sorry." I took a deep breath. "Try not to ask any more questions until I'm done, okay?" I waited for a nod and then I continued. "This kid's pretty depressed because he hadn't gotten a fair break. He died right before his prom and, apparently, his date was going to put out."

"Again, you just knew that."

I ignored her. "Marty finishes his spiel and God moves over to me. I'm thinking to myself, what angle can I play? And then it comes to me. I say, 'God, I know I've made a bunch of mistakes in my life. I know I don't treat people right. I'm selfish and vain and the seven deadly sins are sitting on the top shelf of my refrigerator at home. So, you know what, God, it's all up to you. Whatever decision you make, I'll understand.

"Then, I told Him, 'Personally, I think this kid here deserves a second chance. He's still a virgin.' And God smiled at me. Sure, I'm trying to pull one over on Him, hoping He might like me for being such a good guy, but, Stace, that smile. I've never seen anything like it. And then, He goes, 'I agree with you, Buddy.'

"Sure, I blew the flip, but, at that point, I didn't care. God's smile is spectacular. It makes you think crazy things."

"Yeah, like I said earlier, crazy," Stacey said as her pen hovered motionless over the page.

"You writing this down?"

"Sure." She blew another bubble.

"God rubs His hand on his chin and gets all serious and says, 'You may be just the man I'm looking for.' Of course, I'm thinking maybe He's recognized my talents and wants to put me in charge of something like Head Gatekeeper or Angel Wrangler. But He looks down at me and says, 'I'm going to send you back.' And then, boom, here I am."

"Unbelievable."

"But all true."

"Have you told anybody else this?"

"No, you're the first."

She lowered the notepad to her lap. "I'd keep it that way."

"But it happened."

"Why would He give you another chance?"

"Didn't I tell you?"

"No," she whispered. "Probably the drugs."

"He said He'd send me back under two conditions. I had to change my life. Be a better person. He told me not too many people get another chance, so don't blow it."

"It doesn't sound like much is changing there," Stacey replied. "Besides, I'm still a little hazy on exactly what happened."

"Let the writer worry about that."

"The writer?"

"Yeah, the writer." I pointed at her notepad. "Get your notes into a workable treatment and send it out. What about the guy who wrote *Bruce Almighty*? What's his name? He's with the agency, isn't he?" I rubbed my forehead trying to remember. "If not, somebody else. Let's flesh it out for a feature. At the very least, maybe, we get a TV movie. And remind me to get in touch with Keanu's agent. I think Keanu'd be perfect to play me. And we need a title. How about *Godproof*? Write that down. Gives a hint, but still leaves 'em wanting more."

"Are you sure you're okay?" Stacey said. "How's your head? Are you sure it's not...?" She hit me with a "you know what I mean" look.

Sure, I knew what she meant. It had crossed my mind, but I let it go.

"Never felt better," I said. "How many people can say they talked to God and got a thumbs up? How many?"

"Not many I bet."

"Life is going to be different now. You better believe it."

"Anything you say," she said as she shouldered her purse and stood.

"And remind me to find out if God has an agent," I said. "I think He's ripe for a comeback."

"Sure, I'll get right on that." Stacey stashed away her notepad. "But, how about you get some rest in the meantime. I'll call you later."

That was nice of her. At least, I knew someone cared.

As she headed for the door, she stopped and turned. "Wait, you never said what the second condition was?"

"I didn't tell you?"

"No, that's why I'm asking."

"You might want to sit down for this."

She let out her breath. "I gotta get back to the office, Buddy."

"Okay, here it is." I gave it a three second, dramatic pause and then repeated what I'd been trying to tell my nurse. "He wants me to save the world."

Chapter Two

It had been a couple of weeks since the accident. They pulled the drainage tube from my head after forty-eight hours and said my prognosis was good, but that I should take it easy for a month or so. After one week, I'd had enough of sitting around the house. You can only watch so much TV. I felt fine other than a little soreness from the ribs and a slight limp from the bruise on my thigh so I decided to head into the office.

Of the thirteen years I'd been an agent, I'd spent all of them at Zimmerman Talent. I couldn't complain. Not many get the kind of break I got at only twenty-four. It was a pretty cush job, too, with a nice expense account. Old Man Zimmerman gave me room to maneuver, to do my thing. And it also helped that I was good at my job.

But I was a man on a mission, and I couldn't waste any more time.

"Nice hair," Tommy Bahama said, plopping down into one of my chairs.

Of course, that was only a nickname. He was crowned as such because of his penchant for wearing nothing but Hawaiian shirts. His real name was Oliver Greenblatt so, for him, Tommy Bahama was most likely a blessing. He was my only friend at the agency.

"Still not used to it." I rubbed the semi-bald patch on the side of my head, now filled in with a few bristles. I'd cut the rest shorter to balance things out.

"Gives you a Bruce Willis touch. The chicks will dig it. How's the head?"

Oliver still said 'chicks' and 'dig it'. He wasn't married. I wasn't either, but at least I could say divorced.

"I'm good. Better each day."

"Good thing. The sharks were already circling from the smell of fresh blood."

That's one thing I didn't like about working at ZTA. No honor amongst thieves kind of thing. If one of the agents stumbled, it didn't take long for the others to try to add to their own client list.

"But you kept them at bay," I said.

"Yeah. Yeah." His attention was focused on my Enquirer headshot Stacey had conveniently left on my desk to greet me on my return. She told me I should frame it. "I still can't believe you got front page."

"Remember Madeline Abrams?"

"Mad Maddy?"

"Yeah, she works there now. This," I said, picking up the tabloid, "is payback."

"Teach you to date her daughter."

Madeline and I had a semi-relationship going on when I met someone else at an Industry event. It was a torrid, no last names, call anytime, no strings attached deal, perfect for what each of us wanted at the time. Three weeks later, when Maddy wanted me to meet her daughter over lunch, I discovered the awful and uncomfortable truth. Let's just say I could understand why a picture of me looking like a blowfish, fully inflated, would make the cover.

Tommy and I were sharing a chuckle over that catastrophe when I noticed the open office door and Stacey standing there.

"Oliver, Gloria's looking for you."

Tommy's grin faded as he turned to me. "You teach her to knock?"

"Next story we share'll be about Mad Gloria," I said, patting him on the back. Gloria was his assistant, and she hated his guts. Every day, she made sure he knew it. "Good luck."

I think mine liked me okay. Today.

As he passed by, Stacey edged toward him. "And for your information, I don't need to knock."

He gave her a wide berth as he exited the office, but not without a glance behind.

Before she could escape, I said. "Hey, Stace. Got a sec? I need you to send an email for me."

Disappearing for a moment, she returned with her trusty notepad. She sat and turned to an empty page. "If you hang around people like that, you'll never become a better person."

"Thanks, Mom."

"If you're serious about your promise to you know who." She jabbed a finger at the ceiling.

"Done with the sermon? Can we start?"

A frown hinted at her lips. "Yeah, I'm ready."

"God needs an agent. Do you remember me telling you that?"

"Yeah, but wasn't that the drugs talking? You were acting crazy at the time."

"Crazy like a fox," I said.

"I was thinking crazy like a lunatic. Saving the world and all? Have you told anyone else? If you tell Oliver, everyone'll eventually know."

"You're the only one so far."

A small smile showed. "I held off sending out those notes you wrote up while you were in the hospital," she said.

"That's fine. That's fine. There's something more important I need to do which is why–"

"Let's not repeat the premise." She readied her pen. "You were saying that God needs an agent."

"I don't literally mean God needs an agent. I mean he needs someone on the ground to fix things. An ambassador of sorts."

"Didn't he already do something like that?"

"That was a long time ago. Now is now. I'm telling you, religion could use a makeover. Like if someone claims they're the Son of God these days, they'd be crucified, right?"

"I don't think we do that anymore."

I checked to see if she was serious. She was. "Not *crucified* crucified. I mean crucified in the media."

She bit her lip and then perked up. "I remember reading in *People Magazine* about this guy in Miami who claimed he was the Son of God. They didn't write anything mean about him though."

"How did he come across?"

"Weird, I guess," she said. "I mean he's not really Jesus."

"Exactly! That's how God would seem if He ever reappeared."

"Well, it doesn't hurt to believe in something."

She wanted to draw me off topic. Last year, when I was thinking about repping this family from Utah, some kind of Mormon 'Father Knows Best' reality show, she wanted to become a Mormon. The year before, it was Avon. I didn't offer any help then, and it sounded like she wanted to revisit the issue.

No, she'd have to find solid ground on her own. I had more important things to deal with.

"Remember how I made a promise to God?" I said.

"My friend Jessica saw an angel once."

"Just listen. Last night, I couldn't sleep so I was channel-hopping when I stopped on one of those religious shows where this preacher–"

"She said it was an angel, but from the way she described it, I think it was a big bird or maybe a really fat pigeon."

"Let me cut to the chase. As I watched his show, I had an epiphany."

"What's an epiphany?"

"Think of it like a light bulb going off. All of a sudden, you understand."

"Oh, I guess I just had an epiphany, too."

"Right." *You gotta love her.* "...but you need to stop talking and listen." I waited to make sure we were in agreement; apparently we were, so I continued. "Something appeared on the screen on Channel 562. It was something God had told me to look for."

"Oh! Like a sign?" she said.

"Exactly."

"I hope I get a sign soon we're going to start." She held up her pen. "I've got scripts to read."

I took a deep breath. As much as I tried to keep her on topic, she had a knack for pulling me off as well. Maybe I should invest in a Dictaphone.

"Address this letter to the Right Reverend Oral Hedgins, care of the Breathe Life unto Life Church of the Apostle, Waxahachie, Texas."

Chapter Three

I flew into DFW the following Wednesday and picked up my rental car for the drive down to Waxahachie, a little town about thirty miles south of Dallas. I followed I-35 until I hit 287 and turned east. I didn't have exact directions. They didn't have any cars with GPS, and some rookie behind the desk couldn't find the maps, so I decided once I got close, I'd ask. Turned out, that wasn't necessary. After taking the Waxahachie Exit and driving a few miles, I had to lower my visor to ward off the sunlight reflecting from my intended destination, the Beloved Holy Temple of the Apostle.

An article I read about the Temple said the spires rose hundreds of feet into the air, all eight of them. The building itself was a reinforced concrete behemoth, wrapped with a mirror-like exterior that, from some accounts, on a sunny day, could quick-broil a misguided bird from three yards away. It stood in the middle of two hundred acres of prime governmental boondoggle where construction had begun on a giant Superconducting Super Collider. Five years ago, the Right Reverend Oral Hedgins had bought the hole and the surrounding real estate for pennies on the dollar and established the home for his church and a site for his magnificent Temple.

Following large, colorful signs on a narrow county road, I found the entrance to the complex, a group of low-lying buildings surrounded by a large chain-link fence. A lone guard approached as I pulled up to the gate. When I lowered my window, the outside heat invaded.

"Name," the guard said.

"Buddy. Buddy Price." Given his employer, I expected a much more cordial greeting, but Ernest, as his name tag indicated, was all business. "With Zimmerman Talent Agency."

He scanned a list attached to his clipboard. "Who are you here to see?"

"Reverend Hedgins."

"I'll need some identification."

I removed my license and handed it over. He examined it, then me, and after apparently struggling with the lessened resemblance (due to the hair thing), secured it to his clipboard.

"Stay here," he said.

He disappeared inside his guardhouse where he made a call. I understood the need for security. You never know what kooks are out there.

Soon enough, he returned and handed me my license as well as a visitor's badge. "Be sure to have this visible at all times."

Without even a parting nod, he raised the gate and allowed me in.

The grounds included a number of warehouses laid out like the back lot of Universal Studios. No doubt the original plan had them dedicated to serious scientific work, but from what I could see, that had changed. One warehouse's open doors revealed a more pedestrian function – storage for props. Inside, I caught sight of an over-sized Jesus proclaiming the Dallas Cowboys Number One.

After only one wrong turn, I reached the main building. Adjacent to it was the Heavenly Production Studios, as the large black lettering above the entrance proclaimed. Hedgins had quite the facilities there, state of the art stuff. At least, that's what I'd read.

Outside the perimeter of the fence, maybe a quarter of a mile away, the Beloved Holy Temple of the Apostle reached toward the heavens. I shielded my eyes from the glare, but could still make out a stretch of lawn in front that surrounded a large rectangular pool. Walt Disney would have been proud.

I parked close but still broke a sweat before getting inside. There, the Texas-sized heat gave way to a subdued cool, but the attractive blond receptionist kicked it up a few degrees again.

"Buddy Price to see Reverend Hedgins," I said.

"Did you have any trouble finding us?" she said, running a finger down a list of names.

"No, I saw the light."

"Yes, it's drawn many new members to our place of worship."

Maybe she caught the reference but chose to ignore my attempted humor. I tried a little more of the old Buddy Price charm. "It'd be great to have that window washing contract, huh?"

Her expression didn't change. "I'll notify Reverend Hedgins about your arrival. You can sit over there." She motioned toward a waiting area.

Take rejection without dejection, I thought as I walked away. I guess you could call it my philosophy of life. You pretty much have to have that kind of attitude in the business I'm in.

The people of the Beloved Temple had spared no expense in constructing their own little Eden right in this building. The ceiling ascended several stories above, with a glass dome revealing the bright blue sky; against one wall, a terraced landscape of lush greenery. A waterfall added a melodic refrain as it cascaded over rocks into a shallow pool. Unseen birds chirped. I might have converted then and there, but I caught sight of speakers hidden behind bushes. That killed the illusion for me, although, I have to admit, a masterful bit of manipulation.

After ten minutes, a side door opened and a stacked brunette entered the room. Her heels clicked on the white tile floor, the sound echoing across the expansive room.

"I'm Rebecca, Reverend Hedgins' assistant. If you'll follow me."

Her manner reminded me a lot of the receptionist's so I kept my charm in my pants.

A quick ride on a private elevator brought us to another reception area, this one less overwhelming – I heard no birds – but nonetheless still inspirational with paintings of religious figures gracing the walls and organ music playing lightly in the background.

Rebecca escorted me to washed oak double doors at the end of the room. "He's waiting for you inside."

Hedgins' office featured deep burgundy carpet with plain white walls, a cross-inspired border and topped off with a gilded ceiling. He was not at his desk which rested on an elevated platform, much like an altar. Behind, a picture window offered a view of the Beloved Temple in all its splendor.

Hedgins' desktop was bare except for a telephone and a laptop.

Behind his desk, there it was – the Box – the main reason for my journey to Waxahachie.

I approached slowly as if some hidden trap might spring and catch my advance. Small and compact, maybe four inches by six, the Box appeared to be constructed of lead with worn edges and a rounded top, its surface covered with small pits attesting to its age. The lid contained a sequence of raised numbers, each held in its own little square, ranging from zero to nine. A swirl deco border surrounded the numbers with a flower emanating from the top of the design, a bee hovering above. It was enclosed in a clear, Plexiglas-type container, bulletproof I guessed, set on top of a marble pedestal. A small, flashing red light blinked from a keypad.

A toilet flushed to my right and I took a step back as Reverend Hedgins exited from a hidden doorway in the wall. He wiped his hands with a small hand towel, which he tossed inside before the door closed and blended in.

I squinted against his dazzling grin.

"Mr. Price, I see you made it. Welcome. Welcome." He walked toward me, a slight hitch in his step.

He wore his signature white suit which contrasted with a dark tan, making him look a bit like a photographic negative. I guessed maybe late sixties, but his energy made him seem a man half his age. His voice was strong, as it was on his television show, *The Waiting for God Hour,* but in person, even more impressive. He had me by a few inches.

He took my hand in his and enveloped it with his other. They were still a little damp. "I hope you had no problems finding us."

As if the reflective power of a thousand suns searing your retinas wasn't enough.

"Like I told the receptionist, your church is hard to miss."

"Marketing, my son." He tapped the side of his head with his forefinger. "All in the marketing, but I suppose you know a thing or two about promotion, don't you?"

"I wouldn't be here if I didn't, Reverend."

"I'm always eager to hear from someone interested in spreading the word." He looked down at the box. "So you've been checking out our little miracle I see. Have a seat and let's talk."

Hedgins waited as I found a chair. He then turned his back to me, punched in a code which extinguished the red light. He flipped open the glass cover and retrieved the box. "Have you done your homework?"

"I have, but found mostly rumors about your exodus a few years ago." I paused, not sure if I should finish, but I did. It's why I was here. "And also about what you found."

He sat at his desk. "How about I give you the real story? Truth is always better than fiction."

I nodded although I bet Oliver Stone would likely disagree with that assessment.

Hedgins laid the Box on his desk. "A few years ago, I left the church in search of answers. I journeyed around the world, my travels taking me to places where I lived off the kindness of strangers. I kept hoping one day, somewhere I would find what I was looking for. When my spirit was at its lowest, God must have seen I was ready and sent me an angel. She ran a small, non-descript shop in London selling jewelry boxes. Everyone on the street passed by the shop, but God led me inside.

"She talked with me, and before I knew it, I was purging myself of my transgressions and telling her about my long, arduous search for the Truth. She laid her hand upon mine and told me she had a special curio. Inside it, I would find my answers."

He frowned and pushed at the numbered buttons on the box's lid.

"You haven't opened it." I said after giving him a good minute.

His tan deepened. "No, but the Lord wants us to follow the righteous path which sometimes requires patience." He stood and returned the Box to its position on the pedestal. "Lots of people in my business would like to get their hands on this. They recognize the power it holds within. Our donations went up three percent last quarter." He lowered the glass lid and reactivated the security system.

I wondered if God had told anyone else of His plans. He *had* told me. He said He wanted to end the world, more or less. Of course, I'm paraphrasing, but it was something like, "If you people don't get your shit together, the slate will be wiped clean." He told me to look for a sign. It would be a box and when I found it, I would know what to do. This box had to be that sign.

I'd seen it on late night television, on Hedgin's show. Sure, I still didn't know exactly what I needed to do, but I decided to wing it until that part of the divine message came through.

Hedgins returned to his desk and pulled his laptop over. "Do you tweet?" he said as he typed.

"No, I value my time too much."

"You should try it. It's wonderful."

I had tried it, following a few of my clients at first, but soon grew tired of comments like 'Just ate the best cheeseburger ever at…<insert name of burger joint>', which netted them a few hundred dollars each time. "I'll leave that to the celebrities," I said.

"I find it glorious. I can spread God's word one hundred forty characters at a time." He typed for a few more seconds, closed the laptop lid and focused on me. "Okay, enough of that, Mr. Price. Your turn. Dazzle me."

I planned on doing just that.

"Reverend, as I told you in my letter, the most important thing is to know what your audience's needs are. That's true whether it's creating a hit comedy or a sermon for next Sunday. If it's a comedy, they need to laugh. If it's a sermon, they need to find comfort and meaning in the words. But *we* need something in return, don't we? Let's be honest. We don't do this for free. I'm guessing you have a large overhead?"

He frowned. "So far, I'm not impressed."

"You and I know the way to be successful is to put people in the seats."

He chuckled a bit like a parent tolerating a naive child. "Success comes in many forms."

"But if not for your congregation here in Waxahachie, your message wouldn't be heard at all."

"You haven't done your homework very well after all. I do have a television show."

"I know. It's why I'm here." I rose from the chair. I do my best work on my feet. "Last week, I couldn't sleep. At three in the morning, I'm flipping through channels when I came across *The Waiting for God Hour*. You pulled me in immediately. And that's great, but, the problem was I just happened to find you. We need to make more people aware that you exist and then keep them. Yes, I did do my homework. Last month, your reach was down five percent. Ten percent from the prior year. Reverend, you're not headed in the right direction. You got lucky when I found you, but you can't build a following, the kind of following you need, based on luck alone."

"It's not luck, Mr. Price. It was God's will."

I pointed over his shoulder at the box. "Imagine how big a church you would need to build for all the people who would want to know its secret."

"The church is not limited by physical walls. We help thousands and thousands of people around the world."

"Right, then why not tens of thousands? Why not millions? The world is a messed up place, and we need to reach a lot of people." From Hedgins' expression, I could see that maybe I was getting somewhere.

"All fine and good, but what you propose costs money. Lots of it," he said.

"No, Reverend. All we have to do is reinvent you."

He crossed his arms. "Don't you mean fix me?"

"Not too long ago, you were considered the golden boy of gospel, but then you ran into a little problem."

"Where are you going with this?"

"According to you, the world should have ended. What was it, three years ago? January twenty-first? That didn't happen so much. You tried again, next going for May sixteenth, but again, no dice. You took a beating in the media. Remember that *Time* magazine cover story?"

"Bunch of cowards, waiting until afterward to judge me. What could they have done if I'd been right?"

"And then came the *60 Minutes* exposé on your church." In that interview, Hedgins maintained that God had changed his mind and would let him know.

"My enemies surround me."

"Exactly! Lesser men would have been defeated, but you survived. You rebuilt your following."

"He…" Hedgins glanced toward the ceiling, "gives me inspiration to persevere over all obstacles." He returned his gaze. "And with that in mind, unless you have a point to make."

"My promise to you is to boost your ratings, improve your show and make it the biggest and best out there."

"A gentleman came in last year saying the same thing. And here we are, still stuck in the ratings behind *Father Bob's Kneeling for Grace*." He punched the intercom. "Rebecca?"

"There's a reason you were given the box," I said.

"Tell me something I don't already know."

Rebecca answered. "Yes, Reverend Hedgins?"

"I'm going to use that box to fulfill your destiny," I said. "We promote the hell out of it and the secret it holds inside. Sure, we may need to spend a little, but, in the end, you get it back plus a lot more. Think of who you can help with that kind of money."

Hedgins' hand hovered over the phone.

"You know what I say. Go big or go home." One last chance and I gave him all I had. "When I open that box, your show will save the world."

He stared at me with his cool green eyes. "Never mind, Rebecca." Hedgins punched the intercom off, leaned back and crossed his arms. "So, Mr. Price, tell me more."

I did have one more important thing to say.

"Reverend," I said. "You aren't the only one who has talked to God."

Chapter Four

They put me in an extended-stay corporate apartment. In Waxahachie, that translated to a furnished studio with a Murphy bed, some Corelle dishes and a next door neighbor who liked to play his bass at two in the morning. I would've preferred the Marriott in Dallas and dealt with the thirty mile commute. That's child's play for an Angelino like me, but Oral insisted I get situated nearby in case he or anyone else needed me after hours while I retooled his show.

My idea of spotlighting the box meant big changes, and he needed his top personnel to be briefed. The first week, Oral called a meeting in his office to introduce me to the Advisory Board – Frances Manor, his CFO, James Shockley, VP of Operations, Bill Blanchard, VP of Production at Heavenly Studios and two satellite ministers who looked down on us from a pair of big screen TVs. I quickly learned that the advisory function of the Board was mostly limited to nodding their heads and periodically proclaiming 'Amen'. That was okay by me since I wasn't looking for much advice.

Oral introduced my idea to them but not in the way I expected.

"Everyone, I have glorious news," he proclaimed. "God has sent an angel who will show us the way."

I once dressed as the Pope for Jimmy Cameron's annual Halloween party. That's as close as I'd ever come to celestial status.

"I knew the day would come when God would provide us a way to extend his message to those who languish outside his embrace. If we held strong to our convictions, if we trusted our hearts, if we proved our faith, He would respond. And now, because of this..." Hedgins balled his fist and shook it like an old codger threatening those no-good kids to get off his lawn, "I've been handed a wonderful gift. Soon I will be able to reveal what is inside." He waved his hand toward the box.

In unison, the wall-mounted ministers said, "Praise God."

Oral nodded. "Yes, our prayers have been answered."

"Amen!"

His eyes prowled the room with growing enthusiasm. "As I have warned, the Earth will experience a terrible conflagration. Its surface will be cleansed of all heathen, pagans and unbelievers. It is my duty to warn everyone of this inevitable day, a day which is fast approaching."

Since our initial conversation, he'd been seemingly reassured by the fact that I'd also talked to God, and that my conversation with the Almighty had paralleled his own. Maybe, to Hedgins, it was confirmation that he wasn't crazy after all so he was going all in with me. Personally, I still reserved judgment – about both of us.

"To help in this holiest of missions, a man has come from a place far away," Hedgins said, now waving his hand in my direction.

I guess he means Hollywood.

"His name is Buddy Price, and I want everyone to welcome him with open arms because it is *he* who will guide us over the airwaves to spread the word of the End of Days. And, praise be, Mr. Price will also be my new co-host on *The Waiting for God Hour.*"

Frances Manor, a thin, straight-laced church lady type and the aforementioned CFO of Breathe Life unto Life, eyed me as I stood. She didn't seem as thrilled as the others.

The co-host thing was something I'd pitched Hedgins the first day of the redevelopment process. I suggested that maybe he needed someone who could act like a conductor, a layperson to whom newbies to the 'getting religion' thing could relate, and, more importantly, someone who he could use to deflect potential criticism. I promised him I'd take the heat if things went sideways. Maybe he liked that the most.

For my part, I wanted an opportunity to point things in the right direction. If, and hopefully when, I figured out how to open that box, this show would be a springboard to fulfilling my promise to God, and I needed to be front and center when that happened.

I introduced myself to the Board, gave them a little of my bio, mentioned that I looked forward to an open, working relationship with each at the table and stressed my confidence that I could expand the reach of Reverend Hedgins' show.

After all that, I hit them with my big finish. "The four words I live by," I said, "are Plan, Produce, Promote..." I noticed that Oral paid no attention to any of this, his fingers flying over the screen of an iPhone. "...and Promise. I promise to plan carefully, produce a show you'll be proud of, and promote it until millions are watching." I used this four word mantra to close a deal for a commercial with Pillsbury (except today I swapped out their name with Promise) and thought it fit here as well. "Eventually, everyone will know of the Reverend's message," I said, thanked everyone and sat.

The truth was Oral had caught me off guard. I hadn't expected his pronouncement to the Board that the box would be opened. That's not something we'd agreed to. I'd hoped to hold that off for a few more weeks, or months, as the case may be. True, I had intimated I could accomplish something along those lines, but had he not heard of hyperbole? You know, like he's as big as a house or her brain's the size of a pea. Or, like in my case, I can open your box. But Oral took me at my word, and, as far as these five were concerned, we were locked in for a grand opening for that box.

So maybe five people I could manage.

I cleared my throat to cue him.

Oral glanced up as he pocketed his phone. "I have tweeted the glorious news to our brethren." He hit me with a blazing smile. "The celebration will soon begin."

Okay, more than five, now. I'd been outed.

*** *** ***

As Executive Producer of *WGH*, I concentrated on implementing the new changes in the format. Rehearsals and production meetings filled each day, hardly a moment when I wasn't doing something. We had two weeks before the box would have its premier and the buzz was building. And not just in Central Texas. Word had definitely gotten out. ABC, CBS, NBC, FOX, CNN, you name a few letters and they were banging on our door, wanting to know what we were up to with the Jeremiah Box.

Yeah, the name was one of our major changes. Oral came up with that.

"Jeremiah was a prophet," he had said, "fated always to tell the truth but never to be believed."

Everyone said Amen, and so with that special blessing, the box had a new appellation.

I didn't mind. It was catchy, something the media could latch onto. Something they could use to spread the word. Unfortunately for me, the more attention the box received, the more pressure I got from home.

My cell rang on my drive over to the Temple. It was Stacey.

"Talk to me," I said.

"Your ice-maker doesn't work."

I let her stay at my place in Santa Monica while I was gone. Since I anticipated being out of town for several months, I didn't want it to sit empty. My condo was a few blocks from the beach. Compared to Stacey's apartment in Koreatown, it would be like heaven. I should know. I'd been there.

"I told you that already. Didn't you read my note?"

"Yeah, you got a ton of notes here. Did you expect me to read them all?"

Ton of notes. See, that's hyperbole. "No, I wrote them to–"

"And, my God, your upstairs neighbor like wears cement boots."

Stacey might not know what an epiphany is, but she sure knew her way around hyperbole. "She's big. I think it's a thyroid thing. You oughta say hi."

"Maybe you could call."

"Not on great terms with her myself since my last party. Did you call just to complain?" I asked.

"No, it's about Mr. Z. He's grumbling."

"What's new?" Mr. Zimmerman had two settings, silent and grumble, but he was harmless if you stayed on his good side.

"Are you sure about this show of yours? I mean I never saw the connection. You and religion? Maybe you should come home."

"Life is full of surprises, Stace."

"Yeah, well, uh, don't be surprised if you have no job when you return."

"Don't worry about it."

"I'm serious. People are starting to talk. They say you've gone off the deep end. And those are your friends. You should hear what the others are saying."

"Look, put the Old Man off until next week. Make something up and I'll fly in for a few days to smooth things over. What d'ya say? Can you do that?"

"I don't know," she said. "I'm worried, you know, nobody's hiring right now."

"I'll take care of it and you. Everything's going to be fine." I gave her a chance to respond. Nothing. "Okay, I'll call you tomorrow." I ended the call as I arrived at the front gate.

Security Guard Ernest, adept in the art of recognition, let me through with a wave. I parked and trudged inside, trying to ignore the heat already at ninety-five degrees according to my car's dashboard thermometer.

I also tried to ignore Stacey's not so subtle warning to me. Things weren't going well at the office. I'd amassed a lot of unused vacation time over the years, but apparently, a lack of commissionable sales didn't sit well with the boss. I entered the building and waved at the receptionist who smiled and waved back. Sure, I wanted to act like things were under control, but, deep down, that little voice of reason which intruded sometimes in my life was screaming pretty damned loud. As I waited for the elevator to arrive, I stuffed a figurative sock in its mouth. I had a busy day today and didn't need any distractions.

Before hitting my office, I sidetracked to the kitchen on the second floor where I grabbed my morning cup of coffee. I had checked my email this morning and found one from CFO Manor indicating that she needed to talk when I arrived. From the kitchen, her office was only a short walk to the other end of the hall.

"Good morning, Mr. Price," her secretary said, bubbling over with genuine enthusiasm.

"Morning. Is she available?" I didn't remember the secretary's name or even if I had been introduced, but almost everyone at corporate seemed to know me. I was becoming quite the celebrity.

"Miss Manor is waiting for you. You can go right in."

I approached the meeting as I would ripping off a Band-Aid. I knew she didn't like me. The only question was how much. "Wanted to see me?" I forced a fake smile as I entered, hoping that it might help soften the unpleasantries.

She raised a bony finger while she dealt with a phone call. "Yes. We'll do that. Yes. I understand. Please let me know." She replaced the phone on its base.

I didn't think lips could trace a line as tight as what she showed me – almost as constricted as the hair strangling in the bun on top of her head.

"Close the door behind you," she said.

I did but remained near the entrance. A trio of Banker Boxes lined the console behind her desk.

"Moving?"

"In a manner of speaking." She stabbed at the intercom. "Sarah, hold all my calls, please."

Ah, Sarah, that's it.

"Yes, Miss Manor," Sarah's voice responded through the speaker.

Miss Manor clasped her hands together in front of her on the desktop. "Take a seat." She nodded at a nearby chair and waited until I sat. Then she did something unexpected. She smiled, or attempted something approximating one. "Have you talked with Oral today?"

"No, I came right over to see you. Why?"

"Just curious." She eyed the stapler, lifted the slide to check its load, and shut it. She spun around in her chair and placed it in the nearest box. Turning back, she continued. "Did you happen to attend services last night?"

"I've been pretty busy."

"You should have. It was a lovely sermon." She took a breath. "And how are things going with the changes to our show?"

She said this in a sing-song voice which I doubt she had ever used in her entire professional life.

"Fine," I said, but maybe I was asking as much as answering.

"And your place? I hear there's a delightful pool for you to use."

"There always seems to be plenty of sun," I replied, wondering when we'd hit the real topic of conversation.

"Well." She propped her hands as if she were about to pray.

"Well?"

"How do I begin?"

"What is it we're talking about?" I smiled, all *innocence and peppermint*, as my ex-wife liked to misquote that old Strawberry Alarm Clock song.

"The thing." Her eyes darted off and quickly returned.

"What thing?"

"The thing." She emphasized the two words, each distinct and distasteful. The pale pink in her cheeks rose to a bright fuchsia.

Oh, shit. Now I knew what this was all about.

Last week in the late afternoon, I was working with the stage manager and the assistant director on shot sheets when the video mixer blew. I'd hoped to have a run-through the next morning, but without the mixer, we weren't going to get much accomplished. I jumped on the phone to Hedgins' office to see what options we had. Rebecca must have already left because Oral answered. He sounded in good spirits and remained so after I told him a replacement would likely cost over ten thousand dollars.

"Come up to my office, I'll be here. I can write you a check," he said.

I didn't make it out of the studio for at least a couple more hours, struggling with the new *WGH* Choral Quartet who had arrived late for their practice. No one could remember their cues no matter how many times we went over it. I called it a night, told everyone to get some sleep and we'd start again tomorrow. On the way out to my car, I remembered about the mixer. If Oral were still around, I could grab the check and head into Dallas first thing and take care of it myself.

I ran up to his office, hoping he'd still be there. From the dimly lit anteroom, a light glowed underneath the oak doors, so I entered without a second thought.

It's common knowledge that in times of acute emotional stress, the brain can repress certain memories. With the trauma of an event coupled with the dump of hormones from the body, your neurons never sync and the memory never gets saved to the old hard drive.

In my case, none of that happened.

I remembered everything.

On top of Hedgins' glass desktop, skinny, white legs belonging to CFO Manor wishboned like a 'V' for victory (or vagina, I suppose) toward the ceiling while Reverend Hedgins, with pants around the ankles, pounded away at her lady bits. Hedgins didn't see me, his backside conveniently pointed in my direction, and, if their position had been reversed, he still wouldn't have noticed since his head was kicked up as if looking for an attaboy from on high. CFO Manor let loose with a couple of 'Thank you, Jesuses' before she caught sight of me standing in the office doorway.

I froze like a deer in the proverbial headlights except those high beams were bouncing up and down with each whammo provided by the eager preacher. Our eyes locked and her mouth worked like a landed fish, no doubt wanting to warn Hedgins of the intrusion, yet apparently unable to multitask in her current state of arousal. She closed her eyes, which was enough to break the spell for me. I backed out as fast as my size eleven Gucci loafers could take me.

We hadn't crossed paths or spoken since.

"Look, Frances. Can I call you Frances?" Given our shared experience, I didn't see why not.

"Miss Manor will still do," she answered, her grimace-smile briefly making a reappearance.

"You can relax, Miss Manor. I haven't told anyone."

"Well, I would hope not," she responded in full umbrage, her back rigid as a washboard.

"I know everyone has their little secrets." I nodded, smiling. "This will be ours."

"I don't know what you think you saw…" somehow the washboard got more rigid, "…but I suggest you think again."

There was no confusion about what I witnessed on the altar of Reverend Hedgins' desk that night. I've been to my fair share of strip joints and her leg spread was one of the more popular forms of expression on the pole. Hard to mistake that.

She leaned in. "I wanted to speak with you today so you could see my position."

I already have, my dear, and it was quite remarkable. Maybe a smirk escaped because her fuchsia cheeks spiked to a torrid crimson.

"I'm a good person, Mr. Price. I attend church every Sunday. I tithe my ten percent. I donate my time to help the poor and downtrodden. I will not allow my reputation to be tarnished."

"Frances, please. It's only us here. You can stop the act." Maybe I shouldn't have said it, but I couldn't help myself. She was sitting in the moral nose-bleed section, and I wanted to bring her a little closer to Mother Earth.

"Well, I never."

I smiled and winked in reply.

She stiffened again, her eyes wild and fiery, and then just as quickly, she wilted. Tears glistened, ready to roll. "I–I–I thought he liked me." A single drop crawled down her cheek. "But he was using me." She gulped and fanned her face with a tremulous hand. "Oh my God. Oh my God. I think I'm going to be sick." She turned to the side and bent over, hugging her arms around her waist.

I spotted a trash can by the side of the desk and stretched out my foot to nudge it a few inches closer. "You okay there?"

Part of me wanted to sprint for the door, but instead I drew closer, placing a hand on her shoulder.

She sprang up and wrapped her arms around my neck. "A few days ago, I caught him with Rebecca."

"There. There." I patted her on the back. What else could I do?

"Why did I allow myself to be drawn into his den of iniquity?" She pushed her face into the nape of my neck. "He was so handsome. You can't imagine how lonely I was. When he offered to meet me late in his office, I never imagined what would happen."

She proceeded to drown me in her confessional, the details of which I tried my best to ignore. After a few minutes, I sensed an opening as her rambling slowed.

"He's a bastard," I said. "You just need to put it all behind you."

She sniffed. "I'm not a very good person either."

"Come on." Pat. Pat. "I'm sure you have some wonderful qualities."

"No. No." She exposed some serious Alice Cooper eyes. "You don't understand. I've done a very bad thing."

A strand of hair escaped its bun prison and waved semi-seductively over one eye. I felt a brief pang of empathy for this woman.

Hopefully, it was only empathy.

"You're not a bad person. Look, you're both consenting adults, and everyone has needs. It's a natural thing to want to..." I didn't like where I was headed. "Give it a few weeks, you'll get over it. We all do."

"No, that's not what I'm talking about. I've done something else. Something very, very bad." Her voice sounded deeper now, more remorseful than embarrassed.

I searched her eyes. "What exactly have you done?"

The phone rang. She hesitated and broke her grip on my neck to answer.

"I thought I told you to hold all – okay, give me a second and put him through." She turned to me. "I think we're done here."

"That's it?" She had flipped it off like a light switch. "No, you need to tell me what's going on."

"You'll find out soon enough." The phone beeped with the incoming call. "Now, if you'll please. I need to take this."

Sure, time to go. I'd find out from Hedgins himself.

But a thought nagged at me as I made my way to the door. I turned for one last question. "Frances, you didn't kill him, did you?"

Chapter Five

Rebecca sat at her desk, but today, she kept her head bowed. Normally, she'd perk up at my arrival, not that I warranted any special attention; the cheerfulness factor was standard for all receptionists – sunshine and rainbows allotted in equal portions. A Bible lay open on her desk.

"Morning, Rebecca. Is he in?" I had learned my lesson about impromptu intrusions.

Bloodshot eyes hinted at a bad day. "He won't be coming in today. Did you get my message?"

"No, what message?"

"He wants to talk with you." She pointed at a slight man sitting in a chair across the room. He wore a brown three-piece suit and a John Waters pencil-thin mustache. His eyes were closed, his head tilted against the wall. His hands maintained a tight grip on a briefcase sitting on his lap.

I leaned toward Rebecca. "What's he want?" I whispered.

"He didn't say."

"Tell him I didn't make it in either."

She looked past me and cleared her throat. I straightened and turned.

The man stood a few feet away. "Warren Atterbury, of Winkler, Beechum and Dodge. I'm Reverend Hedgins' lawyer." A wisp of comb-over fell down his forehead, but a practiced swipe placed it back.

"You wanted to see me about something?" I asked.

"Can we go somewhere private?"

"This is so unfair." Rebecca sobbed and rushed from the room.

"Wow. That's the second one today," I said.

"Pardon?" Atterbury said.

"Nothing. I hope maybe you can clue me in on what's going on around here."

"Rebecca is a very loyal employee, and I believe she's emotional about the current status of Breathe Life unto Life. I assume you haven't heard?"

"I've heard something, but I doubt it's what you're talking about."

"Reverend Hedgins asked me to come. He would have met with you, but circumstances are such that it's impossible for him to be here. He sends his regrets and—"

"For God's sake, man, get to the point."

He winced. "Breathe Life unto Life is under investigation by the FBI."

"Really?" That caught me off guard as much as Mark Wahlberg's fake super wiener in *Boogie Nights*.

"Reverend Hedgins, as head of the church, has been charged with committing a variety of offenses."

"Like?"

"Maybe it's best if I showed you something." He paused, maybe checking to see if I offered any objections, which I didn't so he nodded and said, "This way, please."

He led me into an unused annex. Barren offices flanked this hallway, its steel gray rug still showing precisely laid vacuum patterns.

"This was to be the Exhibition Floor."

"For what?"

"You'll see." Atterbury stopped at a door and pushed it open. "After you."

I entered a large room with a rectangular conference table in the center. On its top, little metal easels with rubber-tipped legs held a long, white, tubular structure in place. Portions of the tube wall had been removed, exposing rooms stacked inside, complete with miniature dolls, little people frozen in such mundane activities as reading, eating, and watching TV.

"What do you see?" Atterbury said.

"A dollhouse in a big pipe?"

"Very funny." Atterbury caressed the side of the tube. "Partially correct though, but it's not just any dollhouse. This was built as a model of the Breathe Life unto Life Safe Haven. Think seventeen shafts sunk into the ground. Fifteen miles of tunnels. Lots of wasted taxpayer money. Does that ring a bell?"

"That would be the Super Collider project. Since when did it include timeshares?"

He stepped over to the table and set his briefcase down. "Reverend Hedgins intended on using that space. This diorama represents what would have been thousands of pods designed to provide a safe place for people to survive the End of Times."

"I couldn't help but notice you said 'would have been'."

"Sadly, none were ever built."

"Okay?" I was getting bored. "And?"

"Breathe Life unto Life sold over a thousand of these pods, sometimes up to fifty thousand dollars each." He shifted one of the child dolls closer to an adult one. "Of course, we offered family discounts."

"Of course."

"All the amenities would be provided – private rooms, computers, treadmills, a library, screening rooms, even a pool. Over the course of a few years, pod sales brought in over twenty million dollars, but instead of investing in their construction, Reverend Hedgins decided to focus instead on building his church. The Temple proved a very expensive proposition in its own right, and new things kept getting added, old things kept getting changed, making it bigger, grander, golder." He lifted out an old Grandpa doll and rolled it around in his hand. "The Temple was completed but late and over budget. Problem was there wasn't any money left to build the pods. When January twenty-first came around, they had no place to put anybody."

"Lucky for Hedgins he was wrong."

Atterbury returned Grandpa to the tube. "Reverend Hedgins tried his best to raise more money." He lifted an eyebrow. "I think that's why he gave us another prediction. Frances Manor attempted to hide the problem, but there wasn't enough time. A pod was built in Building Twenty-Nine and used to give tours. That seemed to be working until–"

"Oral decided to share his good 'word'?"

Atterbury nodded. "Miss Manor contacted the FBI to discuss the malfeasance transpiring within the organization. It seems she provided them with a lot of valuable information in return for leniency. Yesterday, Oral informed me of the charges and asked me to take care of a few issues. One of those has to do with you."

I shook my head. "I don't think it matters anymore. As you say down here in Texas, I hitched my wagon to the wrong horse."

"God is a very forgiving horse, Mr. Price."

"Not what I meant." Obviously, I'd misread the sign and picked the wrong box. I have to admit I was a little disappointed. I'd wasted my time and energy believing I was doing the right thing per God's request. But Oral wasn't the man he claimed to be. That was on him. Not seeing it earlier, that was my fault.

Still, I couldn't help but feel a little relief. Stacey had let me know that problems were brewing back home. At least now I could go back with a clear conscience. I'd made the effort and, hopefully, that would count for something.

Atterbury pulled the briefcase closer, flipped the latch and opened the lid. "Reverend Hedgins believes that you are the Chosen One."

"Yeah, I have that effect on people, but still doesn't make it true."

He lifted an object from the briefcase. "Reverend Hedgins wants you to have this."

And there it was, the Jeremiah Box, with its block of numbers on top and little flower decorations. I stared for a few seconds before I shook my head again. "I don't want it."

His eyes dilated and his voice raised an octave. "That's not an option."

"An option implies a choice."

"Reverend Hedgins is depending on you."

"Let him find someone else."

Atterbury took a step closer. "Reverend Hedgins…Oral needs your help. There are those that desperately want this. With him in prison, it could slip into the wrong hands."

"If it's so important, you keep it."

"I'm not worthy. And I've been instructed to give it to you."

"I think it's about time I headed home." I started for the door, but Atterbury stepped in my way, all buck twenty-five of him.

"Reverend Hedgins wants you to have it. Only you."

"Out of the way, Atterbury."

His words spilled out in a rush. "The Devil places obstacles in our way that makes us question our path. You cannot fail this test."

"You talking about me or you now?" I pushed past him into the hall.

He hurried out after me. "What if I told you that it's a matter of life and death?"

"Go ahead," I said. "Try me."

"The future of our world depends on you."

I ignored him and kept walking. He couldn't know.

"Mr. Price." His voice had lost its shrillness.

I stopped and turned.

"If you don't take this, I will be compelled to inform your boss of your recent delusions." He stayed a safe dozen feet away. "Your mental health might be called into question by those more skeptical in nature."

"So Oral told you all about it, huh?"

"I'm not one to question you, but others may not be so forgiving. Trips to Heaven. Negotiations with God. Warnings about the end of the world." He held the briefcase out to me along with a determined smile. "Details you wouldn't want some to know about."

I advanced toward him. "You think you're going to get your way by threatening me?" To his credit, he stood his ground.

"What I'm saying is why complicate your life? Take it for a few months while we straighten things out." He held the briefcase in between us. "What if it wasn't a dream?"

Don't ask how, but the way he asked dissolved my anger. From the sweat dripping off his forehead, I guessed he'd played his last card. Besides, I shouldn't be taking my frustrations out on him. He was right. Why complicate things? Okay, so I take the box with me. I hold onto it for a while. What's the worst that could happen? The world comes to an end? At least then I would know I wasn't crazy.

I let out a long breath. "Okay, I've got a safe at home."

"Perfect." Atterbury's smile made a brief return but quickly disappeared as he glanced at his watch. "I've spent more time here than expected. I have to accompany Reverend Hedgins. He's turning himself in." He shoved the briefcase into my hands and headed for the door.

I felt the weight of the box inside. "Hey, Atterbury. What about you?"

He stopped. "What about me?"

"Do *you* think I saw God?"

His smile returned. "Have faith, Mr. Price. Just have faith."

I suppressed a groan. "Is that all you have for me? Faith?"

"Well, it doesn't hurt to have a little luck as well," he said and ducked out.

If I had only known how much I would need both.

Chapter Six

My first day back at the office, I wanted to catch up with clients who hadn't received much attention lately. Stacey had done a good job covering. I owed her for that, but clients always need that personal, touchy-feely, agenty stuff. However, today wouldn't be so easy to dispense that Buddy loving; I had company catchup meetings scheduled, and to make matters worse, I started off late. My headlights on my new Benz weren't working, and I had to drop the car off on my way into work.

The shuttle service the dealer offered included waiting an hour while they hunted for a driver. One finally showed, unshaven and smelling like stale beer. On the way to drop me off, he regaled me with vivid details of his previous night at a club called Girth, which, according to him, catered to the more latitudinally-challenged of our species. He shared his exploits along with enough methane to kill off half the people in the metro area. I rode with my window cracked to steal a little oxygen and pretended to listen.

When we reached our destination, I guess he must have gotten his first real good look at me.

"Hey, aren't you that 'save the world' guy from Texas?" he said.

"Sorry," I said, opening the door. "I was born in San Diego."

"No, I saw you on TV. You did an interview on the news."

"Really, I'm not that guy." *Anymore.*

"Hey." He caught me as I was about to get out. "But you heard about it, right? That crazy box?"

"Something. A little. Yeah."

"Gives me hope, you know. Maybe there are answers after all. What do you think?"

"Like you said, it's a crazy box." I shut the door.

If I were into metaphors, I'd say that was appropriate. Even though I'd brought the Jeremiah Box back with me, I'd already shut it away in my safe and planned on leaving it and the madness behind.

I passed by the homeless guy who always sat in front of my building, dropped a dollar in his hat and headed in.

When I reached the fourth floor, it was like I'd never left. Everyone at Zimmerman Talent went about their duties without a second glance at me. A few polite nods maybe, but that was about it. Who knows, maybe they were simply keeping their distance in case something might rub off. Self-preservation instincts and superstition run strong in my business.

When I reached my office door, Stacey looked up from threading a brad through holes on a screenplay. "Jake Charmer called about lunch."

"I thought I said no client meetings today."

"You did. This is lunch."

She's a stickler for detail which can be both good and bad. I didn't feel like explaining the difference to her this morning. "Get him on the line."

Jake was a relatively new client. I signed him as a favor to another ZTA agent, Julie Rosenstern, who'd been placed on leave. She had issues and the decision was made a few months ago that she needed an extended vacation. During lunch, she had bolted from Spago screaming something about little Mexicans floating in her tortilla soup. She may have survived that kerfuffle, but she proceeded outside and offered the valet a blowjob if he brought around that shiny new Porsche instead of her '97 Camry. Again, she may have pulled through that too, but unfortunately, Julie was hitting the fifties harder than foreheads at an Enron stockholder meeting, and the valet perceived her offer as an assault on his dignity.

Tommy Bahama got three of her clients, Vincent Talley managed five. Me? I got one.

In most cases, I'd be upset about getting the shaft. Only one client? And what? Vincent's so good he gets five? But, in Julie's case, I'm not complaining. She's not a real firecracker. The best of her bunch? Well, that was Sean Blanc Douchelle whose last credit was playing Captain Stubing in *Love Boat on Ice.*

I got Jake Charmer.

He called before my little accident, worried about his switch to a new agent. He said he'd been with Julie since the beginning of his career, that she had always put him as a top priority and wondered what he could expect from me. I assured him he was in good hands, that he could expect the same personal treatment and promised to take him to lunch one day. Of course, that was a while back and now that long time coming lunch needed rescheduling. I hoped he wouldn't recognize the irony.

I sat at my desk and Stacey's voice came over the intercom. "Jake's on line two."

I punched him on. "Jakey, boy. How are ya'?"

"Yeah, man. What's up?" he answered in a sleepy, surfer-dude voice.

"I'm caught up here at the office so we'll need to do lunch another day."

"Bummer, you know."

"How about next week I give you a buzz?"

"I mean that's a real bummer, dude."

"I know. Feel the same way, but…" I shuffled a few papers on my desk to sound busy, "looks like next week's open. We can do it then."

"I'm in the Valley for a shoot. Can you meet me out here later this afternoon?"

"Another time. Like I said, things are crazy today."

"I have to talk to you, man. It's right off the 405. You can get here in less than thirty minutes."

"I don't know about that."

"What was it you said to me? I was in good hands?"

"Yeah, Jake. You are."

"If you asked me, that box thing you've been involved with seems more important."

"Don't worry. That's all in the past."

"Well, I need to talk to you about the future."

"Jake, I told you. The box was a mistake. It means nothing. There are no secrets to the future inside. From now on, it's just going to be you and me figuring that out."

"No, man. The future of my career. That's what I'm talking about."

"Okay, I get it. We can do that. What about Monday? You can survive the weekend, can't you?"

"I'm thinking about making a major change," he said.

I let the phone slide down my cheek and tapped it there a few times. Although he might not be anything special, I knew he was connected to a few other actors who had some juice and didn't have representation. You never know how things can pan out. Also, this news of a change did bum me out. Jake brought a nice, intangible benefit to visiting the set.

Did I mention that Jake's a porn star?

"Jake?" I heard nothing. "Jake, you still with me?"

He returned, coughing. "Yeah. Yeah." I imagined smoke venting from the handset. "You gonna help me out, man?"

"I'll see if I can take off a little early."

"Dude, you're a life saver. I won't forget this."

Sure you will. "Text me the address and I'll see you there."

Jake "The Snake". That's what he went by in the business, his nickname supposedly corresponding with a part of his body that's highly prized in the world of porn. Not that I'd seen direct evidence. It's not part of my client review process. But I did see his portfolio. Big hands. Big feet. You get the picture.

I made up an excuse to ditch my last meeting of the day, and I drove out to Granada Hills. To get there, I borrowed Stacey's car, a little Korean job that didn't have a working second gear. The address led me to a cul-de-sac hidden in the Knollwood Country Club Estates. At around five o'clock, I pulled in front of the house.

I parked next to a black Vette in the driveway. As soon as I got out, a pimple-faced teen rose from a foldup chair on the high side of the lawn.

"Hey, you can't park there," he yelled at me.

"Looks like I already did," I said and closed my door.

"You gotta move. Mr. Turpin doesn't want anyone parking next to his car."

"I'm sure you're upset that you can't watch them shoot *Hump Along Cassidy* inside, but don't take it out on me."

"Mr. Turpin told me to—"

"How about this? You let me worry about this Mr. Turpin."

"Yeah, whatever." He sneered back with a 'fuck you' face teenagers are so good at.

The front door was cracked and I let myself in. Evidence of filmmaking littered the living room – a couple of light banks, reflectors, and stands, and even a dolly parked next to the coffee table. A dolly in a porn flick?

I sidestepped a Matte Box and a stack of lighting gels. Most of my clients are in movies, so I make it a point to know the technical terms. I'm no stranger to the set. In fact, that's where I do my best work.

Like last year, I was hanging out on the Warner Brothers lot in Burbank where they were shooting some footage for a *Pulp Fiction* DVD re-release. I'm standing next to a catering table and guess who's there but Samuel L. Jackson himself. I know that he's made like a billion dollars acting over the years so I'm paying attention.

I leaned in close and said, "*Motherfucking Snakes on a Motherfucking Plane.* Gotta be the best motherfucking movie ever made."

He couldn't help but laugh. I'm smart that way. He must have used that word about a thousand times in that movie and he knows it and he knows that I know it. So we have this rapport going now. I chatted him up a little more, whipped out my card, and told him if he ever got tired of his motherfucking agent, he could always look me up. He never did call, but who knows, maybe one day. In this business, it's all about networking. Talent can take you places, but it's who you know that keeps you there.

I followed the hallway to the kitchen. Out through the sliding glass doors, I saw the set, though not much of one – two chaise lounge chairs positioned next to a pool. Off to one side, an umbrella extended out to provide a half-moon of shade. I guess you can't have butt cheeks changing from light pink to bright red from one scene to the next.

At the shallow end of the pool, three attractive women dangled their feet in the water. I deduced quickly enough that they must be the talent because of their distinct lack of clothing. Also, I couldn't help but notice that they were built for the business. Their breasts defied gravity, matching the best of a David Copperfield levitation act, and one had lips so full of collagen that she could suction nicely to a plate-glass window. I guess that's the price of admission to the Big Time.

A redhead, a blonde and a brunette. They all glanced over when I walked outside. One gave me a little wave.

Ah, still got it.

I started in their direction before I remembered my purpose for coming here. I spun around and steered toward a big white canopy at the other end of the pool where Jake and another guy lounged in deck chairs. Jake wore an open terry cloth robe with a loose fitting white bathing suit underneath.

"Hey, Jake," I said.

"Yeah?" His eyes fought to stay on the correct side of his head.

"Buddy Price." Getting no spark of recognition, I added, "Your new agent?"

"Oh, yeah. Yeah. Hey, man." He cast his hand off the side of his head in a half-ass salute as he leaned over and retrieved a 7-11 Big Gulp cup, the kind with the dome lid and big hole in the top.

"How's the shoot going?"

"It's the life, man." Jake nodded at his friend. "This is my boy, Wonder."

Wonder (or maybe it was Boy Wonder, as in my Boy Wonder – I couldn't tell) gave me a fast hand wave. He wore a little blue Speedo which fit patriotically with his bright red hair and pale white skin.

"Taking a break?" I asked.

"Recharging the old batteries." Jake stretched out his legs which caused the snake to escape captivity.

Wonder was quick to respond, pulling Jake's robe closed. He looked over his shoulder with a sly smile. "*You* have to wait for the video."

Yeah, I can't wait. "Since I'm out here, how about we catch dinner after you're finished? Did you eat?"

"In a manner of speaking." Jake held out a hand for a high-five from Wonder which didn't immediately come. "Don't leave me hanging, bro."

Wonder finally reciprocated. "Oh, I didn't get it at first," he said, adding a giggle for good measure.

"You wanted to talk, so let's talk." I sat in an adjacent chair.

"Talk?" Jake squinted at me, but it wasn't due to the sun. "About what?"

"Gotta do it today. Those were your words."

"I'm a little busy. We're making a movie if you haven't noticed."

"Jake," I said, shifting to the edge of the chair. "A few hours ago, you were begging me to come out here."

"Begged? That doesn't sound like me." He tilted his head back, the squint more earnest now. "Who'd you say you were?"

"Buddy Price. Your agent." I barked that last bit out more harshly than I wanted, but I caught myself and recomposed. "I'm here to talk about your future, remember?" I already had a hunch where that might lie.

"Yeah, like you control the future, man." He wiggled his fingers in my face. "Where's your crystal ball, secret agent man?"

"What? Are you even–"

Wonder grabbed my shoulder before I could snatch Jake's hand and form a finger pretzel. "Mr. Price? Can we..." He pulled me away to a safe distance. "If you haven't noticed, Jake's a little out of it. I think he took a little pilly or two before coming here." Wonder placed a hand on my arm and hit me with a knowing look. "*He* says it helps with all the pressure." He rolled his eyes. "Well, what I'm saying is this. Maybe you could talk to him another day when he's more, you know, with it."

It wasn't the first time I'd dealt with a client who needed pharmaceuticals to get by. I checked Jake whose lids slid up and down on glassy eyes. "Yeah, I get it. Wasted trip."

Wonder sighed. "You said it." But then he caught my real reference. "Oh, you meant your wasted trip. Right."

"Don't worry about it." I turned to Jake. "Listen, I left my crystal ball at the office. How about we talk later?"

"Your wish is my command." Jake crossed his arms and cast a spell with a quick head bob. "Ha, ha. Genie blink." In the process, he spilled his drink, a viscous, red liquid, down the front of his chest and onto his white bathing suit. "Oh no, that's going to leave a stain."

Immediately, Wonder dove in with a clean towel to blot Jake's lap. "Walter's not going to be happy about that. Jake? Jake?" Wonder patted Jake's face, but he was out cold.

"Who's Walter?" I said to Wonder.

"Try the director from Hell."

Across the way, two guys entered the pool area through a side gate.

"Speak of the devil," Wonder said through unmoving lips as he nodded in their direction.

One man, broad, heavyset with a thick beard paused to take a last drag on a cigarette before flicking it to the ground. The other, tall and thin with wispy brown hair, waited patiently next to him.

"The tall one is Brian. He runs the camera," Wonder said. "The fat turd is Walter Turpin. He's an Aussie. You know..." He switched to a bad Australian accent, "...g'day, mate." And flashed me a playful smile.

"Has he done anything I might know?"

"Well, let me think. Ummmm. He did *One Blew the Cuckoo's Nest*, and let's see, oh, there was *Lord of the Cock Rings*." He ticked each off on his fingers. "And we can't forget *Behind the Red and Green Door: Santa's Cumming to Town*. That was his best. Heard of any?"

"Sorry," I answered, although the second one did sound familiar, but that wasn't anyone's business.

Wonder grew silent as the two men reached our tent. I took a step forward, business cards already in hand. "Buddy Price with ZTA. I'm Jake's agent." I handed one to Turpin and another to the camera guy so he wouldn't feel left out.

Walter shook my hand and turned to his associate. "Brian, get the girls ready." His accent was as thick as Wonder's was bad. "We only have enough sun for a few more takes."

"Okay, Boss." Brian stuffed my card into his back pocket.

He probably cared as much as I did.

"Walter Turpin." The man adjusted his Ray-Bans, and his Hawaiian shirt flapped open exposing a dark rug blanketing his chest. "Since when does Jake rate an agent?"

I was about to explain how I was doing this as a favor for a friend, but he cut me off with a big grin.

"Nah, just being a knocker. I bet you wish you had more clients like The Snake here, heh?" He delivered an elbow to my ribs.

"Well–" I didn't get a chance to finish before his attention switched to Wonder.

"Is he ready?"

"Goddddd, not yet." Wonder hit him with an eye roll. "He came like only fifteen minutes ago."

"That's what I hired him for." Walter crossed his arms. "So get him up."

"I'm not a magician, you know," Wonder said.

"Yeah, but you promised me you were a pro. What d'ya call yourself? The snake charmer, right?"

I knew then Turpin wasn't talking about waking Jake.

"Don't worry. He'll be ready." Wonder's face turned the color of his hair.

"Well, I don't see the cobra rising. Maybe if you took off your budgie smuggler," Walter said pointing at Wonder's Speedo, "he could crack a fat."

"Fuck you, Walter."

"Fuck me? No, fuck you. You begged me to let you fluff." He

continued while mimicking a whiny voice. "Please, Walter, I need the money. Oh, please, I can do this. No problem." He switched back to Aussie. "And what did I say?"

Wonder lowered his head. "You said fluffing is for Sheilas."

"And you go on about how you know ohhhh so much about dongers. Why? Because you have one?" His tone turned accusatory. "You promised me that The Snake here would be receptive."

Jake came to in the middle of this exchange and said in a sleepy voice. "Oh yeah, man. I'm cool with that. No big deal with The Snake. I'm an equal opportunity fucker."

Walter grew more animated with Wonder. "Time is money. In another hour, we won't be able to shoot. Are you going to pay the girls if I have to bring them back tomorrow?"

"No," Wonder said, his brow cringing like Turpin's words literally hurt.

"And it's not like I'm made of money."

I thought of his Corvette parked outside, but, who knows, maybe it was a lease.

"I told you, he'll be ready," Wonder said.

"Well, then, fluff. Fluff. Fluff." Walter raised his hand. "We're shooting in five." He turned and headed toward the shallow end of the pool.

Wonder's lower lip trembled ever so slightly. "Can you give me a minute?"

I, for one, most definitely could so I joined Walter and the girls as they discussed blocking for the next shot.

"Now, Pia, when we start this shot, I want you behind Tammy. Not in front, behind." Walter said this slowly as if talking to a child, moving one of his hands behind the other.

Pia, a dark-haired beauty, nodded, but you could tell from the look on her face, she didn't get it.

"Goddamn. Teach me to take on a Wog." He looked at me. "You speak Greek?"

"Sorry." I'd never heard the term Wog, but guessed it couldn't be complimentary.

"I thought I'd go exotic, but didn't think about the language problem. Crikey, you'd think sex is sex in any language." Walter held up a hand with thumb and finger together making a circle and poked his other hand's forefinger inside over and over.

Pia smiled brightly.

"Now, mate, if I could only figure out the sign for backdoor."

"Listen, Walter. I appreciate you letting me see Jake while you're shooting, but I'm going to take off. I can tell he's a little preoccupied. You know, bad timing." I resisted my instinct to look in the direction of the canopy.

Walter dropped his sunglasses down his nose. "You're leaving now?"

"Yeah. I've got a thing I have to take care of at the office."

"You should stick around for this next shot. Jake's going to do all three at once."

I'd lost the thrill knowing the backstage preparations going on under that white canopy; sort of like going out for hamburgers after visiting a slaughterhouse.

"I think I'll wait until it comes out on video," I said, borrowing Wonder's admonition from earlier.

"Suit yourself," Walter replied. "I've got your card. How about we do lunch next week?"

"Sure, have your people call mine." I had no intention of seeing him again so what did I care?

"Wait, I'll give you my number, too," he said, but his cell went off diverting his attention. "Shit, hold on a second." He answered. "Turpin." He paused, listening, but kept his eyes locked on me so I couldn't go anywhere. "Tomorrow?" Another pause. "No, that won't work. Not one fucking bit." Another pause. "Well, then, you tell that bastard I'll see to it that he'll never work in this business again." He signed off the call. "Goddamn wanker dropped out on me. Now, I'm really screwed. The guy who was playing the pizza delivery boy isn't showing. Shooting tomorrow'll cost me another three grand." He pulled off his sunglasses. "God, everybody's taking a piss on me."

Come on, Walter, pizza delivery boy?

He looked at the canopy where Wonder was hard at work. I forgot and looked, too.

"Let's go. Let's go," Walter yelled. "At least get this scene finished before the sun goes down."

Wonder got up from his knees. "My God, I can't do my job with you yelling at me like that."

"Naw, I don't think that's it."

"Five more minutes," Wonder yelled back.

"That's a wrap everybody." Walter waved his hands wildly above his head. "And Brian, remind me to hold Wonder Boy's check."

Wonder took a few steps toward us. "Oh, my god. You still owe me for the last film, too."

"You should've thought of that before you fashioned yourself as some kind of Penis Pied Piper."

Wonder collapsed to the ground hiding his face in his hands. "Oh, God. Oh, God, no."

"That'll teach that cocksucker," Walter said with a smirk, then adjusted back to a pleasant smile. "Okay, where were we?"

I'll tell you where we weren't – finishing this movie. I've been known to save films before. Take *Inception*, for example. I was on set when they shot the pivotal last scene. I noticed that Jimmy, Leo and the screenwriter argued off to the side while everyone else on set hurried up and waited. I got a chance to edge in a little closer. Apparently, Jimmy had questions about the ending. That didn't surprise me. He's a bit of a perfectionist. I struggled to overhear their conversation, competing with the huge roar of thousands of dollars getting sucked down a dark production hole. When a lull came up in their conversation, I stepped in to offer my take on things.

I don't want to ruin it for anyone who hasn't seen the movie, but I said to them, "Cut on it still spinning." Honest to God's truth, Jimmy's face lit up like a spotlight.

How do you think I got invited to his Halloween Party?

"Did you ever think of letting Wonder play the part?" I put my hand on Walter's shoulder. "Wouldn't that solve your problem? Everyone's happy and you get to finish your movie."

"No way. Once I burn a bridge," he said, "I never rebuild it."

It seemed like a reasonable suggestion to me, but I forgot Walter was no James Cameron. Well, for me, the show must go on especially if it helps keep one of my clients gainfully employed.

"Well then, Walter, I have a proposition for you."

***

INT – KITCHEN – DAY

Well-kept, suburban home. In the kitchen, a woman talks on the phone.

> KITTY
> I don't know, Linda. My husband
> doesn't pay attention to me
> anymore. It's like I don't exist.

The doorbell interrupts their conversation.

INT – LIVING ROOM – DAY

Kitty opens the door to a pizza delivery boy (played by yours truly).

> PIZZA DELIVERY BOY
> Did you order a pizza?

> KITTY
> (licks her lips)
> Did you bring an extra large
> sausage?

> PIZZA DELIVERY BOY
> No, I'm sorry. I only have a
> medium.

> KITTY
> Then you're going to need to
> come with me.

EXT – POOL – DAY

They walk outside where two other girls sun themselves. Raul, the Cuban pool boy, (played by Jake "The Snake") skims the water. Kitty points to a chair.

> KITTY
> You sit there. Your punishment
> is that you have to watch while
> my two friends and I have fun
> with Raul.

> RAUL
> (flashes a smile)
> Hola!

***

And so it goes.

With porn, it's all about getting to the action.

This scene was shot in a few continuous takes, sort of like Hitchcock's *Rope* except this movie's plot revolved around a pizza, a ménage, and the clever use of a pool skimmer.

All I had to do was sit in the chair. Not as much fun as you might imagine. It's not that I wanted to participate, I had a reputation to protect (they provided me a hat and fake beard and Walter promised the pizza boy's credit would go to a Dirk Bendurdict), but you can only watch bumping uglies for so long

Over the course of the next hour, Walter shouted out words like disappointment, despair, longing, excitement, and Brian would swish pan the camera toward me. I would then "emote the sting of your exclusion", as Walter directed me, and Brian would catch my reaction. No doubt there must have been a creative gene somewhere in Walter's body that needed rubbing out.

Jake did himself proud. I was also happy to see that Wonder had successfully attended to business. That was the point after all. I wouldn't be sitting there for nothing. The carnal free-for-all ended when Walter called for Jake to knock off. I think that's Australian for "money shot".

Fade to black.

With everyone happy, I jumped in the Kia and steered my way back onto the 405 and civilization. It was time to get back to reality.

Or so I thought.

My cell phone rang as I was heading into the Pass. It was Stacey.

"There's this guy here says he needs to talk to you."

"Come on, Stace, him and another hundred wannabes. Take his name and put it in the circular file."

"He says his name is Oral Hedgins."

That's when the call dropped.

Chapter Seven

I had worked my way into the Sepulveda Pass, a giant slice cut from the Santa Monica Mountains, and I would have to wait until I made it through before I could get a signal and try her again.

All I knew was that whoever had contacted Stacey couldn't be the real Oral Hedgins. That one was securely incarcerated in a federal prison in Texas. No bail.

I dealt with enough crazies to know it had to be another guy looking for a way to get a little face time with me. Last I checked, the line reached around the block. Stacey knew the drill, but sometimes she'd let somebody slip through.

Almost clear of the pass, traffic slowed to a crawl. I could see red and blue strobes flashing ahead. One lane moved, slowed further by pathetic Looky-Loo's checking out the scene. I progressed nearly to the front of the line, two cars away, when they closed the road entirely to allow tow trucks to remove the damaged vehicles.

I checked my phone; still no bars.

Normally, I'd be upset but not this time.

I eyeballed a blonde in tight shorts, tank top and four inch heels standing near her white Jetta whose front end was wedged under the rear of a Bimbo Bread truck. I made a mental note to get in touch with David

Lynch. That would be a shot he could start a movie with.

All too soon, a CHP officer whisked her away, and I had to find some other form of entertainment while they cleared the accident.

I turned on talk radio, but the topic on the *Tom and Ben Show* wasn't as much fun.

Tom: So, Ben, are you ready for the end?

Ben: I think I'm going to take my chances.

Tom: Yeah, you're the type who doesn't even have an earthquake survival kit.

Ben: Like most everybody here in Southern California.

Tom: So Reverend Oral Hedgins is in jail, but it doesn't stop his mouthpiece lawyer hack from telling people that the end is still coming.

Ben: What a scumbag! Hedgins stole millions from people using this apocalypse scam as an excuse and he's still trying to steal more from the witless boobs who think he's telling the truth.

Tom: And this box of his? The Jeremiah Box? What's inside that's so important?

Ben: Hollywood agent, Buddy Price, who worked with him down in Texas is back in town. Have you heard what he's up to now?

Tom: Probably looking for some other scheme to leech onto.

Ben: Rumor has it he's got the box. Watch out. Hope he doesn't open it and let out all the demons.

Part of me kept listening in case there was something new on Hedgins, the other out of morbid curiosity. I switched off the radio when I realized I was a Looky-Loo to my own accident.

With the renewed silence, my mind wandered back to the other Hedgins at my office. "Oh, just kidding, Mr. Price," he would say. "I wanted to show you my new screenplay about the end of the world, you know, since that's your specialty." I wondered how many of those I'll have crossing my desk. If he was still around, I'd lay into him for sure.

I tapped my steering wheel as I watched the tow truck extract the Jetta. My stomach growled. Should I stop for takeout or wait until later?

My mind kept wandering back to Texas. What had Atterbury said? Have faith? He said good luck, too. That's what I needed more than anything. And maybe some inspiration to help me decide what to do with the box.

Or maybe I simply needed another sign.

My stomach growled again. Close enough.

I'd grab a Chubby Burger.

It took another twenty minutes before the lanes opened up. Descending into Westwood, I had bars, but when I tried Stacey, she didn't answer. I picked up the pace as I headed east on Sunset and, after a quick run through the drive-thru, I arrived a little before seven. The elevator doors slid open on the fourth floor, but I didn't get a chance to get to my office before a voice yelled out.

"Price."

No mistaking who that might be – my boss, Hal Zimmerman, head honcho at ZTA. He passed by, moving at a fast clip.

"Walk with me," he said over his shoulder.

Hal walked one hundred laps every morning. The agency had the entire floor so he would do his walking by circling the corridor adjacent to the outer bank of offices. He did the same thing again every evening. Usually, his assistant would accompany him in case notes needed taking or an important call came in. Tonight, he walked alone, decked out in his dark blue Nike sweat suit, the same one he wore every day. It didn't surprise me he was still here.

I matched his pace.

"You actually... eat that shit?" he said.

I'd brought my Chubby bag with me. "Bad habit."

His words came in short bursts. "Should be a habit... to eat right... that's a good one... to have... stays with you... keeps you alive." He pumped his arms up and down as if beating a punching bag attached to his chest.

"I don't like to cook," I said.

"Know how old I am?"

"Not exactly."

"Take a guess."

From my failed marriage, I learned always to guess low when it came to things like age or weight. "Sixty-two?"

"Not even close... Seventy-five... Could pass... for fifty-two... right?"

"You're in better shape than most here." Well, certainly better than me. We'd completed one circuit together, and I was already winded. "Leg's acting up, Hal." We approached my office. "I'm going to leave you to it. I've still got some work to tackle."

Hal stopped with me, checking his pulse watch. "You need to get a life,

Price. You're still young enough. Good looking guy. You can remarry. Maybe have some kids. You don't have any, right?"

"Not that I know of."

"Funny, Price. I can get Lois to set you up. Get you out of the office. Hell, it's Friday."

Everyone knew why Hal worked late. I certainly didn't want his wife touching my love life in case some of it rubbed off.

"I'm okay for now."

He fixed me with an icy stare. "Why'd you say that?"

"Say what?"

"For now. What's that supposed to mean?"

"I don't know," I said.

"It's your shit about the world ending, isn't it? Goddamn. Can't you let that go?"

"Hal, I was talking about dating."

"You're lucky I don't fire your ass like I did Rosenstern. You may be as nuts as she is."

"Don't worry. Interest'll fade soon enough."

"Think so? Did you see that article in the Times yesterday?"

"It's old news."

"Since that preacher friend of yours got locked up, it's new news," he said. "It's brought out every kook in the country who thinks they know how to open that box of yours."

"It's not my box, Hal."

"You need to do some damage control. All the publicity doesn't paint you in a good light. Explain yourself. Tell 'em you're sorry if you have to. Act like you care. Hollywood's a lonely whore," he said. "She'll float you a freebie if you act like you care."

"I'm not looking for a freebie from an old whore."

"Lonely. I said lonely." Hal pulled an energy bar from a fanny pack secured around his waist. "Don't kid yourself. We're all looking for one, lonely or otherwise." He ripped off the wrapper and took a bite. "You've gone soft, Price. Soft, I tell you." He chewed slowly, staring at me the whole time. "What do I say around here?"

That was easy. "Commit or quit," I said. You were indoctrinated with that maxim the moment you were hired at ZTA.

"I'll give you one more week to prove it – that you're fully committed."

"It isn't a problem."

"Show me. Don't tell me." He looked at Stacey's empty desk. "And about your assistant…" He snapped his fingers as he fought to remember her name.

"Stacey," I said.

"Right." He tore another bite off his energy bar. "Get rid of her. I don't like her. I know she was giving me the runaround while you were gone. Don't like it when my people give me the runaround. Not one bit."

"But she's–"

"Don't fail me, Price. Commit…" he swallowed and waited.

I reluctantly completed his sentence. "Or quit."

He punched a button on his watch and took off with a backward wave. "Maybe there's still hope for you yet."

I pushed into my office hoping to see Reverend Hedgins waiting patiently for me, but I knew that wasn't going to be happening. It wouldn't have made sense, but what did these days?

Commit or quit?

Of course, the office was empty.

At my desk, I spotted dozens of little notes. I think Stacey was getting back at me for mine.

I picked through a few to see if she'd left something new regarding our visitor. The first one – Don't forget to get your dry cleaning. Another – I sent myself flowers for Secretary's Day and you're welcome. Then the one I was looking for – I'm heading to Club One for Happy Hour. She neglected to tell me anything about Hedgins or rather the person claiming to be Hedgins. I knew I'd have to go there to find out more, plus I still had her keys. And, of course, there was the small matter of Zimmerman's directive.

I tossed the unopened Chubby bag into the trash.

I'd lost my appetite.

Chapter Eight

Club One was only a few blocks away on Franklin Avenue so I walked. It gave me time to consider my options. Who was I kidding? What options? Commit or quit. Those were the only options I had.

Commit or quit.

And I couldn't quit.

Being the hottest nightclub in Los Angeles this week, Club One already had a long line running down the sidewalk and around the corner – cute little party girls in their tight black dresses that barely covered their baby makers, and guys decked in skinny jeans and affliction shirts, intent on eventually unclothing the aforementioned makers of babies. They were all corralled behind a red velvet rope waiting for a nod of approval from the club doormen.

There was no way I was going to wait in line. I whipped out my phone. After the fifth ring, it seemed I was headed for voicemail, but Stacey answered. Loud noise spilled out.

"Hey, Buddy? Are you here?"

"I'm outside."

"Okay, see you soon." And she hung up.

Did she hang up on me? I hit redial. "Stacey, I'm not going in. I need–"

"Hurry. Lisa's here."

Ah, the lovely Lisa. She ran a sex toy business, think Tupperware parties except with products like nine inch sex aids called "The MANitoba". Not someone Mrs. Zimmerman would ever set me up with.

Focus, Buddy. You know what you have to do.

"Come outside. I need to talk to you," I said.

"What?"

"Come outside."

"I can't… hear… you…" Her voice faded away from the phone and the line went dead.

I tried her one more time, but she didn't answer.

I repocketed my cell and approached two muscle-bound bouncers manning the entrance. I read the name tag of one. "Hey, Ed. Buddy Price." I held out my card. "I need five minutes to talk to my secretary. She's inside. That's not a problem, is it?"

"Sorry." His voice sounded like he'd swallowed Hulk Hogan with a gravel chaser. "You'll have to wait in line like everyone else."

He didn't have the courtesy to even look.

"I don't think you understand." I poked out the twenty I had hidden behind my card, but he didn't catch the hint. Either that or it wasn't enough.

He swept a massive arm in front of me. "Step aside, little man."

A group of four girls queued up giggled at that remark. Not that the "little man" comment wasn't warranted. Ninety-nine point nine nine percent of the people in this world would be little compared to this guy.

Okay, maybe I needed to find a different way to filly with my new droog.

I stepped forward. "Hey, No Neck. That's no way to treat a customer."

"What was that?" He took one giant step forward, positioning himself so my face stared directly at his no-neck.

I reconsidered my choice of names. Maybe I should have gone with Ace or Dog or maybe Amigo in case Ed happened to be short for Eduardo. I dipped my shoulder to him while making the twenty more visible.

"Eddie, baby." We were two close friends sharing a secret. "How about I give you this? I go inside for a couple of minutes. And then I come out. You keep the Jackson and everyone's happy. That works for you, right?"

Eddie baby considered the offer for a moment and held out his hand.

There we go. Now we're talking. I could tell we'd be able to look on this later and have a good laugh. Remember the time when…

Grabbing my hand, he squeezed it hard, and proceeded to twirl me around like a ballerina doing a fast pirouette. After I'd lost a little urine, he snaked his other arm under my armpit and up behind my neck, locking me in tight. I had as much control as Mel Gibson at a routine traffic stop.

He dragged me away from the entrance to the amusement of all. At least, that's what I assumed that noise was. I couldn't tell because my face was crushed tight to Ed's chest. We reached an alley, and the lights of the street faded away as he dragged me into the abyss. At a dumpster, he released his hold and pushed me against it. My head boomed against the side.

Like I needed another head trauma.

He held me there with a single meaty hand on my chest. "So let's discuss your customer complaints."

I gave him my most sincere, apologetic look, because I was now most utterly sincere and apologetic. "I'm sorry. Really I am. Believe me, I completely misjudged the situation. It's been a long day and—"

"How about I teach you a little something about treating people with respect?" He drew back his fist.

I stepped back, and crouched, prepared to use my one year of Karate training (from which I had acquired a limited knowledge of self-defense along with a broken toe), but before the hammer came down, the dumpster shifted behind me.

The lid raised and a shadowy figure popped up. "Chipmunk chaddywack. Give a dog a bone?"

Ed cocked his head. "What the hell?"

The fist hovering in front of me slowly lowered as the man from the dumpster rolled over the side and landed on the ground.

"I asked you," the man stumbled toward us, "you gonna give a dog a bone?"

"Get outta here, bum." Ed waved him off.

"Cheddar cheese, I didn't hear please."

"Get lost or I'll whip your ass, too," Ed shouted as he released his hold on me.

"Whip my ass? I got three. Three I say. And what you got there? Fried chicken, that's all. Come on! Put your money down." Dumpster Man danced around, boxing at an invisible opponent.

Off the radar for the moment, I took a couple of steps, but Ed grabbed my shirt and brought me front and center. "I'm not finished with you."

His walkie-talkie beeped. While still keeping an eye and hand on me, he pushed the receive button. "Copy."

"Let's go. Three rounds. Put your money where your big mouth is, Chunky Brewster," the bum yelled.

Ed took a step toward him, pulling me right along, but a staticky voice halted his advance. "Disturbance in VIP lounge. Need you inside."

"Be right there," Ed said and pointed a fat finger in my face. "You're banned. Don't come back. Understand? If I see you again, anywhere near, you're meat." He glared at the bum. "You, too," he said and headed back for the club.

I smoothed out my shirt as my new friend busily stomped on unseen cockroaches swarming the area.

He looked up from his efforts. "He gone, huh?"

"Yeah, thanks for helping out there," I said.

"No problem, Mr. Price," he said with no apparent mental defect now.

"What?"

"I said no problem."

"How did you know–? Who are you?"

"Oscar Mayer Johnson, at your service."

When he stepped forward, I recognized him. It was the homeless guy who hung out in front of our building most days, the very one who I'd dropped a dollar for this morning.

"You're the guy who–" I didn't know what else to say.

"Who just saved your ass. Always act a little crazy with the big ones. Throws 'em off their game." He did a little soft shoe, his layered set of coats flapping about him.

"How did you know my name?"

"It's my responsibility to know all my peeps." He mimicked holding a cell phone to his ear. "Buddy Price here." Pause. "One million?" Pause. "No, that won't work. My client won't accept anything less than two." He flipped the invisible phone closed and placed it in an imaginary breast pocket. He pinched the air in front of his face and bowed slightly. "And scene."

"Nice." I held out my hand which still somehow clutched the twenty mashed into a small ball. "Here. Take this. You earned it."

After Oscar plucked the bill from my hand, he unwrapped it and hit me with a smirk. "Is this the way you gonna treat your guardian angel?"

I regretted giving him anything. "How about if I catch you later?"

Oscar shook his head. "Maybe later will be too late."

"Your choice."

As I walked away, he yelled after me. "Maybe you're banking on the world coming to an end. Won't have to settle up with old Oscar then?"

Even the homeless guy had heard of me. Sure, I wanted to tell him how wrong he was, but I didn't have the energy. "Like I said, thanks for helping. I gotta go."

I didn't look back until I reached the street. Oscar hadn't followed and the alley was empty.

Good.

I poked my head around the corner to check out the club and see if the Incredible Bulk had gone inside. He had, and I spotted Stacey and Lisa outside. Stacey stretched on tiptoes while Lisa roamed the line. I waved and caught Stacey's eye. She waved back, grabbed her friend and they both ran over.

"Hiii, Buddy." It seemed she'd had a few, evidenced by sideways steps on too high, high heels.

"Hey, Buddy," Lisa said with a little smile.

"Hey, Lisa." I pried my eyes from her plunging neckline and zeroed in on Stacey. "Why didn't you answer your phone?"

"But I did," she said.

"You hung up on me."

"Is something wrong, Buddy?"

Zimmerman's voice echoed in my head. *Commit or quit. Commit or quit.*

"Yeah, something *is* wrong. I called you and you hung up on me." If I was going to pull this off, I had to work hard to conjure up the negative.

"But I couldn't hear you."

Focus, Buddy. Focus. "And another thing. What's with you leaving tonight? Didn't you tell me someone wanted to see me?"

"But Buddy–"

Don't think about it. "I come to the office and he's nowhere to be found."

"Why are you so mad?" Her upper lip gave a little tremble.

Almost there. Just get it over with. "And you leave me these crazy notes all over my desk. It isn't acceptable." I'd riled myself to the proper frothy state.

Now or never. "I can't stay organized. It's impossible. Stacey, I'm going to have to let you go."

"What?"

"Yes, you heard me. Don't bother coming in on Monday. And, uh, and here are your keys." It's hard being delusional. Rational thought keeps intruding. I should have led with the keys. She stared at me with those big blue eyes of hers, and I started to lose my grip on insanity. "Thanks for letting me use your car, too." I was definitely running out of steam.

"Buddy? But why?" she said, her eyes welling.

I wanted to tell her "It was all Zimmerman. He made me do it." Of course, that wasn't true. Who was I kidding? I was the asshole who couldn't say "no". I was thinking about telling her to forget the whole thing as a bad joke when good friend Lisa intruded.

"You bastard. She'd do anything for you and this is how you repay her with your petty bullshit and lame excuses," she said, her 38DD's pressing against my chest. "You are the most vile, self-absorbed man I have ever known." She pushed her face inches from mine. "You're a piece of shit who doesn't deserve to breathe the same air as her."

Before I got a chance to calculate my future dating prospects, Ed emerged from the club. He spotted me as if I had a large neon arrow pointing down on my head. "Hey, you. What did I say?" he shouted.

Stacey and Lisa stepped aside to make room for the Beefmaster's fast approach. I stumbled off the curb and sprawled flat on my back in the street. As I pulled myself up to a sitting position, I thought of what I'd be soon telling God, something along the lines of "Boy, I really blew it."

But behind me, tires screeched and a taxi skidded to a stop. The backdoor flew open and my new guardian angel, Oscar, leaned out.

"Need a ride?"

I dove in with Ed only feet away.

Chapter Nine

Stacey stood on the sidewalk with her head buried in Lisa's shoulder.

I am such a schmuck.

Ed lumbered after us in the street, but we turned the corner and I lost sight of him.

I don't think I'd ever be able to find anyone like Stacey. And I had let her go. For what reason? Zimmerman had his panties in a bunch? I should have ignored him and simply talked it out. I'm good at that. It's what I get paid for. Instead, I took the easy way out.

Well, maybe not as easy as I thought.

"The big dude had it out for you," Oscar said. "What'd you do?"

"It wasn't right. It wasn't right," I muttered to myself.

"What's that, Chief?"

I looked at Oscar, a man who'd saved me twice so far tonight – this homeless man who I'd previously acknowledged with pitifully small handouts, mostly to make myself feel better. I was never concerned with who he was or how he had landed on the streets. I never saw him as a human being before this. And here I felt like pouring out my soul as if somehow he could make it all right, that he'd magically make me a better person when not even a trip to Heaven had brought about a change.

"I fired the best assistant I ever had. She was loyal and always had my back. And you know why I fired her? Because I didn't want to lose my own job."

"Damn, ain't that something," Oscar replied.

"She puts up with me. I'm not that easy to get along with. I've got issues. And… and…" I coughed. "She makes me… a better person."

"You seem all right."

"No, I'm a raving…" A cold sweat coated my forehead. "Megalomaniac."

"Who isn't in your business?"

"Stop trying… to make it right. I'm… I'm…" I coughed again and tried taking a breath which felt like pulling air through a straw.

Oscar edged closer. "You okay?"

My lungs shut down. Something gripped my heart and squeezed tight. I collapsed across the seat and the ceiling of the cab slowly lifted away. Stars filled the night sky which telescoped to the end of a long, dark tunnel.

"Maybe it's your conscience?" Oscar remarked from somewhere far away.

I wanted to shake some sense into him. Tell him a conscience was located in your head, not your chest. And hadn't I proved I didn't have one. Look what I had done to Stacey. I stretched my arms out, but he was too far away.

"I think your friend needs a doctor," the cabbie said.

"Nah, he's okay."

I willed my lips to part so I could yell that Oscar wasn't a freaking doctor, no matter how many lab coats he wore, and yes to take me to the hospital. Instead, all I mustered was a small burp.

Oscar's face flew down my tunnel and back out, then returned again. His mouth moved, but I couldn't hear anything other than a terrible roar. Suddenly, I shot away into pitch black and felt a familiar rush of wind.

I'd taken this ride before.

On the way, I checked behind me. At least this time I didn't have a tail.

The pain subsided as I flew toward a growing light ahead. It flashed and…

I rolled onto soft ground, my eyes shut from the brilliance of the light. Finally, I sneaked a peek. I lay in a lush field of green, felt the tickle of soft grass on my cheek and inhaled its fresh fragrance. I didn't know where I had landed, but for some strange reason, it didn't matter.

A whirring sound drew closer.

I tried to focus, but couldn't quite get a fix. I heard a click and footsteps crunched the grass near my head. I pulled an arm underneath and raised my other hand to block the light.

"Here, these'll help," said a familiar voice.

Something hard nudged my hand. A pair of sunglasses hovered near my face. I slid them on and got a better view of my benefactor.

God, dressed nattily in pressed black slacks and a dark red shirt, helped me to my feet. He wore a white Titleist golf cap on his head. "Seventy-five," he said.

I shook my head. "Seventy-five?"

"Yards." He pointed ahead. "About seventy-five yards to go."

I recognized the familiar darker green of a putting surface. A small yellow flag flapped from a pole marking the hole. Behind it, magnificent brown mountains with hints of white on top lined the horizon.

He walked to the rear of the golf cart and pulled out a wedge. "You play?"

"Fifteen handicap, but wouldn't you already know that?"

"Good." He pointed at a golf ball ten feet away. "Your turn."

I brushed blades of grass from my shirt and coughed out some very important words. "Am I dead? Did the taxi crash?"

"It drains to the right so hit left of the pin."

"Am I dead?" I repeated as I took the club, but I didn't move toward the ball. "Because, you know, this *would* be my idea of Heaven."

"Take the shot and we'll talk."

I backed toward the ball, hoping for an answer by the time I hit.

"Remember, go left," He said.

I hit the shot perfectly and landed my ball where I needed. As predicted, it rolled to within three feet of the pin. "I've got to be dead. That hardly ever happens in real life."

"My turn," God said, taking the club from me and positioned himself over another ball. His shot pulled far right and into a bunker. "Look at that. You have an easy birdie, and I'm lucky to make par." He jumped into the cart. "Coming?"

Of course I was.

In the cart, I closed my eyes and let the cool air caress my face. "So, what are the rules here?"

We rode in silence until we pulled up to the green. God got out, extracted a putter from the bag and handed it to me. "I'm far so I go first. How about that for a rule?" He removed a sand wedge, stepped onto the sand, positioned himself and hit a nice smoothly arcing ball within inches of going in. He walked over, tapped in with the back of his club and pulled the flag for me.

I had a three-footer. I could make these in my sleep, even with a fifteen handicap. I knocked it toward the hole, but it lost steam inches away. "Come on!"

"That give you a clue?" God said, laughing.

"I have no idea what you mean." I couldn't see the humor in missing a gimme. I was dead, but I wasn't dead, if you know what I mean. "How about explaining?" I said.

"Think about it. If this were Heaven, you'd have made that putt."

"Well, this can't be Hell," I said. "There's too much grass."

"There you can't even get a tee time." He wiped sand from the wedge. "Think of this as a way station. Not too bad, but not nice enough. Besides, this time you're not dead. More of a panic attack."

"Could have fooled me."

"Those things just make you feel like you're dying, but, believe me, you're not dead."

"So if I'm not, why am I here?"

I followed him to the cart. After bagging his club, he faced me. "Buddy, ask yourself this. Do you want to spend Eternity missing three footers?"

"No, but–"

"It won't be so easy when you get back. Your work isn't done. From what I see, nothing has even started."

"Can I help it if you sent me on a wild goose chase?"

"Don't close your eyes to possibilities." God extracted a score card from his back pocket. "The more you put off your destiny, the harder it's going to get for you. Keep that in mind next time you have a choice."

"I didn't sign on for this," I said.

"No one does." He penciled in his score and tucked the card in his pocket. "You got a par on that hole. Try harder next time."

He reached over and removed my sunglasses.

The sun fast-forwarded below the mountains, dropping me back into darkness. God and the golf course launched away from me. I felt the wind again rushing past my head. I hurtled through empty space, struggled in nothingness, trying to draw a breath. I gagged, swallowed through a dry throat and drew air in. I opened my eyes, now back in the cab. Wind whipped against my face from an open passenger window.

"Hey, Chief." Oscar said. "You okay?"

"No, I was dead." I grabbed him by the collar, but my hands fell away, too weak to hold on. "And all He was interested in was the score on the last hole."

"Calm your jets." He pushed me back. "You're sounding crazier than me. You sure you're okay?"

"Want me to take him to the hospital?" the cabbie offered.

"It's a little late for that," I yelled. My head was killing me. "Take me home. It's on Placid Place."

The cabbie didn't let me give the address. "Yeah, we're almost there."

Oscar handed over my wallet before I could ask the obvious. "It fell on the floor while you were passed out."

I checked inside to make sure everything was still intact. "You know what I think, *Chief*," I said. "I think your guardian angel days are over."

"Hey, bub," the cabbie interrupted. "Which one's yours?"

I checked out the window and saw familiar surroundings. Finally, home sweet home. "On the right, there at the corner."

The driver turned off the meter as we came to a stop in front of my condo. "That'll be forty-two fifty."

I pulled out the last of my money, three twenties, from my wallet and handed it over. "Keep the change."

As I stepped out, the cabbie swung a long arm over the top of the seat and frowned at me. "What about him?" He pointed at Oscar.

"Take him wherever. I gave you extra."

"Hey, Chief." Oscar chimed in. "Do I have a say in this?"

"I already stopped the meter," the cabbie said to me. "We're starting fresh now, pal."

"You're kidding."

"Does it look like I'm kidding?" His frown lengthened to Fu Manchu proportions.

I checked my wallet again in case I'd overlooked a folded bill. Nothing. Then I remembered. "Oscar, if you don't want to walk, cabbie needs you to pay. Use the twenty I gave you."

Without waiting for a response, I slammed the door and started for my condo. Behind me, the cab door creaked followed by a solid chunk as it closed.

Keep walking, just keep walking. Don't look back.

"Hey, Chief. Wait up."

Fifteen more feet. I fished for my keys in my pocket.

"I know you can hear me."

I spun around. "Yeah, I can hear you."

Oscar halted in his tracks.

"Go home, will ya'?" I said.

"Funny. Ha! Ha! Go home he says to a homeless man."

"Okay, bad choice of words."

"I thought maybe you could spare a bed tonight. You know, after all I did for you?"

"That's not going to happen," I said.

"Just one night. The ground gets hard." He rubbed his back to emphasize the point.

"There's always a catch, huh? Someone does a good deed and there's always something wanted in return."

"No, I only thought—"

"The shelters are over on Wilshire." As I said this, the cab drove away.

Oscar noticed as well. "Maybe I could stick around in case you needed someone. And this won't do me any good now." He held up the twenty.

The golfing God flashed in my head telling me I needed to start doing my job, but I was tired, tired of getting manipulated and intimidated. As far as I was concerned, a simple act of kindness wasn't going to get things rolling. "Sorry, the inn's closed."

To my surprise, Oscar didn't argue. "Okay, Chief. I got two good legs. I can walk." He nodded his head. "See you on Monday." He watched me for a few seconds and must have seen I wasn't going to fall for the guilt trip. He shrugged his shoulders, turned and trudged toward the street.

Of course, he was right. I'd see him on Monday, and the day after and the day after.

I stared at the door to my condo, at two silver angels complete with fancy little harps framing the window. Funny, I'd never noticed those before. I shoved my hand in my pocket, searching again for my keys.

Today, I'd filmed a porno, fired my assistant, almost been pounded by a meathead, and played golf with God. Had I taken one moment to consider what I was doing? What anything really meant? If I'd never noticed those angels before, what else did I need to wake up to?

My head began to ache. I couldn't think about it. I only wanted to get inside before Oscar changed his mind.

The first key I tried, of course, was the wrong one, and I fumbled for the other.

Never fails. Two keys and I always pick the wrong one.

Behind me, footsteps approached. Oscar had changed his mind and returned after all, but this time, I'd let him know who was in control. I spun around. "Come on! If you think–"

I didn't get a chance to say anything else when I was jumped.

Chapter Ten

"I don't have any money, I swear. Check my wallet." I struggled to say those words flat on my back with a forearm pressed against my throat.

But the forearm didn't belong to Oscar.

A young muscular kid sat on my chest while the other, a tall, gaunt older man, bent over and picked up my keys from the ground. "We don't want your money." He selected a key and unlocked the door.

Wouldn't you know it? He got it right the first try.

He pushed open the door, flicked on the light and motioned to his colleague who by then had me on my feet. "Put him in there, Flex," he said, pointing toward my den.

Now, if there ever was an appropriate name. Young, I was betting not even twenty, Flex filled the room with muscles, testosterone, and with his overalls, a healthy dose of *Deliverance*. He wore dark green work boots whose steel-tips brought attention not only to the shoes, but also to his pants that rode high in serious flood mode. An ever present grin on his darkly tanned face belied the fact that he enjoyed his enforcer role in all this. Flex pranced me inside and tossed me onto the sofa.

"What do you want then? My TV, stereo, the laptop? Don't waste your time looking. I'm not a jewelry guy." I lied a little on that last one.

The skinny one smirked. "I can tell."

Before I was tempted to rebut that comment (*he doesn't know me*), the doorbell rang.

"What should we do, Marlin?" Flex said.

Marlin was apparently the brains of the bunch – how much, still to be determined. "You expecting anyone?" he said.

I shook my head.

At this time of night, the only person I could think who might complain about noise was Mrs. Wheeler upstairs, but since she weighed over four hundred pounds, I doubted she would have gone to all the trouble to struggle downstairs to find out what all the commotion might have been. More likely, she would have simply called and yelled at me over the phone.

My persistent bell ringer tried a few more times and stopped.

"Well, there we go. Problem solved," Marlin said.

His smile didn't last long when loud banging and shouts came from the other side of the front door. "I know you're in there. Open up." It was Oscar. He'd returned after all.

Marlin nodded at me. "Keep him quiet."

Flex covered my mouth with a ham hock hand, both in size and smell.

"Who's at the door?" Marlin asked.

I waited for Flex to figure this one out, but he needed some guidance.

"Ah, hell," Marlin whispered, "take your hand away so he can answer." Flex lifted his hand.

"It's just some guy I shared a cab with," I said. "He'll go away."

The banging intensified.

"You need to answer it," Marlin said, "but get rid of him. And no funny business."

As Flex escorted me to the door, he reinforced Marlin's warning. "No funny business."

Were these guys for real? Funny business? Who says that anymore?

Flex took a step over to stand behind the door when I opened it. "Don't let nobody in; your life depends on it," he said.

I unlocked the deadbolt and cracked a small opening.

"Sorry, Buddy. Emergency." Oscar shifted from one foot to the other. "I gotta take a leak. Don't want to spoil the neighborhood."

Asking for money, maybe a ride downtown, or a bed for the night, all of these I could say no to easily. But how do I refuse a request to use the facilities even if it was only a lame excuse to get inside? Still, I couldn't let him in. I could hear Flex's heavy breathing just feet away.

"Uh, sorry there, Oscar. Toilet's all plugged." That was the best I could manage on short notice.

Oscar squinted at me with an *are-you-kidding-me* look. "Are you kidding?" *What did I say?*

"Man, you are one fucked up dude. You can't let a guy in to take a piss? What's your problem?"

"No, seriously. It's been a real bad day. I can't–"

"You've had a bad day? Well, try my life." He pushed past me into the condo. "Let me use the john, man."

He barely got inside when Flex jumped out and body-slammed him to the floor. Oscar proved no match for the over-sized gorilla bearing down on him.

"Had to call in reinforcements? Couldn't take on old Oscar yourself, huh?" he yelled.

I glanced at the open door, beckoning for me to escape. Two steps and I'd be outside before they could do anything. Two steps and... Oscar grunted as Flex yanked his arms behind his back.

"Flex played football." Marlin watched me from the foyer, arms folded, bushy eyebrows raised in anticipation. "He can still run a respectable forty, in case you're wondering."

At best, I could do three pull-ups in high school, and my capabilities had declined from there. And these days, I got winded doing a lap around the fourth floor of ZTA with old Hal.

I shut the door for them.

* * *

They'd come prepared. Marlin rummaged in a backpack and extracted a roll of duct tape while Flex dragged two kitchen chairs into the den. Flex used the tape to secure us, wrapping our arms tight on the arm rests, the same with our legs to the chair legs, and a few dozen loops around the chest. I could move my hands up and down, my head side to side. That was about it.

While Flex was hard at work, Marlin poked around and discovered my bottle of thirty-year-old, single malt Macallan. I planned to break it out for some extraordinary occasion which hadn't yet occurred. This wasn't exactly what I had in mind.

He unscrewed the cap and tipped the bottle my direction. "Here's looking at ya'," he said before taking a slug.

What a waste.

He tested the tape securing one of my arms. "Good work, Flex." He checked Oscar as well and sat on the sofa. He took another drink, wiping off leftover dribble with the back of his hand, and set the bottle on the coffee table.

"Mind using a coaster?" I ticked my head toward a small stack of cork coasters.

Not surprisingly, Marlin ignored me. "Let's do this quick, and we'll get out of your hair." He eyed me for a few seconds. "We came for the Jeremiah Box."

"The what?" I couldn't keep the astonishment out of my voice.

"You heard what I said." Marlin took another drink accompanied by an annoying exhale of breath. "Don't make things harder on yourself and your friend here."

"No, Chief, don't give it to 'em," Oscar said. "Don't give 'em anything."

"What do you care?" I said to Oscar, but didn't wait for his response before returning my attention to Marlin. "That's assuming I know what you're talking about."

"I read the paper when I can." Oscar answered anyway. "I know what's going on. That's some powerful shit you're playing with."

"Ah, a true believer," Marlin said. "You could join us if it wasn't for one small problem."

Flex, standing directly behind Oscar, pushed at his head. "Yeah, you picked the wrong parents, mud man."

I let loose with a nervous laugh. "Mud man?" I'd never heard that particular invective before, but it sent chills down my spine.

"Genesis 1:25. And God made the beasts of the earth according to their kind." Marlin rose from the sofa. "That's what we call abominations like him. Get it now?"

"Uh, no. Not exactly," I answered.

Oscar clarified it for me. "They're a couple of racist motherfuckers."

Marlin smirked. "We're all creatures of God, some of us more deserving than others."

"I got no qualms where God stands on the matter," Oscar said.

"We're His chosen people fighting a war against Satanic forces." Marlin's face glowed a bright crimson. "…whose army you belong to. God will rain down hellfire upon you and your kind before you will stand in our way. He will smite down all those who choose the wrong path."

Marlin started around the coffee table, but his shin connected with its edge. He stumbled to the side, rubbing his leg. "Goddamn, son of a…"

I winked at Oscar and whispered. "Let the smiting begin."

"You all right there, Marlin?" Flex asked.

Marlin waved him off and limped over to Oscar. "It was pre-ordained when you were begat by the unholy union of Eve and the Serpent. You can't help the color of your skin. It's your affliction."

Oscar tilted his head at Flex. "Then how come your boy here spends so much time working on his tan?"

"Shut up, you." Flex hovered menacingly. "I work outside a lot."

"Ignore him." Marlin made sure Flex was back in neutral and then turned to me. "And you, don't you realize that the Jews, blacks, communists, and homosexuals have seized control of America? Our holy duty is to regain the land for the people and for God, because He is a vengeful God and He wants us to join Him and wage war on all those that oppose Him."

I shook my head. "No, really, he's laid back. We've met."

"Blasphemer!" He poked a finger in my direction. "You are a heathen and a blasphemer!"

"I'm just saying," I said.

Marlin grabbed my face and squeezed. "It is our sacred duty to protect the Jeremiah Box. It is so decreed." Spittle bounced on his lips as he spoke. "You will not mock us." He let me go and stepped back. "Tell me where the Box is."

"I don't know what you're talking about." I didn't want to keep it, but on the other hand, I couldn't simply hand it over, as Oscar so aptly put it, to *a couple of racist motherfuckers*. I would make my stand here for God, for country, for the lives of all people on Earth. This was a test and I would hold strong for principle.

Flex stepped over and backhanded me across the face.

"Hey, man," Oscar yelled. "What the hell?"

"Tell us where it is," Flex shouted.

My cheek felt like it was on fire, and I tasted blood at the corner of my mouth. "Isn't there some rule about counting to three?"

"Are you going to cooperate?" Marlin said.

"I'll count to three this time." Flex raised his hand again. "One."

Was this my reality check? I'm sitting here all wrapped like a second-rate mummy in a Roger Corman movie, trying to protect something that might simply be the extension of severe psychotic visions I'd been experiencing. And I'm going to let myself be pounded on by Junior from *Hee Haw* because of it? Maybe the reality was that *I* was certifiable.

Flex continued. "Two."

"I made it up. It's all made up for ratings. Don't you get it? The Jeremiah Box. Who knows what's inside? I certainly don't. It's only a stupid box. I took the delusions of an old Texas preacher and put a name on it. And now you think it's got the secrets of the future of the world in it? Don't you see what's going on? You've bought into the scam."

"You know what, Flex?"

"What's that, Marlin?"

"It's time we introduced him to Betty."

That sounded promising. Maybe she'd be more reasonable. I like women. And sometimes they like me. But I had second thoughts as a weird grin spread across Flex's face.

"Yeah." Flex extracted a large hunting knife from a sheath hanging from his side pocket. "Say hello to Betty, Mr. Hollywood."

"Don't worry," Oscar voiced encouragement. "He doesn't have the balls."

I saw the crazy in Flex's eyes. It wasn't *his* balls that concerned me.

Marlin sucked on a yellow snaggletooth and instructed Flex on what to do next. "Let's start with the tips."

"In my bedroom… behind the painting… above my bed!" I blurted out. "There's a safe!"

"Damn, man," Oscar said under his breath. "I been with hookers that don't give it up that fast."

"Sorry," I said, maintaining my gaze on Betty. "I like all my tips attached." I gave Marlin the combination and watched him disappear in the back with Flex.

As we waited, Oscar wouldn't look at me as if I'd personally betrayed him. He sat shaking his head until I couldn't take it anymore.

"Will you stop that?" I said.

He glared at me. "You betrayed a trust."

"Believe me. It's not that big of a deal." I could see he wasn't buying it. "Sure, at first, it was the principle of the thing, but let's be realistic. I'm a bleeder."

"It's the Jeremiah Box. It's what everyone is waiting for."

"My bread box holds as much about the end of the world."

"So you're a fraud then, like they say about Hedgins?"

"I never claimed I was anything special."

"No, but you played along. Did that make it easier to pretend?"

I didn't have an answer for him.

We sat in silence for a few minutes. I could hear muffled voices coming from my room, but the earlier bitch slap still had my ears ringing.

"They get it yet?" I asked.

"Wait." Oscar seemed to be straining to hear what they were saying.

"What's going on?"

"Chill. They're coming." Oscar relaxed in his chair and seconds later Marlin and Flex returned to the den.

Marlin held the Jeremiah Box securely in his hand, a wide smile covered his face. "Thank you for your cooperation, gentlemen. The good Lord is smiling in heaven again." He picked up the backpack and dropped the box inside.

"Hey, man." Oscar struggled in his chair. "I still need to take a piss."

"I'll be in the truck," Marlin said to Flex as he retrieved my bottle of Scotch. "Take care of 'em." With a nod, he walked out the front door.

I pulled at the tape binding my arms to the chair. "Take care of what? What are you going to do? You got what you wanted."

"Cool your jets, Hoss," Flex said. "You'll live to see another day. Just gonna make sure you're all situated." He tested my tape and then glanced at Oscar. "What you got there, boy?"

"Who the hell are you calling boy, boy?"

Flex reached over and fingered a gold cross hanging from a chain around Oscar's neck. "Who'd you steal this from?"

"None of your damned business." Oscar struggled at his bindings, but like me, it didn't do him much good.

Flex snapped the chain from around Oscar's neck and bounced it in his hand. "Don't worry. I can put this to good use."

"That's one big mistake you're making. You take that and I'm coming for you," Oscar said.

"Shut up, mud man!" Flex said. "You don't scare me."

"Then, take this tape off, and we'll see what you got, you piece of redneck shit."

"You can't talk to me like that." Flex's arms hung taut by his side.

"I'm coming for you, fat boy. I'm coming for you. Keep that in mind while you're slopping the hogs."

"I'm telling you."

"Don't make him start counting," I warned.

"Let's go a couple of rounds. Take the tape off and give a dog a–"

Oscar didn't get a chance to finish. His head lolled off to the side, the result of a solid right cross. "You got anything to add?" Flex said, glaring at me.

"If it's not too much trouble, can you turn the TV on when you go?" I gave him a cautious smile. "I get bored easily."

"Go figure." He retrieved the roll of duct tape on the coffee table and proceeded to pick at the end trying to get a strip started. "After all this and you wanna watch TV. I'll never understand you Hollywood types."

He toyed with the end, not quite getting it free. "I got a question for you." He found the end and pulled out a six-inch strip. "I been a Christian all my life and never heard a word." He peered down at me and ripped the tape free. "You really talk to Jesus?"

"If you let me go, I promise to put in a good word for you."

"You got a mouth on you, dontcha?" Flex frowned and mashed the strip across my mouth. He did the same to the unconscious Oscar. He stepped back and inspected his handiwork. "Y'all have a good night."

Flex adjusted his overalls and headed for the door. But on the way out, he did something totally unexpected.

He turned on the TV.

I wish I had kept quiet. My 59" Plasma HDTV blazed away in all its glory but not the way I had anticipated.

The spokeswoman on screen held a ceramic baby and hit me with a dazzling smile. "And you can get this baby Jesus figurine for only $99.95 in three easy payments. There are three hundred thirty-one left, and we won't be leaving you until all are gone. Call before it's too late."

Chapter Eleven

I must have nodded off during the night because, at some point, I jerked awake from a nightmare of being chased by cherub Christmas decorations riding ceramic horses. They shot arrows at me as I ran through a forest of hand-crafted Polish stoneware and flameless candle trees.

Daybreak sliced through the breakfast room blinds in bright shafts of light – a nice way to wake up if it weren't for the duct tape binding me to a chair and the stench of urine wafting from Oscar.

I was starting to feel sorry for myself when God entered the room.

He carried a steaming cup of coffee in one hand, the LA Times in the other. His brown and blue-checked robe reminded me too much of my dad who wore one every morning of his life. He parked himself on the sofa and rested his feet on the coffee table.

"Good morning," He said as if everyone wakes up with God in the room.

The duct tape still covered my mouth so there wasn't much I could say in return.

"Rough night, I bet."

I nodded.

God placed his coffee cup on the table. "Didn't see that one coming, did we?"

I shook my head.

"Well, maybe I did, but what can I do?" He lifted the cup and slid a coaster underneath. "It's not like I can intervene everywhere. What fun would that be?"

I appreciated the coaster, but He didn't seem too concerned about removing the tape.

"I heard what you said last night. Not your best moment."

He was right, but I didn't want to give him the satisfaction by nodding. He probably knew anyway.

"I'm here to give you a little pep talk. Reinvigorate the faith again. You understand what I'm saying?"

Or else he'll *wipe the slate clean*. I think those were his exact words. Yeah, I understood.

"I think I've been patient." He hunted through the paper and extracted a section.

I nodded.

"But I understand; you're having doubts." He eyed the paper and something caught his attention. "Ah, the Lakers lost? I might have to do something about that." He laid the paper down and saw my surprised expression. "Well, sometimes I do get involved. Like Noah. Don't worry, I'm not asking you to build a boat." He picked up his coffee and took a sip. "I'm letting you know that I get it. Noah had his doubts, too, but he came around. We had a talk and look how it turned out for him." God checked his wrist watch. "Buddy, I'm running a little late for this thing. You understand how it is. I get pulled in all directions with my schedule."

Sure, although I didn't quite get the watch.

He extracted a thick document from the robe's pocket and dropped it on the table. "How about we have one more agreement? An addendum to the original contract. Article Twenty-three, Paragraph Fifteen, Section Five." He laughed at my reaction. "Kidding. Just trying to keep it light. You should have seen your face." He retrieved the contract and stashed it back in the robe. "Remember, I'm not the one who does contracts." He gave me a wink. "Let's agree that there'll be no more backsliding. Simple enough. Three words. No more backsliding. Can you do that?"

I nodded.

"I'm giving you one more week? I think that's fair. One week to get everyone shipshape or I, well, you know."

He stood and headed for the door.

One week? Would you please take the duct tape off so we can talk about this? I moaned through the tape, desperate for him to look. *I don't remember negotiating a deadline.*

He turned at the TV for one last word. "Is something wrong, Buddy?"

I gave up. What good would it do anyway? I mean, he's God, right? I shook my head.

"Just remember," He said. "That box is more important than you think." Glancing at the screen which showed sequined glass hummingbird feeders for sale, He waved his hand and the screen blinked off. "Don't say I never did anything for you."

✱ ✱ ✱

I opened my eyes.

Natalia, my weekend housekeeper, stood next to the darkened TV screen and replaced the remote. "Mr. Buddy, what have you done?"

I moaned and shoved my face up toward her. She took the hint, came over and carefully removed the duct tape from my mouth.

"What happened you?" she said.

"I don't want to talk about it." I licking my lips, trying to remove leftover stickum.

A hint of a smile played on her face. "Oh. Some kind wild sex party last night?"

"More like a home invasion."

Oscar stirred next to me.

"You want me call police?" she said.

"No. No. That's not necessary. You mind?" I arched my shoulders to show her I wasn't exactly going anywhere.

"Then it was wild sex party." She pouted and moved behind me. "Why you not invite Natalia?"

Ever since she had seen Lisa's sex toy catalog sitting on my kitchen table, she had me pegged as a sexual deviant. I knew it was her dream to join in these imagined festivities and, apparently, I had let her down once again. I would continue to do so given that a) it was entirely her imagination, b) she had twenty years on me, and c) a penchant for bondage which she was so kind to share with me one day.

As she worked on freeing my hands, she sniffed the air. "What I smell?" She sniffed again.

She freed my left hand, and I leaned over to remove the tape from Oscar's mouth.

He was fully awake now and frowned. "Don't look at me like that."

Natalia inspected the stain under Oscar's chair. "I get cleaner."

As she headed for the kitchen, I started removing the tape binding Oscar's arms.

"I figure they got a few hours on us," he said, "but we'll catch 'em."

"Who's talking about catching anyone? We're lucky to be alive."

"Come on, Chief. You aren't gonna let 'em get away?"

"That's exactly what I'm going to do." I finished unwrapping one of his arms.

Oscar went to work freeing his other arm. "Don't you want to get your box?"

"Why do you say that?"

"Don't you? Someone takes something from me, I'm getting it back."

"I haven't decided," I said.

Oscar pulled the last of the tape off his other arm and started on his legs. "I bet they have some deal going with it. The sooner you go looking, the better, so it's not used the wrong way."

"I didn't know it came with instructions."

"And for me, well, Baby Huey took something of mine that I can't let go. He's gonna learn the true meaning of holy retribution."

"I hate to break it to you, but they're long gone."

"Sure about that?" He flashed me a smile. "I know who they are."

"You *know* them?"

"I heard them talking in back. The kid said something about Vandy."

"Good for him." The only Vandy I knew was that university in Tennessee.

"I put two and two together. I spent some time in the pen up at Lompoc. That's near an Air Force base, Vandenburg or as it's also called, Vandy. There were a few guys incarcerated in my block who belonged to a survivalist group. They were religious fanatics and skinheads all wrapped into one. Sound familiar?"

"That's a stretch to conclude –"

"It's damned obvious is what it is. It's where we got to go."

"When did you become we?"

"It became we when I saved your ass in the alley last night, and when you invited me into your condo for a beat down."

"You wouldn't take no for an answer," I said.

"You owe me, Chief."

"I owe you?"

"That's twice I –" Oscar cut himself off as Natalia returned and inserted herself in between us.

"I clean now," she said, but her expression turned to shock. "Oh, no, Mr. Buddy." She held out her hand, caressing my cheek. "You have hurt on lip."

"It's okay. I'm fine."

"No, Natalia kiss it. Make feel better."

Natalia leaned in, but I held her off. "It's nothing. Please, the rug."

She pouted again. "Make feel better, no?"

"No!"

With cleanser and rag again in hand, Natalia angrily waved Oscar off his chair. "Move now, Mr. Pee-Pee Pants." She glared at me. "Natalia must clean rug."

Chapter Twelve

Highway 101 sliced along the coast between narrow, rocky beaches to the left and gentle sloping mountains rising to the right. I rolled down my window and inhaled a healthy dose of dimethyl sulfide. No, not ozone like we'd always thought. I found that out attending a screening of a pilot called *Good Science, Bad Science*, a show which highlighted scientific misconceptions like the Earth being the center of the universe or how the liver circulated the blood. Being a Hollywood agent does have its benefits. You learn a lot.

Unfortunately, I hadn't learned how to decline a homeless man's heartfelt appeal to drive him to Central California. He told me how the necklace was a gift from his dying mother. I agreed to take him, but only if he promised me he would make the trip back on his own.

Negotiation is an art, not a science.

So is denial. And when it comes to that, I'm Pablo Freakin' Picasso. This trip would give me a chance to clear my head and forget the countless requests for interviews about the Jeremiah Box and the highly anticipated end of the world. And I also wanted to forget I'd screwed over Stacey (who wasn't taking my calls). But most of all, I wanted to forget I'd had breakfast with God, a God who, for some reason, wore my Dad's robe.

I hoped this drive up the coast was the answer.

Traffic was light, and we made good time. With the Benz still in the shop, I had to call up Hertz and have a car brought over. I asked for a hybrid. If God wanted me to make the world a better place, how about I start with emissions? Baby steps, you know.

Other than a quick lunch in Santa Barbara at one of those Mexican takeout joints, the kind that has the little flames next to the menu items, we didn't stop. I wanted to get there and back before beach traffic built up in the afternoon.

I tried calling Stacey again. Still no answer. I left another voicemail. Maybe by the time she called me back, if she called at all, I could figure out who to blame.

One hundred fifty miles and a little over three hours after leaving L.A., a sign indicated we were ten miles from Lompoc.

"Almost there," I said.

Oscar pulled himself up in his seat and stretched. I'd convinced him to change into something less attention-grabbing. He now wore a pair of my khakis and a blue shirt he'd selected from my collection of failed TV pilot memorabilia. The one he'd chosen came from a reality show called *Animal Test Farm*, the concept being individuals competed head-to-head against animals to determine who could solve puzzles the quickest. It tested off the charts, but no networks picked it up because PETA complained about using animals in such a humiliating manner. I didn't see a big problem because, most of the time, the animals won.

"Do you know where we need to go?"

"Of course, Chief. You think I came all the way up here without knowing that?"

"Sure I do."

"Take the next exit," he said, sounding a bit disgruntled.

We left the freeway and headed west on Route One until reaching the outskirts of Lompoc. Signs pointed north to Vandenburg Air Force Base, but Oscar directed me to take a street called Ocean.

"Why Ocean?" I said.

"Because their camp's near the ocean and since…"

Blah. Blah. Blah. I tuned out the rest. He had no clue. Instead, I concentrated on finding a place where I could dump him and go home.

About five miles down Ocean, he had me turn on a road that headed into the mountains. Before long, we were well into steep terrain following a narrow winding road.

After a few more miles, I couldn't hold back. "You don't know where you're going so why keep pretending."

"Almost there, Chief. I feel it."

Actually, what I felt was my partially digested lunch in earnest discussion with my lower intestines. I didn't want to delay my return any more than I had to.

I spotted a gas station/country store cleaved into the side of the mountain. "I need gas."

A small deceit, I was driving a hybrid after all, but necessary to set the stage. This would be where Oscar and I would go our separate ways.

The store maintained a tortured façade of battered brick with a weathered, shake wood roof which sunk dangerously low in one section. Two rusted gas pumps, hopefully operational, stood guard out front. I would top off the tank, grab a soda and unload Oscar. He could fend for himself from here. As far as I was concerned, I'd earned my good citizen merit badge.

"You pump, I pay," I told Oscar as I pulled up.

"No problem," he replied.

When I went inside, I discovered that the general store aspect of the establishment proved as worn and weary as the exterior. There were three short aisles, with inventory seemingly an afterthought since shelves displayed at most a few items. I nodded to a teenage boy behind the counter who declined to acknowledge my existence. The refrigerated display case in the rear was empty and the glass warm to the touch. An old Amana refrigerator hummed off in one corner and upon opening it, I discovered a six pack of soda, three pre-packaged pimento cheese sandwiches and two six-packs of beer. I snapped off a Pepsi and headed up front.

A teenage girl in shorts and a pink tank top rested on a stool behind the counter with the boy. She smacked her gum as she flipped through pages of a Vogue magazine.

"I'm filling up. Shouldn't be too much." I laid a twenty on the counter.

"Which pump?" The boy sidestepped to the register. "I need to turn it on."

Of the two available pumps, my car was parked in front of the pump that displayed a big red number one. And we were his sole customer. I could have said something, but an image of Flex jumped in my head, wagging a finger at me, "You gotta mouth on you, dontcha?"

I played nice. "Number one."

"All right. Twenty on one." With his tongue partially protruding, he punched a couple of buttons on the cash register, and the cash drawer sprang out. "The pump don't have the space for dollars so I'll have to add it up for you."

"You should try to get on *Antiques Roadshow*."

He stared back with a dull, blank expression.

"Never mind," I said.

He placed my twenty in the drawer and turned to the girl.

"Hey, Sheila. Turn on Number One."

The exaggerated boredom emanating from her eyes was matched only by the herculean effort she used to roll them toward the ceiling. She flipped a switch on the wall behind her. She shot me with a withering stare and cracked her gum before returning to her magazine.

"Thanks, kid," I said to the boy and motioned through the window for Oscar to start pumping.

I was about to step outside and inform him of our new travelling arrangements when something caught my eye on the counter. Pictures of homes on a cardboard display were positioned next to the cash register. Each one had a caption, such as "SPACIOUS OFF GRID", "MONDO SURVIVAL CONDO", and "BACKYARD BUNKER BEAUTY".

"You sell real estate here?"

"My mom does," the boy answered.

"These seem to be off the beaten path."

"You want me to call her?"

"Get a lot of people asking?" I said.

"No, they're a…" When Sheila moved next to him, he hesitated, and then let the last words dribble out. "…favor for some people."

"Hi, Short Stuff," I said to her with a forced cheerfulness.

She couldn't have been five feet with chubby legs squeezing out of her shorts like thick icing from a pastry bag. She made up for her lack of height with an inexplicably lofty attitude.

"What business you have here?" she said.

I'd dealt with some of the toughest executives in Hollywood; this shrimp cocktail didn't intimidate me. "You know of any camps nearby?"

The boy stiffened, but she kept her cool. "We don't know nothin'."

"Well, I'm thinking about leaving the old rat race behind." I stretched my neck to one side. "Want to escape the Man, you know. He's bringing me down. I want a little more freedom. Get back to God and Nature. Seems like–"

"I said we don't know nothin'." Her eyes challenged me to say otherwise.

I felt a slight rumble in my lower abdomen. "Maybe if I could talk with your–" I bent forward as a stronger contraction interrupted my reply.

"You all right, mister?" the boy said.

Another one doubled me over. No, I was definitely not all right. Taco Blow was in full revolt.

"Bathroom?" I said through gritted teeth.

For some reason, they both seemed to have lost the ability to process English.

"Where's your bathroom?" I shouted.

"Out back," they said in unison.

"Errp." That's the sound you make when your guts thrash around as if caught in a washer's spin cycle. I stumbled out the door as I headed toward full dilation.

"Hey, Chief." Oscar stood by the car, waiting for me. "You okay?"

"Errp."

Behind the store, I found a door with a large penis scratched on its paneling. I took the hint. Inside, I splashed through small puddles of brown water into the stall and gave brief thanks that the toilet at least had a seat. The place stank as bad as an old Ed Wood movie. I didn't care. I ripped down my pants right before the explosive diarrhea hit. Any carbon credits I'd earned using the hybrid were immediately counterbalanced by a massive methane cloud venting from the bowl.

With each convulsion, I promised myself I'd never eat another four-flame burrito. As I mulled the possibility that this might be another, and heretofore undisclosed sign from God, the bathroom door slammed open.

Someone coughed.

I clinched my butt cheeks. What's more embarrassing than taking a dump in a public restroom? No one should be subjected to the sounds and smells of your colon in action. Oh, and, of course, if you have little kids, because I remember when Dad farted, it was always hilarious.

He addressed the urinal adjacent to the stall, his shoes visible from just under the side. I looked away and did a double take. Dark green work boots with steel tips. I'd seen shoes like that only fourteen hours before. I now had a much better reason for remaining unnoticed. Unfortunately, I'd already left my calling card hanging in what was left of our breathable air. As Denzel said in *Training Day*, "King Kong ain't got nothing on me."

"Shit, what crawled up inside you and died?"

It was definitely Flex. Instead of answering, I relaxed and let nature and gravity take its course. That proved enough for him to surrender.

"Wait 'til I go." He banged on the side of the stall. "That's just sick."

Seconds later, he zipped up. "Damn, I can't even breathe." After a few more choice words related to my family tree, personal hygiene and unspeakable acts he'd perform on my mother, he vacated the premises.

With Flex here, I guessed we were in the right place after all. Good for Oscar, bad for me. I wanted to drop him off and be done with it. Let him find Flex and the gang on his own. Now, they'd found us.

Actually, Flex hadn't exhibited any outward agitation, other than from the assault on his olfactory senses, so chances were good they hadn't spotted Oscar. But I wouldn't find out until I had finished my business.

A few minutes later, with my lunch duly recycled, I crept over, cracked the door and listened. No shouting, no gun shots, only the chirping of nearby birds and, as I stepped out, the soft rustling of blessed fresh air moving through the trees.

I ventured to the corner.

Flex leaned against a dull brown pickup truck. They were on my end of the lot, nearer the road, about thirty feet from where I hid. The rental car remained at the pumps, but no Oscar.

I hoped that was a good thing.

Another man, definitely not Marlin – in fact, far from Marlin-esque in stature, this one short and wide with a substantial beer gut – exited the store holding the two six packs of beer from the Amana and a bag of pretzels. The two loaded into the truck and took off in a shower of gravel.

I walked out front and considered possibilities. Maybe I'd been too quick to assume Oscar's continued health. The truck had a tarp in back. Maybe his lifeless body had been dumped underneath.

The bell from the store door dinged. "Looking a little pale," Oscar said.

"Not for the reasons you're thinking." I was glad to see him. "How'd you make out?"

"Fatty seems to steer around folks from *Animal Test Farm*, no matter what their color." He shot me a smile.

Of course, I hadn't given the acronym any thought, but there emblazoned on his shirt was the reason. ATF. It was a good choice after all.

Oscar was first to the car. He jumped in the driver seat and pushed open the passenger door. "Coming?"

"Not with my car. I brought you up here. The rest is up to you."

"No man. He's got my cross, and he's not going to get away with it."

"Not with my car," I repeated.

"And your box? You gonna let 'em get away with it?"

"Maybe that's exactly what I'm going to do."

"Sorry, Chief. I've got different ideas."

"Get out, Oscar. This is the end of the road."

He started the car and revved its engine which offered only a high pitch whine.

But, hey, good for the environment, right?

"I'm going without you then," he said.

"No, you're not." I grabbed the door handle.

"Makes no difference to me." He pulled ahead a few feet, dragging me along. "Last chance, Chief."

I did what any intelligent human being would do who didn't want to be left behind where girls with stubby legs dream of being supermodels and boys with no sense of humor don't know anything about quasi-intellectual reality shows on PBS.

I jumped in.

This was the second time I'd joined Oscar in an automobile, hastily and with no consideration to consequences. The first time, it ended with me duct-taped to a chair.

I'm not sure what made me think this time would be any better.

Chapter Thirteen

Oscar maintained a distance of several hundred yards behind the truck. It's hard to blend into traffic when there isn't any around, but we were far enough back not to draw attention in Flex's rearview mirror. After several miles of this hide and seek, we topped a rise. Billows of dust rose to the right.

"I bet we're getting close," Oscar said.

"Good, pull over. You can walk from here." According to God, the world would end in one week. I wanted to last at least that long.

Oscar slowed enough to make the turn. "Not yet, Chief. Close, but not close enough." We drove into the cloud.

The road was narrow and rutted, and the steering wheel juked wildly in Oscar's hands. Though visibility was low, he kept up a steady twenty miles an hour.

"How about backing it down a little?" From what I could see through the dust, we had closed the gap.

My cell phone rang. I checked the display and knew I had to answer. "Hey, Stace. Look, I'm a little busy."

"I heard your voicemails." Stacey emphasized the plural with a hiss like a snake. "What do you want?"

"Not a good time. I'll call you back later."

"This is your one chance. Speak now or forever hold your peace, Mister." Her tone reminded me of the ex-Mrs. Price right before she was about to lay in on me for some oversight, real or imagined. Well, maybe mostly real, thus the 'ex' designation.

"Stacey. Please."

We edged closer to the truck. "I said back it off, Oscar."

"You tell whoever Oscar is that you have something more important to deal with," Stacey said.

"No way he's shaking us this time," Oscar shouted back.

"Like why the hell you fired me last night," she said.

"Forget it. It was all a big misunderstanding." I caught a glow of red from Flex's tail lights through the thick dust. "He's slowing."

"How can I forget something like that?" Stacey said.

Oscar ignored me and accelerated.

"Don't be an idiot," I screamed.

"Oh my God. You're such an asshole."

"No, not you, Stacey."

"He's trying to get away," Oscar yelled back.

"He's braking, don't you see?" The car hit something in the road that bounced my side high in the air. "And watch the car! I want my deposit back." We hit a deep rut and bottomed out. "You're screwing me." I brought the phone up. "And, Stacey, that wasn't meant for you."

"Yeah, well, you're still an asshole," she said.

"How about this? You're not fired. Okay? That's what I wanted to say. I'll explain everything on Monday. Gotta go."

"Buddy! What are you doing?"

"Truck!" I yelled as we rounded a blind curve.

The road directly ahead of us was blocked. Oscar swerved and slammed on the brakes sending the car sideways.

"Stacey, you still there?"

"What's going on?"

"Call 911!"

Flex and his corpulent pal marched toward us. I noticed a tire iron gripped in Flex's hand.

"Where are you, Buddy?"

"Reverse," I shouted at Oscar. "Let's go. Reverse. Reverse." Then into the phone. "Call the police, Stacey. We're in big trouble."

Oscar slammed the gear shift into reverse and punched the accelerator, but he hadn't noticed the ditch behind us into which the rear tires promptly plunged.

Flex reached my door, but I flipped the lock in time.

I pushed at Oscar. "Bail out. Bail out. Go." It would have to be his side.

He shoved at his door. "I can't. It's jammed," Oscar yelled. But it didn't matter. A beer gut now blocked the view from his window.

"Stacey, call the police!"

"Stop yelling at me. You're making me nervous."

She was never very good under pressure. For that matter, neither was I.

My window shattered and Flex snatched the phone from my hand. He hung up by smashing it to the ground.

Stacey got her wish.

I wouldn't be yelling at her any time soon.

* * *

The wind blew hot and sharp like a slap across the face. Supplies crowded the forward part of the truck bed, some partially hidden under a light blue tarp that displayed a bright orange, checkerboard design. Oscar and I, along with the guy with the huge beer gut, rode in what space was left in back. Our semi-diligent host munched on his bag of pretzels and sipped a beer as he eyed us, but mostly he kept his head held up and into the wind as dogs tend to do when riding in cars. A shotgun lay across his lap, his free hand resting on top.

I eyed Oscar. He motioned with a quick tick of his head toward the tarp. Its edges flapped like a bird with a broken wing. As it lifted, I caught a glimpse of what lay underneath – a makeshift crate, its slats set wide enough apart that I could see its contents clearly – off white, rectangular blocks. If that wasn't enough, someone had scrawled 'BOOM' across the side (with smiley faces in each 'O'). I glanced at our guard, but he hadn't noticed me looking. I preferred to keep it that way and kept my eyes trained on the passing scenery.

We drove a few miles, turned on yet another dirt road, crossed a bridge over a dry creek bed and then travelled about another mile before nearing a dead-end. A quick honk caused the bushes blocking our way to part, carted off to the side by a couple of camouflaged hunter-types.

A large, open compound spread out in front, appearing to cover at least a few dozen acres. Green canvas tents the size of mobile homes dotted the site. Although mostly barren land, one section showed efforts to establish crops of some kind as the ground had been tilled in neat rows. There was also a barn with a couple of swayback horses lazily feeding from a trough.

At the far end, a two-story house held the high ground and commanded a full view of the area. A man wearing a green, sleeveless flak jacket dashed down the stairs as we parked in front.

Flex appeared at the back and lowered the gate. "Out!"

I stumbled onto the hard-baked earth. Oscar landed next to me. Beer Gut clambered out after us.

"Go tell him we're here," Flex told Beer Gut, who nodded and headed for the house.

The guy in the flak jacket had reached us by then, a video camera raised in front of his face. "I'm going to get a wide shot first, go to a close up on you, Flex, and then pull out again. Okay? Ready?"

Flex grunted and pointed at the ground. "On your knees, hands behind your head."

I caught him looking at the camera.

"Oh, for God's sake," the guy with the camera yelled, "don't look at me. Cut. Cut." He motioned with a finger across his throat. "How many times do I have to tell you? Okay, we'll need to take it from the top again."

Flex kicked at the dirt, cursed and headed back toward the cab.

"Keep doing what you're doing." The cameraman knelt down in front of me. "You're a natural." He shot out his hand. "Joe Drako."

"Buddy Price." I kept my hands behind my neck.

"Yeah. I know." His eyes shifted to Oscar. "But I don't know you." He looked back at me. "Who's this?"

"He's Oscar."

Drako turned toward the truck. "I need a reason he's here." But Flex was already inside the cab. He turned back. "Are you Fed?"

He must have noticed the shirt.

"Fed up, more like it," Oscar mumbled.

"Doesn't matter, man." He placed his hand on my shoulder and patted it like I was a good dog. "We can fix the video in post."

Flex poked his head out the window. "Hey, hands off."

"Just having a little convo here." Drako raised his hands in surrender, waited for a moment and leaned closer. "Such a prima donna. Put a camera in his face, man, and he starts busting everyone's chops."

I couldn't help but notice Drako's shirt as well. It had an image of a sneering Statue of Liberty presenting the middle finger. Underneath, four words were printed – "Freedom is a bitch."

"So what are we doing?" I said.

Drako stood and bounced back and forth on the balls of his feet. "Can't tell you. Sorry about that. Rules are rules. Stay with the program. Don't do anything stupid, man. Follow instructions. You know the drill." He winked and headed for the truck.

"No, I don't," I said after him.

Not only did Drako have enough nervous energy to power a small city, something else about him kept nagging at me. I couldn't quite put my finger on it.

"Okay, everyone." Drako spun around. "Places. Let's knock this out of the park."

Flex leaned out the truck window again. "What's my motivation?"

Drako closed his eyes briefly and held his hand parallel to the ground. "Gentlemen, stay cool. Back in a sec. Little inspiring to be done before we make the magic happen." Drako took a step and stopped. "I've got to say. This is so golden, you showing up like this. I didn't have an ending until now."

"What's that mean?" I said.

Drako winked. "You'll see."

My knees ached and I plopped down cross-legged in the dirt to wait as Drako conferred with Flex at the truck. Oscar sat beside me.

"Did you see it?" Oscar said, keeping his voice low.

"No, and you didn't either."

"They got enough C-4 to blow up the–"

"I said you didn't see anything. The less they know we know the better. Got it?"

"Sorry about all this." He poked a rock near his foot. "Not exactly what I was expecting."

I didn't answer him.

"I guess I owe *you* one," he said.

"Way more than one," I replied.

Drako stepped back from the truck. "Okay, are we ready?"

I rose to my feet. "Well, it's show time," I said and threw out a pair of half-hearted jazz hands for effect. Oscar stood with me.

"Okay, everyone." Drako raised his arm. "And–"

I stopped him before he could say 'Action'. "What do we do?"

"Hold up. Hold up, everybody." He took a few steps toward me. "Go with the flow. You get told to do something, do it. Okay? Okay." Drako backed away from the truck and raised his hand again. "And…Action."

Flex exited the truck and headed toward us with an exaggerated John Wayne swagger. He stopped and pointed at me. "Man, you ain't on your knees. What the hell?"

"Cut! Cut!" Drako said. "What's the problem now?"

"They're standing. Ain't they supposed to be kneeling?" He pointed at me. "He's supposed to be on his knees."

"Sorry. Sorry." I struggled back down on my knees, pulling Oscar down with me. "My bad. Okay, we're ready." I wanted to be as helpful as possible to get this little cinematic nightmare over and maybe talk with someone who had some sense.

Drako folded his arms and shook his head. "No! No! This isn't going to work at all."

"What's amatter? They were kneeling before." Flex argued like any reasonable script supervisor would.

"No." Drako shook his head. "We need to start with them back in the truck."

"Ah, horseshit," Flex said. He waved his arm at us. "Get in the goldarn truck."

"No!" A deep voice boomed out from the porch. "Forget that for now." An imposing figure stood at the top of the stairs. "Bring Mr. Price to me."

Chapter Fourteen

The man was broad shouldered with a stiff, imperious posture. He held his hands clasped firmly behind his back. A handlebar mustache completed the portrait of authority.

"Yes, sir, Major King. Right away," Flex said, making a couple of quick bows like a pretty, little Geisha linebacker.

The Major motioned to Beer Gut, who stood dutifully beside him. "Don't just stand there. Go help 'em."

He turned and disappeared inside.

"Gotta be the head dude," Oscar said.

"Nothing gets by you, does it?" I said.

"Be sure to ask him about my cross."

"Tops on my list, Oscar. Tops on my list."

Flex pulled us both to our feet. "Take him to the barn." He pushed Oscar toward Beer Gut, who had now joined us. He maintained a firm grip on my arm. "Smartass is mine."

"Stay strong, Chief," Oscar said as Beer Gut escorted him away.

Flex guided me toward the house while Drako hovered by my other shoulder. He spoke in a low voice. "Don't let the Major throw you. He'll come at you hard, man. Like he's some kind of sumo dragon, but he's a prophet. Listen to his words because they're full of truth. He's been to the mountain top and he knows, man. He's been to Heaven and back and will show us all the way." Drako leaned in close. "There's not much time, man. That's what he's saying. *You* know that. You've been there."

I snapped my fingers. "Hopper. Dennis Hopper."

"What?" Drako said.

"Hopper. That's what this whole pseudo Sixties' psycho-babble is for, right? That's been bugging me since I got here."

"I don't know what you're talking about, man."

We reached the stairs. "You're just an errand boy sent by grocery clerks," I said in my best (some would say worst) Brando impersonation.

Drako fell back a few steps. "No, man. I got this gig on my own."

He had no idea what I was talking about. Maybe he didn't know Film as well as he thought he did.

We stepped onto the porch, and Flex pushed me through the front door. The foyer was simple but clean. White-washed walls with terra-cotta tile floor emanated a coolness that didn't exist outside. Our footsteps echoed on the floor as Flex directed me toward a room on the right. Along with the same plain tile floor, the room held a simple oak desk with two blue-padded chairs positioned in front.

Major King rose. He appeared to be in his late seventies but strong and vital. He reminded me of a Wilfred Brimley without the stomach and diabetes.

"Take a seat, please." The Major waved me to one of the chairs.

To my right, a Confederate flag, on the left, a Swastika flag. Pictures on the wall showed Klan meetings, cross burnings, WWII Nazi rallies, and a large poster of the Aryan Nations Constitution.

"You can go, Flex," King said.

Flex nodded and headed out, dodging Drako who remained at the doorway.

"Close the door, Joseph. We can talk later."

"Yes, sir." Drako backed out, shutting the door behind him.

"Major Bartholomew King of the American Federal Reservists, at your service." King gave me a quick nod. I could have sworn he clicked his heels, too.

"Buddy Price."

"Yes, I know. You've become quite the celebrity on God's channels." He sat, clasped his hands on the desktop and took a deep breath. "You're probably wondering what this is all about."

"The thought had crossed my mind."

"Want anything? Water, tea."

"Scotch? I could use a drink."

King shook his head. "Liquor only weakens us to the temptations of life."

I took that as a no. "Water will do. You got a lot of dust."

"Yes, it *can* kick up." King lifted a walkie-talkie and double-clicked the button. "This is Major King. Send some water to my office. And I'd like some of that lemonade."

After a brief burst of static, a voice replied on the other end. "Ten-four."

"The girls make the best pink lemonade. You should try it," King said.

"Maybe I will." I crossed my legs, still waiting for an explanation.

"I want to show you something." He turned around and leaned down, fooling with a drawer in a credenza behind his desk.

I've learned over the years that it's often the small things kept close that give the true measure of a man. An old black and white, framed photo caught my eye. Six men dressed in varying degrees of battle fatigues, several in shorts, no shirt, all smiled for the camera. I took a closer look. One on the far right bore a distinctive handlebar mustache.

"Khe Sanh, '68. Tet Offensive." King had turned back and caught me looking. "They threw everything they had at us, rockets, mortars, artillery."

"That's you."

"Never got used to the pounding, but we held. Seventy-seven days until they relieved us. Pure hell." King shook his head. "After we left, they let the base go two months later." He cleared his throat as if trying to rid himself of a bad taste. "They were good men. None of 'em made it out." He pulled out his desk drawer and fished out a key. "Did you know we have something in common?"

I considered the flags behind his desk and thought of the hate they represented. Sure, I hated some things, but mostly it was telemarketers, Monday mornings and reality TV with manufactured drama. King, on the other hand, took the hate thing to a new level.

"No, not really," I said.

"You and I, we've both seen God. He's warned us that the end of the world is coming, and we need to do something."

"I think you've got the wrong idea about me."

"Think so?" He slid his desk drawer shut. He returned to the credenza, used the key and slid something from a drawer. He spun back, placing the Jeremiah Box in front of me. "The way I look at it, we're both true believers."

Apparently, he had no problem flaunting the item he just stole from me. "I'm not sure what you mean."

"You believe in God, don't you?"

"You can say I've had some personal experiences."

"I know, but do you believe?"

"Major, I don't know how you've–"

"God told you the end was near. You've already made that perfectly clear." He patted the Box. "He's spoken with you, but the question remains, do you believe?"

"I don't know what…" He was going all Barbara Walters on me, and I didn't want to fall for it.

"Well, I do. That's why we're here, preparing for what's to come. That's why you're here, too. That's why you're sitting in that chair talking with me. God sent you to help us prepare."

"No, if you haven't been told yet, I was kidnapped."

King held up his hand and let out a long breath. "God works in mysterious ways."

I wanted to ask him what was so mysterious about two guys forcing their way into my home and duct-taping me to a chair. Sounded more criminal to me, but I decided to keep it to myself. "I would have given them the Box if they'd asked."

The smile remained on King's face. "Not what I heard."

"I'm willing to overlook things." I forced a smile as well. "Let bygones be bygones."

"It's not a mistake."

"Well, let's agree to disagree." I cocked my head toward the door. "So if you can give me a ride to–"

"It's all about spreading the word." King leaned forward, banging his fist on the desk. "You tried, but failed. It's a job that requires more than one man. I've assembled others who believe, and we'll spread the word for you to those that deserve to survive. It's *all* about spreading the word. We're both on the same page about that, are we not?"

I stood in a room filled with racist flags and Nazi memorabilia, a virtual museum of crazy. We were not only on different pages; I was in a completely different book. "We each have our own way of doing things," I answered diplomatically.

He frowned, rose and walked to the window. "The race war will begin soon, Mr. Price. We will overthrow the government and replace it with true representatives of the people. And God will recognize what we have done and vanquish to Hell all other groups he finds impure. We will stand side by side with him." He turned back to face me. "We will stand strong with our brothers and sisters for what is right and white." I caught a gleam in his eye. "We'll survive, by whatever means necessary. The question is, will you?"

"Oh, don't worry about me. I'll get by somehow."

The Major's eyes tightened. "God says that the time is coming soon. I can offer you sanctuary. A man of your talents and your background with the Jeremiah Box will come in handy for our cause."

A knock at the door interrupted us.

"Enter," King said.

The door opened and a slender, attractive girl entered. Wearing a simple print dress, her blonde hair pulled under a little white linen hat, she carried a wooden tray with a pitcher of pink lemonade, water and two glasses. She placed the tray on a side table.

"Thank you, Mary. Please, two lemonades," King said. "You should try it," he said to me and, with a nod, put her to work.

She carried one to King, and as she brought mine, I caught sight of something hanging from her neck – Oscar's cross.

"May I ask a question?" I said to her as I took my glass.

She kept her eyes on the floor.

"Mary," King said. "It's okay." He nodded at me. "Go ahead. Ask your question."

"Your necklace, where did you get it?"

She froze, a painful expression playing on her face. She answered in a soft, low voice. "It was a gift."

"Recently?" I asked.

She nodded.

King walked from behind his desk. "What's this about?"

I could tell she was scared so I tried to calm her. "It's no big deal. The cross belongs to someone I know." I turned to King. "My friend had the idea we could come here and clear things up."

"Is this true, Mary? Did you take the cross?"

"No." That seemed all she would say but finally added, "Flex gave it to me this morning."

The Major picked up a Bible and proceeded to thumb through it until he found a particular page. "The Good Book asks us to live by certain rules – Thou shalt not steal." He held the Bible under her downturned face and pointed at a passage on the page. "If a man gives to his neighbor money or goods to keep safe, and it is stolen from the man's house, then, if the thief is found, he shall pay double."

So if there were two thieves, does that mean I get a quadruple payout?

"We live by these rules; otherwise we'll be nothing but savages and misanthropes. Isn't that right, Mr. Price?"

"Look, all I…" The last thing I wanted to do was get this girl in trouble. "It's just that this cross has serious sentimental value and–"

King snapped the Bible shut which caused Mary to jump. "If we find that one of my men has taken this cross without permission, I'll see to it that he's punished accordingly. We're a God-fearing outfit, and my men are sworn to abide by God's laws." His voice trembled in that preachy emotional way, reminding me a lot of Hedgins giving one of his sermons. "Hand me the cross, please."

Mary removed the necklace and handed it over, her eyes still trained on the floor.

"You may go now."

After she left, King returned to his desk and hung the cross over his desk lamp. He placed the Bible in front of him, folded his hands over it and lowered his head, seemingly in prayer. After a few moments, he raised his head "This is very unfortunate."

"Well, we didn't come up here to cause any problems. And, you know, everything else…" I waved at the box. "…no big deal."

"No, it is a big deal. It plays a key component in my plan. You can be a part of that."

I wasn't sure if that was a question so I waited for one to come.

"I believe you've met Mr. Drako already?"

I nodded.

"I hired him to make a movie warning everyone of what is to come. He's thought of a very catchy title. It's called *Apocalypse How.*"

Now that was the first thing that made sense all day. It explained a lot about what went on outside, even if Drako didn't have a clue. "Very catchy. Coppola would be proud."

"Perhaps that would be of interest to you as well?"

"Sorry, Major. My client list is full these days."

"The end of the world is coming." King's voice boomed out, strong and defiant. "Whose side do you want to be on?"

I had held my tongue as long as I could. "With all due respect, my intentions weren't to exclude more than three quarters of the population of the Earth."

"It's survival of the fittest and we know who that will be."

"If it's all the same to you, I'll take my chances," I said.

King stood. He ran his hands along his long sleeve shirt to straighten the fabric, all the while, his eyes drilling deep into mine. "That's too bad. I would've enjoyed working with you." He came around his desk, motioning for me to stand as well. "It was a mistake for Flex to bring you here. I hope you'll accept my apology if we've inconvenienced you."

"Already forgotten."

"So tonight, you'll be our guest and–"

"No, we don't mind going–"

"I've been informed you wrecked your car," King said as he walked me to the door. "It won't be ready until tomorrow."

"Oh." That seemed to be that.

He placed his hand on the doorknob and said, "Tell me something. The Box, did you ever find a way to open it?"

I shook my head. "I wanted to drill it out, but Hedgins said that would destroy whatever was held inside." Sure, I didn't want him to have the satisfaction of knowing I had no idea how to open it, but on the other hand, it seemed I was going home, so why complicate things?

King smiled. "Well, Mr. Price, I've found someone who can."

Chapter Fifteen

Staying the night hadn't been on my agenda, but it didn't seem like the issue was up for debate. Flex led the way up the stairs and, once at the top, pointed me down the hallway. At the end, he opened a door to a nicely appointed bedroom. A king-sized, four-poster bed with hand-carved oak columns stood against one wall, its canopy brushing up against the ceiling; next to it, a nightstand and across the room, a high profile chest of drawers. In the center of the room, there was a throw rug with a raised spiral pattern which reminded me of one of similar style from my grandparent's den. Another door opened to an adjoining bathroom while French doors led out to a balcony. A large fan hung motionless from the ceiling. Not exactly what I had expected; racists with taste although a little outdated for mine.

"Any chance my car'll be finished today?"

"If the Major wants you to stay the night, you stay the night," Flex said.

The acrid air in the room made me wonder where the dead body had been stored. I pulled the chain attached to the ceiling fan, but nothing happened.

"All the comforts of home." Flex grinned. "Almost."

I noticed a kerosene lamp sitting on the nightstand. "So no electricity?"

"It's the way of the future after the war. Might as well get used to it."

"War?" I said, but Flex had already turned toward the door.

The floorboards creaked from the hallway. "Come on. I don't have all day," he said.

Seconds later, Mary, the refreshment girl from the Major's office, appeared at the door, carrying a bucket of water in one hand and an armload of linens and towels. I was surprised to see her after what had gone down back at the office. I'd have thought given King's apparent penchant for hellfire, he would have banished her somewhere.

She squeezed past Flex, drawing back so as not to touch him. I noticed that. Flex, the resident genius on tenderness and affection, did not. She made her way directly to the bathroom, her eyes trained on the floor.

"You'll get some chow later on after everyone's eaten," Flex said to me.

I smiled. "Hospitality is making your guests feel at home, even when you wish they were."

Flex's face scrunched. "What's that supposed to mean?"

"It means..." Footsteps echoed from the hall. "You know, just forget it."

Beer Gut appeared at the door. "Hey."

"What you want, Chuck?"

Chuck didn't answer, instead choosing to stare at me. "Ain't you just something now?"

"You talking to me?" I said. No, I wasn't launching into De Niro. Honestly, I couldn't tell. He had a wandering eye, which made it hard to judge.

"Yeah, I'm talking to you."

"What's something?" I answered.

Flex put his hand on his friend's shoulder. "Don't get into it with him."

"It's hard to believe that the Good Lord would waste his time with someone like you," Chuck said, ignoring Flex.

"Let me tell you, God and I are like this," I said twisting my index and middle fingers together. "We had breakfast yesterday. And you know what he told me?" I skipped the part about the Lakers. "We're running out of time, and if idiots like you two don't get their shit together, he's going to hit erase. You think hurricanes and earthquakes and floods are bad, wait until you see this action. So, yeah, talk all you want, but I'm the guy who could save your ass. That is if I thought it worth saving. Maybe I'll tell God to go ahead. And there's nothing your Major King can do about it."

"Naw, man." Chuck squared his shoulders. "You don't know shit."

"I told ya'." Flex held Chuck back with a hand on his chest. "He'll try to flip-flop your brain."

"God's going to make one helluva entrance. And you know why?" I'd worked myself into classic Price. "Because of bozos like you." Maybe I didn't believe half of what I was saying, but well, when I get annoyed, I let it all out.

"Uh, yeah, well same to you." Chuck stared at me like I had sprouted alien ears.

"That's the best you can do?" I said.

Flex nudged Chuck. "What the hell you come up here for anyway?"

"Uh." He blinked, trying to recover. "To tell you I got the other one all tucked away. And the Major wants to see you."

"Okay, soon as Mary's done."

"He said ASAP."

Mary exited the bathroom.

"I got to go downstairs," Flex said to her. "When you're finished here, go on to the kitchen. Dinner needs fixin'."

"Okay," she said, her eyes rising to meet his for the briefest second before dipping away again.

Flex shoved Chuck ahead of him out of the room, and they disappeared down the hall. I was glad to be rid of them. I took a deep breath and tried to remember what I'd been ranting about.

Mary placed the linens she still carried onto the bed and tiptoed to the doorway. She peeked out and closed the door.

She straightened her posture and turned, her eyes no longer surveying the floor. When she walked across the room to the balcony door, it was with an assurance that hadn't existed a few seconds earlier. She fished in her skirt pocket and extracted a lighter and a pack of cigarettes, patted the bottom producing a single cigarette which she popped in her mouth and quickly lit. She shut her eyes as she inhaled and blew out a cloud of smoke, making sure to aim it outside. "God, I was going to go crazy if I didn't have one soon." She opened her eyes. "Smoke?"

I shook my head and retrieved my lower jaw from its resting place on the floor.

"Good for you," she said. "It's a bad habit. One of these days, I'll quit, but haven't found the right day." She flicked the ashes outside on the balcony.

All I could do was nod. I hadn't seen a better transformation since Naomi Watts' audition scene in *Mulholland Drive*. Of course, the lesbian stuff later on wasn't too bad either.

"That was quite the performance you put on," she said. "What were you going for?"

"Nothing. That was… that was me." I stared at her like she'd stolen my alien ears. "Nice change yourself. What's your angle?"

"Survival. You adapt to survive." She laughed. "Isn't that ironic? At a survivalist camp."

"Yeah, love that irony. What are you doing here?"

"Long story. Bad boyfriend, bad choices. I wouldn't want to bore you. I mean, who really cares?" She flicked the cigarette over the edge of the balcony.

"I'm sure somebody does," I said.

She nodded slowly as if coming to a realization. "You, know, maybe today is the day." She pulled the pack out. "Time to get rid of the things that are no good for me, right?"

"Right."

She tossed the cigarettes over the side and took a deep breath. "To new beginnings."

"To better choices," I said.

"Okay, better choices." She headed over to the bed. "Now, my first better choice is to make your bed or my fiancée will get upset."

"King?"

"Ha! He's old enough to be my grandfather." She ripped the bedcover down and began putting on the fitted undersheet. "Flex."

I helped pull the sheet under the mattress, first on one end and then the other. "Sorry for saying so, but I don't see it."

"Oh, me neither. Flex and I, we've been *arranged*," she said, derision dripping from the word. "We women aren't capable of making such important decisions so Major King has final say. You know what I think?" She stopped her bed-making.

"No."

"It's the only way these idiots could ever get a girl."

"Well, getting and marrying, there's a big difference."

"I'm not too worried. I have another year before it happens. I'm spoken for, but…" She fluffed my pillow. "…he can't touch me until we're married. It's the rule."

"Probably why he seems so angry."

She laughed loudly with that but quickly slapped a hand over her mouth. "You're funny," she said as she pulled the bedspread up to finish the bed.

"Look, maybe it's not for me to ask, but why don't you leave?"

"It's not easy getting in. It's harder getting out."

I didn't like the sound of that.

Just then, Flex burst through the door, red-faced, fists clenched. "What's the idea of shutting the door?"

The meek Mary immediately rematerialized. She held her arms wrapped around her waist and stared at the floor.

"I asked you a question." Flex advanced on her. "And I expect an answer."

"Hey! Hold on." I grabbed at him as he passed.

Flex shrugged me off and glared. "Now, ain't that sweet. You think she needs protection?"

"Nothing's going on. The wind must have blown it closed."

"Get on downstairs." He pointed a finger at Mary. "I'll deal with you later."

She hurried out, carrying the wad of sheets she had pulled from the bed.

Flex turned to me, pushed close, his face inches from mine. "Nobody puts their hands on me."

I took a step back, but that was as far as I could go because of the wall behind me. "Why do I get the feeling we aren't hitting it off?"

"Maybe because I don't like you and your smart mouth." He grabbed my collar.

"Couldn't tell."

"You…" He shoved me against the wall, jabbing his finger into my chest, "…you think you're better than me?"

"Obviously —"

He pressed a big hand against my neck.

I should have started my reply differently. "…a big misunderstanding." I barely coughed out those three words.

He relaxed the pressure. "Yeah, must have been."

"I think we have a different perspective on things."

"One thing's clear to me." He squeezed harder again. "You think you can take my girl."

I barely shook my head from side to side, just enough to communicate my disagreement. Truth was I thought she was hot in an Amish kind of way, but that part I didn't plan on sharing.

"No?" Flex pulled his arm away. He took a step back, apprising me. "No, I ain't gonna let you get me all riled up. Nope. You're already sitting on the high side of a long fall."

"Meaning I'll be burning in Hell after a long fall from grace?" I guess I'd read too many manuscripts where I look for some kind of foreshadowing in everything.

He didn't answer; instead, he turned and headed for the door.

"Or something equally apocalyptic?" I called after him, wanting some kind of hint. I hoped he was only speaking metaphorically.

He stopped at the doorway. "Don't worry, you'll be safe. We got security all over the place.

Chapter Sixteen

Dinner never showed which was okay by me. I'd have given my left nut for a couple of Tums though. And my right one for some aspirin. I had a huge migraine.

Sleep came slowly. The 'you'll be safe' assurance I'd received from Flex didn't make me feel so safe. I was more worried about those inside the perimeter than outside. And, no matter what a pain Oscar had been up to this point, I couldn't help but worry how he was doing. Where was he? What had Beer Gut said? *He'd been tucked away.* That didn't sound too ominous.

Eventually, I did fall asleep. I awoke from a nightmare and saw glowing, red eyes staring at me from the balcony railing. With a blink, they disappeared. Seconds later, a horned owl materialized on the dresser and slowly pivoted its head like Linda Blair in *The Exorcist.* "Hoo. Hoo. Hoo." Its red eyes glowed brighter. "Who's going to save the world, dickhead?"

I jerked up in bed. I could have sworn I heard the rustle of feathers, but a quick scan of the room revealed no unwanted visitors. I rubbed my eyes and made sure I was awake this time.

The owl's question played over and over in my head. Why did everything seem like a message from God, although I seriously doubted He would employ the word dickhead? I checked the time. It was almost four. I also checked my internal calendar. How long did I have to fix things? Five more days? And here I was out in the middle of nowhere. Maybe the owl was right.

I was a dickhead.

Stumbling my way through the darkness, I reached the facilities. At least they had a toilet on the inside. It was one of those high tank types with the pull chain. As I went about my business, I understood the reason for the bucket of water carried in earlier. Flush and refill.

When I finished, I walked onto the balcony. There I considered my chances on making a run for it. I could jump the ten feet to the ground, somehow elude the guards and escape the compound, run however many miles to the main county line where I'd head for civilization and freedom. I went back inside. After all, running was involved.

A dark figure stood in the middle of the room. "Time to wake up," it said.

I'd have crapped my pants if I hadn't just gone. "Damn it, Flex." I recognized the voice. "Ever hear about knocking?"

"Sleep well, your highness?" He lit the lamp next to the bed.

"Not hardly."

The soft glow shadowed his face making his grin appear almost ghoulish. "Room not good enough for you?"

Boy, this kid had a huge self-esteem problem. "Are we going?"

"Yeah, we're going." He backed up to the door and waited for me to get dressed.

After I slipped on my shoes, he escorted me downstairs and out the front door. A panel van idled in front, the sliding door already open, waiting for my entrance. Chuck sat in the passenger seat.

Flex gave me a little extra shove inside, and I hit my head with a resounding thud on the far interior wall. "Sorry about that," he said and slid the door shut. I don't think he meant it.

Inside it was pitch black and smelled like a sewer. I rubbed the ache from my head and found a seat on top of something, which wasn't the hard metal floor of the van. The ceiling light blinked on as Flex opened the driver door, and I found the source of the smell. My seat consisted of several of those flattened bags of manure you can get at a Home Depot. Farmer Toledo's Family Manure, it said, complete with a smiling cow that seemed happy she'd provided you with a few weeks' worth of her shit.

Considering my situation, completely poetic.

Flex closed his door and the interior was cast back into darkness. "Where's Oscar?"

"He's at the annex," Chuck said.

He and Flex both laughed at that one.

"Why's that funny?" I said.

They laughed again and we took off, squeaky springs arguing with the suspension about which would fail first. We bounced along for not more than thirty seconds when the van came to another halt. They got out with Chuck opening the sliding door.

I could now see Flex wrestling with a lock and chain outside a small shack adjacent to the barn. The Annex, no doubt. They say people find humor in the funniest places. I guess that depends on how racist you are.

Flex opened the door and disappeared inside. Quickly, he reemerged pushing a dazed Oscar ahead of him.

They reached the van, and with a shove, Oscar joined me, but at least I caught him so that there was no thud this time. I watched through the door as Flex headed back to the barn.

"You okay?" I pulled him up.

"Yeah, you?"

"Looks like we're going home." I said loud enough for Chuck before whispering to Oscar. "I don't have a good feeling about this."

"Wow, you do have psychic powers." He whispered back, then shouted at Chuck. "So, how's it going to go down?"

"Shut up in there," he said. "No talking."

I grabbed Oscar's arm and pulled him back. "What the hell are you doing?"

He shrugged me off and focused again on Chuck. "Know what I think. I think you'll take us for a little drive. Our car's parked a few miles up the road, right? You'll have it all fixed up and ready to go. So you'll hand over the keys, maybe Flex'll apologize for breaking my friend's phone. We'll get in, you'll wave goodbye, and we'll wave goodbye. We'll drive on home, and life will go on like nothing ever happened. Isn't that the way it's going to happen?"

"Yeah, how'd you know?" Chuck said with a smirk.

"Got to have a happy ending, right?"

"Yep."

Oscar prodded further. "How stupid are you?"

Chuck turned and poked his head into the van "What did you say?"

"I asked you how stupid you were. I bet you gotta dig deep to find your IQ."

"Hey, you better shut up or things'll get really hard for you."

"That's what your Momma said last time I was with her."

It was another of Oscar's "come on, let's go" act, and Chuck was falling for it.

He gripped both sides of the van door opening, ready to hoist himself in. "I'm gonna crush your sorry −" he started to say, but a hand slapped down hard on his shoulder and pulled him out.

Instead of Chuck, a cinder block landed inside.

Flex poked his head in. "No time for games this morning, Mr. ATF." And he slid the door shut.

* * *

The van jerked to a stop. We'd travelled about ten minutes, without hitting any level, paved road which meant we were still in the middle of nowhere and totally screwed.

I edged close to Oscar. "We'll have to make a run for it."

"No shit, Sherlock," he replied.

Apparently still a little cranky from last night.

Chuck opened the sliding door, brandishing a shotgun. "Get on out."

Oscar glanced over at me. "After you, Princess."

Very cranky.

We stepped out into a narrow passage, similar to a back alley but instead of buildings on either side, there were sheer rock walls.

With a pistol held by his side, Flex met up with us at the front of the van. "Your car's on up ahead."

From behind, Chuck prodded me along with the barrel of his shotgun.

"Wanna watch that?" I said, feeling a little cranky myself now. Eminent doom will do that to a person.

Chuck laughed. "We wanna make sure you make it to the drop off point."

They marched us into a miniature Hollywood Bowl-type enclosure, sheer rock walls surrounding us on all sides, the area inside a large grassy slope leading down to a natural rock platform. It seemed to serve as a stage of some sort because on the slope, wooden benches had been placed in row after row, grouped on either side of a wide, middle aisle. It was the setup usually reserved for spiritual retreats and vigorous renditions of *Kumbaya*. A pervasive darkness fell like a large backdrop behind the platform.

My rental car was positioned on stage with two light stands shining brightly onto it. Drako waited next to a camera set on a tripod. Chuck led us down the center aisle and up a gravel ramp to the stage where Drako met us.

"Beautiful, isn't it? Last testaments before you go. Nothing big. I need a small show of appreciation to the Major for his hospitality." He handed me a piece of paper. "I jotted down a few words."

I scanned the paper and noted key words like inspiring, humanitarianism and godly. "Seriously?" I said.

"Do this and they're gonna let you go, man."

"Nobody's getting let go," I said. "Since when do you need a gun to get a performance?"

Flex stepped up. "Hell, I told you he wouldn't do it."

"Let me talk to him," Drako said.

"No, we're gonna go ahead and do this our way."

Flex grabbed my hand and wrenched it behind my back. Searing pain coursed through my bent wrist. I felt a thin band zip tight. He quickly repeated the process with my other hand and linked the two together. Chuck slammed Oscar against the car and gave him the same treatment.

"But I need this last part," Drako said to Flex. "Otherwise I have no ending."

Flex grinned back. "Don't you worry. We'll give you an ending." He opened the back door. "Get in. Y'all going for a ride." He made a skipping motion of one hand off the other and whistled as the hand dropped toward the ground. He glanced at Drako. "That good enough for you?"

Drako pursed his lips and then nodded. "I can work with that." He headed back toward the camera.

I remembered Flex's words from last night. Eyeing the dark drop-off, I wasn't so wrong about that foreshadowing thing after all.

"You don't have to do this." I said. "We won't tell anyone. I promise."

"I know you won't." He pushed Oscar in and shoved me after him. "Did ya' bring the cinder block?" He said to Chuck.

"No."

"Hell, do I gotta do everything around here? Watch 'em," Flex said and started the hike up the slope to where the van was parked.

I shifted my hands toward Oscar and whispered. "Can you get these off?"

"No, man. They gotta be cut off."

"Try."

"Come on, Chief. I know about these things."

I lay back in the seat and tried to think of something, anything. "Hey, Chuck. You don't honestly think this is going to work?"

He scowled at me. "Yeah? What's not to work? You two took a wrong turn and drove off this here cliff into the quarry below. What's so hard about that?"

I could see Flex returning down the slope with the cinder block already. "There's going to be an investigation afterward. You don't think a cinder block doesn't look suspicious?"

Flex let the block fall onto the platform with a loud chunk. "What y'all talking about?"

"Nothing," Chuck said. "Let's get this over with."

Flex slammed the door, so I yelled out the open driver side window. "It isn't going to look like an accident. Oscar and I in the back seat, our hands tied behind our backs, cinder block on the accelerator? If you want it to look like two people taking a wrong turn, you have to rethink things."

Flex ignored me, but Chuck pawed the platform with his boot. "Hey, Flex. Major King said we had to make it look like an accident, didn't he?"

"Yeah," Flex answered. "That's what we're doing."

"Well…" Chuck leaned a hand on the car. "They got cuffs on."

"No one's going to find 'em before they're all rotted anyway."

"Hey, Chuck." I yelled. "Ask him about the cinder block."

"Shut up." Flex jerked open the driver door and laid the block on the front floorboard. "He ain't listening to you."

"Why not put us both up front?"

"I ain't stupid," Flex leaned in, slipped the key in the ignition and started the car.

"You've got a gun," I said. "Besides where can we go. The van is blocking the exit."

"Maybe he's got a point," Chuck said.

"Yeah?" Flex shot back. "Who's in charge here? Huh? Who's in charge?"

"You are, Flex, but Major King's sore already about what you did." Chuck ran his hand through his hair. "We can't screw this up."

Flex stared out into the void. I hoped he didn't realize all he had to do was put the car in Drive? We'd creep over the edge as sure as George Constantinesco invented the torque converter.

I learned that from Top Gear.

With a glance at us, he pulled Chuck off to the side. They conferred for a few minutes before Flex returned to the car and stuck his head in. "If you don't do what I say…" he unsheathed Betty and held the knife up in front of my face, "…I won't be caring whether it looks like an accident. Understand? Now, get out."

When we were out of the car and on stage, Flex sliced off the cuffs. "Okay, get in front," he said, avoiding eye contact.

As I rubbed my wrists to get the circulation flowing, Oscar took the initiative and jumped into the driver's seat. "I'll drive."

Flex grabbed the steering wheel. "Only driving you're gonna be doin' is straight ahead. Got that?" He pointed at me, but spoke to Chuck. "Take him on around and be sure he don't buckle up." As Chuck dragged me to the other side, Flex motioned to Drako. "You want your shot? You're gonna get one chance at it."

"Yeah, man." Drako nodded. "I'm ready. I'm ready."

I thought Oscar was a little too eager getting back in the car. I wanted to delay things as much as possible. I had no Plan B yet. "Hey, what good is filming us going over the edge?" I stumbled a bit to slow Chuck. "You won't be able to use it," I yelled to Drako. "First degree murder won't play well at the Academy Awards."

"Don't worry," Drako said, aiming the camera. "I've got enough to edit around."

"Not what I was thinking."

Chuck shoved me in the passenger seat and slammed the door.

Flex stepped back and leveled his gun at us. "All right, then. All ya' have to do is put the car in drive and press the gas. Understand?"

Oscar nodded. He shot me a quick glance and said under his breath. "Don't worry, Chief. I got this." He put the car in reverse.

"Whoa. Whoa. Whoa!" Flex leapt forward and pressed his gun against

Oscar's head. "Did we already forget?"

"I was going to back it up a little to get a running start. You want us to make the water, don't you?" Oscar said.

The gerbil wheels turned and soon enough Flex nodded. "All right, but nice and easy like."

Oscar backed up the slope with Flex and Chuck pacing us on either side. Half way up the slope, Flex patted the fender. "Okay, that's far enough."

Oscar pressed the brake and put the car into Drive.

I whispered to Oscar, "When you said you got this, you meant you had a plan?"

"Actually, I was waiting for some divine inspiration."

"Okay." Flex stepped back and raised his gun. "Floor it now or I shoot you where y'all sit." Before I could really get pissed at Oscar, Flex slapped a hand on his shoulder as if he'd just been stung. "Yowww. Sunuvabitch."

Chuck took a step toward him. "What's amatter, Flex?"

This time I heard it coming. A quick whizz and Flex jerked his head back, a red gash appearing above his eye. The gun fell off to the side.

"Good enough for me." Oscar mashed the accelerator. We flew down the slope and up the ramp, but instead of heading straight over the side, he swung the wheel hard and drifted left across the platform. Drako dove out of the way, but the camera was not so lucky. We connected hard with it and the two light stands, shattering all into countless pieces and sending the bowl into darkness. The car bounced off the left edge of the platform and grass churned behind us as Oscar accelerated again.

"Where are you going?" I yelled.

"Hell if I know." He switched on the car lights.

Oscar hung another left and sped up the side of the enclosure. Flex and Chuck sprinted up the middle aisle, their guns blinking bright flashes in the darkness. I ducked down as bullets plinked stars across the windshield. A blast from the shotgun exploded out the back window. Oscar clipped an outcropping as we swung another left at the top of the bowl.

"Don't count on getting that deposit back," Oscar yelled.

"Ya' think?"

Ahead, the only exit was blocked by Flex's van.

Oscar glanced over. "We bail out here."

"What?"

"You wanted a plan? Bail out."

The exit and the van rushed toward us, and I didn't give it any more thought. I jerked open my door, rolled out, and checked up against the rock wall, staying low. The car swung wide, aiming toward Flex and Chuck. High beams flashed on blinding them.

Oscar was still in the car.

Chuck's shotgun roared blotting out one headlight. Oscar floored it and sped toward both of them. Flex dodged the front fender, but the car's rear quarter panel connected with Chuck and bounced him hard into the benches.

The car jerked right, aiming down toward the rock stage. It accelerated away from Flex who had picked himself up and squeezed off round after round. If Oscar could make the stage, maybe he could jump out there. But something was wrong. The car didn't slow. It sped across the platform. The engine whined as it left solid ground, and its taillights arced up and dropped down over the edge, out of sight. A few seconds later, a faraway splash.

I lay on the ground, my breath coming in sharp gasps, my heart pounding hard in my chest. Unlike many of the things I'd experienced lately, this was very real. They had killed Oscar, and I was next if they found me.

Flex yelled for Chuck. "You okay?"

"Damn!" Chuck yelled back. "I think he busted my arm."

"Come on. Let's get outta here."

Drako ran up to them. "What about my camera? Who's paying for my camera?"

As their confab went on, I crawled along the rock wall, looking for the exit. In my favor, they thought we had both been in the car.

"Fuck your camera." Flex said. "We're going back to camp."

Shadows drifted toward me, but I kept moving forward.

"Woooweeee!" Flex shouted. "Did you see that thing go? Damn!"

The wall curved out and I could see the nose of the van. I kept moving, edging along the side. As I was about to clear it, a figure materialized ahead of me.

I froze.

Voices closed in from behind.

I had nowhere to go.

A flashlight blinked on and off. It was Mary.

"Come on." She grabbed my hand and pulled me back into a small crevice in the wall.

A portion of it had eroded away and provided a way out. I followed her, matching each handhold and foothold. We climbed a few dozen feet where we reached a small ledge. She pulled me close, holding her small hand over my mouth. A faint scent of vanilla washed over me and felt her cool breath on my cheek.

"What are we gonna tell the Major?" Chuck said, his voice cracking from directly below.

"Hell, man. We tell him the sons of bitches had an accident just like he wanted."

"What about my arm?"

"And my camera?" Drako added.

The van door slid open and the interior light flashed on.

"Y'all quit your whining. I almost got my eye put out." Flex wiped blood from the side of his face.

"What you suppose that was?" Chuck said.

"Maybe a bat diving around. I don't know. Get on in."

The van door slid closed and the engine roared to life. Headlights flashed on and the van slowly reversed out of the hollow. Soon, the sound of the engine melted away into the darkness.

Mary removed her hand.

"How did you know we'd be here?" I noticed we remained pressed together.

I guess she felt something, too. She cleared her throat and stepped back. "Well, Flex tells me everything."

"You sure took your time."

"I was having trouble with the distance." She produced a slingshot from her back pocket. "Let's go. We have to get to the highway before daylight."

"And then what?"

She shrugged. "I don't know about you, but I'm going home."

Chapter Seventeen

"Do you have room?"

"Where you going?" The burly trucker inspected Mary from underneath the hood of his eighteen wheeler.

"To Vegas."

"I'm headed south." He laid down his screwdriver. "Maybe I can help."

From my vantage point behind the cab of an adjacent eighteen wheeler, I could see the slight inhale and straightened posture of a hoisted gut.

"I've got a friend. Can you take two of us?"

He lifted the bill of his gimme cap back with a crooked finger. "If she's as cute as you, darlin'." The hat displayed in simple bold lettering "My Wife Said No!" Little doubt who did the shopping in that family.

The guy was putting on the charm. He lowered the hood with a resounding chunk, his Virgin Mary hood ornament vibrating from the impact.

Mary winked. "Maybe not as cute, but friendly as they come."

Why did I take offense at that?

She ran her hand through her long, blonde hair. That was my cue. When I appeared from around the corner, the man's eyes clouded. "Sorry, little lady." His face reddened, he quickly climbed up into his cab and slammed the door.

"Hey, what would Jesus do?" I yelled up at him. Maybe the next time I saw the Big Guy, I'd ask.

I caught up with Mary who was already heading for the truck stop restaurant. "Told you it wouldn't work," I said.

"He looked like a nice man," she said, without looking over.

"You've been camping too long."

"We'll try again."

"First I need to make a call," I said.

Now she looked. "You don't want to do that."

"How do you know who I'm going to call?"

"Back at the camp, they think you're dead."

Okay, she did know. "Look, they just killed my friend."

"I know and it's horrible. And you want justice, but trust me, let them think that you're dead at least until you get out of the area. Then you can call the police."

I slowed at a phone booth outside the restaurant. I wanted to call now. They had killed Oscar. Sure I didn't know the guy, but for some strange reason, I felt like they'd taken somebody I'd known my entire life. It ate at me and I needed to do something about it. I fished in my pocket for change I didn't have. Mary placed her hand on mine.

"By now King knows I'm gone," she said. "It won't be safe for either one of us."

"But the police will protect us," I said.

"For someone in your line of work, you sure are naïve." She turned to go inside.

"Wait." I grabbed the door. "I saw something else when they brought us in, under the tarp in Flex's truck."

"I know. Flex told me about that, too." She removed my hand from the door handle. "I want them to pay for everything they've done and to make sure they don't do anything else, but now's not the time."

"I'll call the FBI instead."

"Sure, you do that." She opened the door. "I'm going to get something to eat." With that, she went inside.

I never liked negotiating without knowing at least a little about the players involved. Here, I was outside my element, with no information and hungry as hell. Okay, I didn't know the local law enforcement. And maybe the FBI could wait, too. Putting things off until later today would hardly matter. As soon as I got back to Los Angeles, I'd contact my lawyer and let him handle things – Oscar's death, the attempt on my life, the explosives.

I followed Mary inside and found her already seated at a table.

"Shouldn't we be keeping a low profile?" I said as I sat across from her. "You know, in case?"

"You're the one who's dead. Not me."

"What if the police–?"

"Just don't make a scene and we'll be fine."

"And you know that because?"

"Wow, if I knew you'd be this much trouble, I would've left you back at the quarry." She raised her menu. "Hmmm. This all looks so good. I haven't had real food for months."

From that first transformation in my room at the lodge and then with her selfless act of deliverance at the quarry, she both surprised and amazed me. She possessed a self-assurance that seemed to transcend her age, which I pegged at late twenties, and had proven she could play any role – from the Stepford wife to the quavering waif to the hot chick jonsing for a hit of nicotine. I couldn't help but wonder if I'd been introduced to the real Mary yet.

"Thanks again for what you did," I said.

She pursed her lips, still looking over the menu. "I was a little worried he was too far away."

"Why did you help?"

She glanced up. "You helped me make the bed." Then back down at the menu. "I'm just sorry I couldn't help your friend, too."

"I should've remembered that door was stuck." I shook my head. "I knew him for just a few days, but he always seemed to be there to help me. And, this morning, he did it again."

Mary reached out and squeezed my hand. "He must have had his reasons."

If she only knew what her words meant. Honestly, I didn't want to dwell on the fact Oscar had died to help me. My biggest sacrifice to date was giving up chocolate for Lent. What did that say about me?

"So, what are you having?" Mary said.

"Pancakes, maybe. You?"

Mary's eyes focused over my shoulder toward the entrance and stiffened. It had to be Flex. They'd hunted us down and were heading for our table. Before I could overreact, a slight smile graced her lips.

"That's so sweet," she said.

I glanced back. The waitress led four women toward a table near ours. I didn't give much thought as to why they might be so special, but the little girl sitting across the aisle from us clarified things.

"Mommy, why are those men dressed like ladies?"

You'd think I'd have a better eye for those things considering where I worked. Mary said hello as they passed.

"Good morning, dear," one said in a Monty Pythonish falsetto.

On closer inspection, I could see the hint of whiskers fighting through heavy makeup. Another passed who easily topped six feet five. She walked with the square gait that men use when walking in high heels. I'd seen Russell Crowe try to pull off Marilyn Monroe at that Halloween party. It hadn't been pretty. Neither was this.

A muscular black woman rocking three inch, yellow platform shoes and a thin Asian in a tasteful sundress brought up the rear. As she passed by, she stumbled slightly and a broach dropped from her dress, landing on the floor next to the little girl's table.

The little girl nudged it with her foot and then bent down and scooped it up.

"What do you have, Tammy?" her mother asked.

The little girl showed it to her. "Can I keep it?"

"Where did you get that?"

"I found it on the floor."

Mary must have noticed, too. "I think one of them might have dropped it," she said, pointing to the table of new arrivals.

Mom took the broach from her daughter, glanced over at the newcomers and simply laid it near the edge of her table.

The little girl pleaded. "Can I keep it?"

"Eat your oatmeal," Mom said.

Mary cleared her throat and stared me down. "Well?"

"Me?" I said.

"That would be the nice thing to do," she said.

I chewed the inside of my lip. "Pardon me," I said to the mom. "Uh, if you would like me to return that for you?"

"Yes, by all means, please." She picked it up and held it out like it was contaminated. "I wouldn't feel comfortable."

"It won't be a problem." I took the broach from her and muttered, "They aren't contagious." I don't know. Maybe I was in a mood, but I had to say it.

Her face deepened to beet red. "I… I didn't mean… I didn't… That's not…"

She couldn't find the words, but her little girl knew how to get the message across. She stuck her tongue out at me.

With the broach in hand, I approached their table and tapped the Asian woman on the shoulder. "I think you dropped this."

She patted her chest where the broach should have been. "Oh my God! I didn't notice."

"You're a doll," her tall girlfriend said with a deep timbre to her voice. "I'm Marcia."

"Nice to meet you, Marcia. Price. Buddy Price."

"This is Aja who I believe will now be a friend of yours for life."

"Yes, I will never, ever, forget this." Aja popped up and laid a big kiss on my cheek. "Ever."

The Monty Python aficionado joined in the conversation. "And I'm Chris-Tina and this is Lacreisha."

Lacreisha wagged a finger at Chris-Tina. "Make up your mind, girl. Is it Chris or is it Tina? You can't do this forever."

"Today it's both," Chris-Tina replied, her nose held high. "Don't pay her any mind," she said to me. "She always acts like she's got a broomstick stuck up–"

Marcia cleared her throat. "Let's not go there, ladies."

Aja took my hand. "Anyway, thank you again."

"You ladies have a nice breakfast," I said and returned to my booth.

"That was very nice of you," Mary said, clapping her hands lightly as I sat. "For the past six months, all I've heard is hate. It's nice to see some civility for a change."

The waitress came over and we ordered. I got my pancakes, Mary the bacon, eggs and toast. We were halfway through our breakfast when things got dicey.

A group of four teenagers were brought in and seated in the booth directly behind us. With their baby faces, relatively large size and letter jackets, I guessed high school football players. At the time, I didn't pay much attention to them. Typical kids, a little loud, but no big deal, that is until one of them noticed the women sitting nearby.

The first remark wasn't too loud, meant primarily for the gang, but it was loud enough for me to hear.

One nudged his friend with an elbow. "Look over there." He cocked his head.

Mary had her back to their booth, but I could see from her expression that she heard, too.

His friend looked, shrugged, and did a double-take. Word travelled fast in harsh whispers that I couldn't pick up. Soon, they all giggled like a bunch of girls talking about their latest crush. It didn't take long before the shared private joke went public.

The lanky one on the end turned around and leaned toward the women who had already been served their food. "Excuse me. You know, you're insulting the cook."

Aja looked over and answered. "I'm sorry. Insulting who?"

"The sausage they serve here is good. You didn't have to go and bring your own."

The boys' laughter filled the diner like a bunch of braying donkeys.

Aja slowly turned away, a look of horror in her eyes. Marcia started to rise from her seat, but Aja grabbed her arm and pulled her back down. "It's not worth it," she said.

Mary had other ideas.

She turned and tapped one of the boys on the shoulder. "I think that was very disrespectful of you. Why don't you all grow up?"

"And why don't you go fuck yourself?" he answered.

He happened to be the biggest at the table, which, in his mind, probably afforded him certain rights and privileges normal-sized people didn't have. That included hurling profanity at a perfectly wonderful human being to whom lately I had found myself extremely attracted.

"Nice one, Ricky," another said.

I tended not to agree. "That's the only way *you'd* ever get any," I said. Like with Ed at Club One, the words came out without me giving them much thought.

"What did you say?" Ricky slowly emerged from the booth.

I didn't have time to feel intimidated, besides, he was a kid. I clarified my previous statement. "I said the only way you're ever going to get any is if you fucked yourself." I slid out of my booth as well.

"Buddy?" Mary said, gripping my arm to hold me back, but I pulled away.

"And while you're at it, like she said, how about a little respect?" I pointed over at Marcia and the crew. "Is that too much to ask?"

Ricky placed his hands on my chest and gave me a little nudge. "And what are you going to do about it?"

Mary started out of the booth, but another one in the bunch held out an arm and blocked her exit.

"Maybe you need to be taught a lesson about respect." Ricky pushed hard this time, and I stumbled back a step. "Maybe we'll teach your girl a lesson, too."

I'm basically a peaceful guy. I can't remember ever having been in a fist fight in my life. And, frankly, if I had, I most definitely wouldn't have picked a fight with a guy twice my size. But one is not always afforded such luxuries in life, especially when it comes to protecting the dignity of a woman.

"Whaddya think of that?" Ricky said.

I knew exactly what I thought. I kicked him in the balls.

Two of his friends were on me before I could do any more damage, not that I was capable of that. They tossed me onto the floor next to Ricky who still rolled around, clutching his family jewels.

The tall one yanked me to my feet. His first punch glanced off the side of my head. The second one never arrived. A stylishly manicured hand intercepted the blow from behind. Marcia wrenched his arm around, grabbed him by the hair and pulled back. Aja appeared and delivered a strong sidekick that sent his friend bouncing off the booth.

One remained; all alone staring at his fallen brethren. He raised his hands up in desperate surrender as Mary held her slingshot cocked and loaded with a salt shaker.

"I'm sorry. I'm sorry. We didn't mean it," he pleaded.

Marcia shoved him toward his fallen comrades. "Damn right, you didn't."

I fell back into friendly territory as the boys regrouped.

"Wouldn't you say it's time to leave?" Chris-Tina said in her high falsetto which made it that much more embarrassing.

Ricky struggled to his feet, still groaning and gripping his groin. "The hell with you. Let's go."

They limped out of the restaurant to scattered applause from the other patrons.

Mary rushed up to me and gave me a hug. "Are you okay?" She pulled back and stroked my hair.

I don't remember answering.

The restaurant tilted and everything went dark.

* * *

I stared at playing cards laid out on a green felt table, a Three-Ace-Eight, all hearts. I looked around in a smoke-filled room. Four other players flanked the table in a game of Texas Hold 'Em. Across from me, I could have sworn was Albert Einstein or at least a man whose hair had never seen a bottle of hair conditioner. To his right, a man wearing a cowboy hat, to his left, a man in full military uniform sporting a dark beard. I couldn't tell exactly who. They all looked the same in those old pictures. However, I couldn't mistake the player sitting next to me – God.

He puffed on a Swisher Sweet and gave me a sideways wink. "I'll be just a second."

"Two hundred thousand," Einstein said pushing in a large stack of purple chips.

No one at the table seemed especially surprised or worried that I had manifested at the table. At least, that was what I assumed I had done. Maybe that was a common occurrence here, wherever here might be.

God pushed all his chips into the middle. "All in, Al."

So it was Einstein after all.

"And I don't have time for any of your theoretical positing," He said. "Put up or shut up."

"The odds, this time they are in my favor." Einstein pushed his remaining chips in with the rest. "Aces and Eights," Einstein said flipping his cards. "I have you this time."

"Dead man's hand." God flipped over his cards, revealing a flush.

Einstein's face turned red and he pushed away from the table. "No, you can't win forever."

"Who at this table defined insanity as doing the same thing over and over again expecting different results?" God pulled the chips over.

"Next time I *will* win." Einstein stood, shook his fist and marched away.

"He's impossible," God said. "The man thinks he knows everything."

"What am I doing here?" I picked up a wayward chip and rubbed my fingernail along its perforated edge.

On the far end of the room was the bar where Einstein and the others had retreated for drinks. Near them, large doors swung open and bustle of activity – loud talking, ringing bells – flooded in.

"What is this place? A casino? What are *you* doing here?"

"Now, Buddy. You know what I say about judging others."

"Am I dead? Really dead this time?"

"No, take a couple of aspirin when you wake up." God smiled and patted my hand. "That's all you need."

"Is it the Jeremiah Box? Is this another reminder?"

"Unlike Mr. Einstein," God said with a sideways nod toward Einstein, "have you ever thought that maybe what you're *not* doing is driving you insane?"

With that, he pushed. I felt a rush of wind as I fell back.

* * *

I came to in a hazy world with Miss Nurse Universe hovering over me once again. I'd been here before. Finally, some place familiar. I understood. All of this had been a bad dream. I had never left the ER. I reached out to grab those huge gazangas...

Weird. They don't feel right. Mushy, like foam rubber. When I squeezed again, the stylus ripped from the record.

Marcia removed my hands from her breasts. "I think he's coming to," she said over her shoulder and leaned in closer. "Is that anyway to treat a lady?" but she said it with a smile. She slid a strong arm behind my back and helped me up to a sitting position.

"Welcome back, Sleeping Beauty," Aja said, poking her head above me.

Chris-Tina hovered in front. To my left, the world flashed at high speed. I jerked up in my seat.

"Where the hell are we?" I shouted.

"Mary?" Marcia said over her shoulder. "We need you."

Mary appeared over the back of the seat next to Aja. "Hey, Buddy."

"I think we should switch now," Marcia said.

They traded seats within what I quickly recognized as a minivan.

"What's going on?" I said.

"We're going to Las Vegas, silly," Aja said. "We're going to put on a show."

Marcia joined her in back as Mary slid in next to me. "It's more like an audition," Marcia said. "Nothing definite yet."

Aja disappeared from view for a moment and reappeared wearing a Carmen Miranda-style fruit hat that scraped the ceiling of the van. "Isn't it exciting?" she said.

"Slow down everyone. " Mary said, taking my hand. "Buddy, they go through L.A. so they can drop you off. Don't worry."

"No." I shook my head. "I'm not worried."

"Are you feeling okay now, honey?" Aja sighed and stroked my hair. "You're so lucky to have a man who stands up for you," she said, looking at Mary.

Marcia pulled Aja away. "Let's give the two love birds a little privacy."

I shifted in my seat as they disappeared from view.

"Are you feeling bad again?" Mary said. "Do you want some water?" Her eyes swallowed me up.

"No, only a headache. Par for the course these days. It'll go away." I shifted again, this time not because of the seat, but because of what I was about to say. "Sorry about that."

"Sorry about what?"

"That little love bird comment. I didn't say anything to her to make her think–"

"Of course, you didn't."

"And I don't want you to feel uncomfort–"

"I'm not uncomfortable. People like to make assumptions."

I looked out the window, but after a few minutes, the streaking scenery started to make me dizzy. I laid my head back.

"You can use me." She raised her shoulder slightly.

"Thanks," I said, trying to bring my heart rate down to under a hundred.

I closed my eyes, and after a few minutes, I found myself drifting away.

As I did, Mary's soft voice asked, "You want me to wake you up when we get to Los Angeles?"

I may have said yes.

***

I woke up in the same position, but with Mary's head resting on top of mine. I inhaled, enjoying the sweet scent of her hair. My headache had subsided, but I felt bad nonetheless. I still had a decision to make.

"Mary?" I brushed her arm.

Her shoulder moved and I raised my head.

"Hello, sleepyhead." The stylus ripped again. It was Marcia. "Have a nice nap?"

I retreated back onto my side of that imaginary line. "Will you quit doing that?"

"Doing what?" she said.

"Never mind. Where's Mary?"

She nodded toward the front passenger seat where Mary snoozed. "She needed to nap." Marcia's gaze touched on me and darted away.

"Something wrong?" I said.

She remained silent at first, then like water coming to a boil, she bubbled up and overflowed. "What do you think?"

Vague memories of the ex-Mrs. Price invaded my head. A little voice screamed I should already know what was wrong, but, like back then, I still drew a blank. "Let's make it easy for both of us, and you tell me what I'm supposed to think."

Marcia let out an exasperated huff. "Men."

"Good for you. How about a hint for the Neanderthal here?"

She grabbed my hand. "Why aren't you going to Las Vegas?"

"What?"

"She wants you to go. She'd never say it, but I know. I can tell."

I cocked an eyebrow. "Because of your feminine intuition?"

"Well, it doesn't take a rocket scientist."

"I said something wrong?"

"It's what you didn't say," Marcia said, still huffing.

"When I say something, it's the wrong thing. When I keep my mouth shut, I'm still in the doghouse."

"You like her, don't you?" she said.

"Well, sure." I mumbled. "I mean, we only met a couple of days ago, but…"

"She saved your life. Not her words exactly, but she told me."

"So that obligates me?"

"I can't believe I spent so much time playing for the other team. Go with her." Marcia fixed me with a steady gaze. "Is there something more important?"

It took only a few seconds for me to determine that it wasn't such a hard question to answer after all.

Chapter Eighteen

"I will miss you, Buddy Price." Aja held me tight.

We congregated outside an off-Strip motel called The Two Jacks. Mary had already said her goodbyes and waited in the backseat of our taxi.

"You need to let the poor man go," Marcia said and pried her friend loose.

"I know. I know." Aja stepped back. "Linked for life," she said while holding her hands together in a little heart shape over her chest.

Marcia gave me a hug as well and then held a card out for me. "You're part of the club, now. This has my cell. If you need anything at all, like advice on how to treat a woman, call." She choked back a sob. "Oh, I'm going to cry now." She turned and fanned her face. "Go on before I really make a scene."

I didn't want to do that so I ducked into the cab.

"I think they like you," Mary said, squeezing my arm.

"Well, you know, I do have that effect on women."

She squeezed again and laughed. Somehow it reassured me about my decision to come with her.

We headed north on I-15 and then east toward what she said was part of North Las Vegas, to a street called Thistle Down. From the looks of it, the street had never known a thistle or any other living thing that relied on water. This is where she had grown up, she said, until she ran away from home at fifteen, a year after her mother's passing. She'd eventually returned to Vegas but hadn't set foot at home.

The street was in bad shape, too, potholed asphalt bordered by broken sidewalks when there were any. Many houses not only had cars parked in front but major appliances as well.

Mary leaned over the front seat and pointed for the benefit of the driver. "At the end, on the right."

Our destination stood out from the rest of the homes and not in a bad way. There it was at the end of the street, on a small cul-de-sac, a seeming residential oasis. It featured a bright, green lawn with a large fountain situated in the center. Two small children drifted back and forth on a swing set.

As we neared, I noticed that the idyllic picture had been a mirage after all. When the cab pulled up to the curb, I stepped out onto an artificial lawn, its long-range, brilliant green having morphed into a close-up dirty olive. The fountain proved equally unimpressive; no water flowed from the stork's broken beak perched in the middle. The swing set was rusty and the shriek of the metal chains stopped when the kids jumped to the ground and ran to Mom who had appeared outside the front door. They clutched at a large, imposing woman who watched us with unbridled skepticism, arms folded under massive breasts.

Mary grabbed for my hand. I knew no matter how brave she had acted in the van when she first told me of her sister – how she needed to see her to make amends, how it was something she had to do – she wanted me to lead the way.

"Ready?" I said.

She nodded so we proceeded up the driveway, across the chipped cement walkway and up to the first step of the small slab that served as the porch. We stopped there and faced her sister, with the children hiding behind her tree-trunk legs. I squeezed Mary's hand and let go. The rest was up to her.

"Hello, Alice," she said, her voice carrying a slight vibrato.

Alice, who appeared much older than Mary, maintained her composure, but her eyes darted back and forth between us. Strands of blonde hair mixed with gray framed a tired, oval face. Large dark circles under her eyes reinforced the theme. I'm sure we didn't present a pretty picture either. A little splash of water in the restaurant bathroom wouldn't wash off much of the hard road we'd just travelled.

"Hello, Mary. It's been a while." She said this with a resignation which I guessed registered at least a 7.9 on the despair scale. She pushed open the front door and shooed the kids, a boy and a girl, inside. Then, turned back to us. "Well?"

We followed, entering into a living room which had one worn afterthought of a stuffed chair and nothing else. We hung back to let her lead the way through the den which appeared to be the room where the family lived and where, at least, there was furniture. Toys were strewn about the floor between matching recliners fronting a big screen TV. A bright yellow sofa positioned between them provided some balance to the walls, which were covered with dark wood paneling.

Alice directed us into the kitchen where we sat at a creaky wooden table covered with plastic, sporting green fern-like designs. She busied herself at the refrigerator where she extracted a large pitcher holding a bright purple liquid. The two children appeared at the kitchen door. The boy seemed slightly older, or maybe he was just big for his age. He looked at us as he gravitated toward his mother. His sister followed.

"Who wants some?" Alice said.

The kids crowded next to her and she gave each a filled glass. She placed hands on hips. "What do you say?"

The boy screamed, "Yay, Kool-Aid."

His sister took the more politic route. "Thank you," she said with a little curtsy.

"Grey-Jay!"

His next words were drowned out in his drink.

"I think that was a thank you," Mary said with a little smile.

Alice approached the table, her children following close behind, faces deep in their glasses, but their eyes still watching our every move. She pulled them over to stand beside her. "This is Maggie and Grey, Junior. We call him Grey-Jay. Say hi to your Aunt Mary."

I couldn't help but smile at the look of wonder that crossed their little faces. At first, they melted back against their mother, but Maggie soon proved the more adventurous of the two and took a step forward.

"Pleased to meet you," Mary said, offering her hand.

Maggie's boldness ended at handholding so Mary transitioned nicely and pointed to me. "And this is my friend, Buddy."

I could see that Maggie wasn't impressed. She focused on her new aunt instead. "I have a dollhouse in my room."

"That's wonderful. I had one when I was about your age, too."

Grey-Jay, apparently energized by his sister's bravery, stepped forward. "It's my room, too. And I have a Transformer there. It's Optimus Prime. Wanna see him?"

"Sure," Mary replied with a sweet smile.

Grey-Jay streaked from the kitchen.

"Don't run in the house," Alice yelled.

Maggie chased after him. "Wait. No fair. She wanted to see my dollhouse first."

"No matter how much you tell them, they never listen." Alice looked back to her sister, her features melting from overtaxed mother to concerned sibling. "Where have you been?" she said and sat.

Mary's face reddened. "How's Daddy doing?"

"It would have been nice," Alice looked away, "if you had at least called once in a while."

"Alice, is he…?"

She looked back. "Yes. Six months ago."

Mary inhaled sharply.

"I couldn't find you, to tell you," Alice said.

Tears began to stream down Mary's cheeks. Her shoulders sagged slightly. Seconds later, I found Mary in my arms. She held me tight, the wetness of her cheek brushing my neck. I let her stay there, let her work it out. Normally, I get an allergic reaction to raw emotions, especially when it comes to tears and women. This time, for some reason, it felt okay.

A high-pitched scream arose from the back of the house. Serious shouting ensued. Alice cleared her throat, placed hands on knees and pushed herself to her feet. "I'll be right back," she said and left to referee.

Mary released her grip around my neck.

"You going to be all right?" I asked.

She wiped her eyes with the backs of her hands. "Of course."

"I'm sorry about your father. I can see how it would be tough, you not being here, I mean, you would have been here, but you were somewhere else, but then you're here and she tells you. Tough, you know, that's… that's…" I gave up. Like I said, tears and women.

She sniffed. "He's why I left in the first place."

"I don't understand."

"I'm just mad I didn't get a chance to tell the bastard off."

Chapter Nineteen

Maggie and Grey-Jay quickly assimilated their new aunt into their lives and had dragged her out front to play. I was left to my own devices so I crashed on the sofa in the den and was out within minutes. I needed it.

Minutes or hours later, I don't know, I woke to the clink of glass. A largish man hovered over me, holding two beers in his hand.

"Beer?"

I took it. "Thanks."

"I'm Grey."

"Buddy. Buddy Price." I pulled myself up to a sitting position and shook his hand.

"The little woman says you're travelling with Mary."

"You could say that."

He collapsed into one of the recliners which sagged with the man's weight. From the wear and tear of the chair and the positioning of the side table that contained the remote, an issue of Sports Illustrated along with a few other magazines, and an empty beer bottle, you could tell that was Dad's territory. He searched in a side pocket and lifted out a TV Guide.

"In town long?"

I didn't get a chance to answer before Alice yelled from the kitchen. "Grey, I need you."

"Never fails," he muttered to himself.

"Grey!" she shouted louder.

"Can't live without me."

"Yeah, I know how that is." I said without the slightest idea of what that meant.

"Coming." He pushed from the recliner. The chair creaked and moaned in complaint, and after a brief struggle, let him leave. "We'll talk later."

I took a long drink of the beer. It felt good going down, and I hoped more would be available. I'd had a rough few days. I started to take another drink when a growling noise grabbed my attention. Grey-Jay poked his head above the cushioned arm from the other end of the sofa and eyed me. With a red Matchbox car in hand, he proceeded to run it along the arm and up the back of the sofa, adding that strange noise for special effect. He disappeared behind me, I felt the slightest flick of my bristled hair as he passed the car over my head, and then he reappeared by the sofa arm on my side. A chartreuse booger fell halfway from one of his nostrils.

"You got a little thing there, kid." I wiggled my finger under my nose.

He squinted, no doubt wondering what evil trick this stranger was trying to pull on him. He sniffed and drew his hand across his face, snagging part of the offending snot, and then hoovered the rest inside.

We stared each other down for a good minute before he broke.

"I had a pet fish once," he said.

"Good for you."

"His name was Buddy, too."

"Good name." I shot him a smile.

"I flushed him down the toilet when he died."

"How do you know it wasn't a girl fish?"

"Because his name was Buddy, duh?"

I conked my forehead with the palm of my hand. "Why didn't I think of that?"

"That *was* stupid."

"You like girls yet?" I asked.

"Ugh, they're gross," he said.

"Too bad. I met the perfect girl for you." I said, thinking back to the little girl at the truck stop restaurant.

"Grey-Jay, time for dinner." Alice stood at the door to the den. "Go wash your hands."

He turned his back to his mom and made a face at me. "Okay, Ma," he said and then turned to skip into the kitchen.

Alice remained at the door. "Is that any way to talk to a child, filling his head with such nonsense?"

I could tell why Grey-Jay was the way he was now. She didn't let him have enough nonsense. I kept my smart mouth shut, doffed my beer toward her and then took a long swig.

Alice shook her head. "You're a lost soul," she said and disappeared back into the kitchen.

I lay back on the sofa trying not to give her comment too much thought. How could she know that after meeting me only a few hours earlier? Not that it wasn't true, but–

"Swimming in a fishbowl." Mary's voice from the other side of the room startled me. She stepped into the room. "I didn't want to interrupt."

"That would be 'two lost souls' to stay true to the song," I said. "I should know. I practically have that entire album's song lyrics memorized."

"Alice used to listen to Pink Floyd a lot, too." She cast her eyes down to the floor and back at me. "Do you think you and I are two lost souls?"

"I think your sister suffers from depression."

"What about you?" Mary asked.

"In the beginning, everyone's a lost soul. It's as you get older, live life, that maybe you get lucky and figure a few things out."

"Have you had enough?" She walked closer to the sofa.

"Hey," I said, holding my arms out from my side. "I'm the guy who gets to save the world, right?"

Mary shrugged her shoulders and proffered a smile. "Ready for dinner?" She held out a hand and led me into the kitchen.

Dinner consisted of meatloaf, mashed potatoes and English peas with a large basket of rolls. I hadn't eaten meatloaf in years. It's not a dish I normally would choose, but Alice did herself proud. Of course, the kids picked at theirs, struggling to swallow each bite. Alice reprimanded them, but it didn't help.

Dinnertime conversation stayed in safe territory, revolving mostly around the children, for Mary's benefit, to catch her up on the years that she had missed. I found out Maggie had an imaginary friend named Geraldine who lived in her room and had tea with her at noon every day. Grey-Jay told everyone about the lizard he'd caught and put in a glass jar out on the back porch and how the next day he came outside to play with it, and it had turned into a stick.

He received a "not during dinner" from Mom for that one. Out of the corner of my eye, I thought I caught a flicker of a smile from Dad. The little guy might have a chance after all.

After dinner, the plates were cleared. Alice filled up bowls with vanilla ice cream and sent Maggie and Grey-Jay with theirs into the den to watch TV. As she returned to the table, I could tell from her expression that the adult conversation was about to begin.

"You would have been okay if you'd stayed. I had it under control," Alice said as she sat.

Mary poked at the ice cream with her spoon.

Alice turned to me. "So, how long have you known each other?"

"A few days," I said.

"And already bringing you home to meet the family? You must be something special."

I grinned. "My mother thought so."

Mary dropped her spoon in her bowl, now providing a delayed answer. "But *I* didn't have it under control."

"What was that, Baby Sister?" Alice said.

"You can be mad at me as much as you want, but you weren't the only victim."

"You shouldn't have left."

"By then you had Grey. All I had was a boyfriend who hit me like–"

"Hey, whatcha say Buddy?" Grey cleared his throat and rose from the table. "How about a beer outside?"

Alice snapped. "He should hear this."

"If it's all the same to you, I know how the story ends." He looked at me. "Sorry." He grabbed his beer and exited through the back door.

"Did you know what you were getting yourself into?" Alice asked me. "I mean, there's not much you can learn about a person in a short period of time."

"Leave him alone," Mary said.

"No, I don't think I will. You come back here after ten years with hardly a word, bringing a perfect stranger around my kids. Well, he's going to hear all there is to know about the acting out, the quitting school, the running away. He's going to hear about all of it."

Mary froze.

"Alice, do you want to know how your sister and I met?" I said.

"Save me the soap opera," she replied. "I'm sure it's like all the rest."

"This one's an original. Long story short, she saved my life. How's that for a soap opera? She risked her life to save mine. She didn't expect anything in return, but she did it anyway because it was the right thing to do. I'm proud to call her my friend. Maybe you should take some time to get to know her again. I've known her two days, and I bet I know her better than you." I stood. "Thank you for dinner. The meatloaf was wonderful."

I took my beer and followed Grey's escape route out back.

* * * *

Later that night, Mary entered the den dressed in a hefty-sized, white nightgown.

"Who's missing their parachute?" I said.

"Oh, this old thing. Don't you think I'm sexy?" She put her hand on her hip, lifted the gown to show a little leg.

"It doesn't do you justice."

I extended Grey's recliner's footrest and tried to get comfortable. Mary had the sofa and she crawled up under the sheet.

"Is everyone all set?" It was Alice in the hallway. Her words fell kinder and gentler than before.

"I think so," I said.

"Well, if you're up early, there are fresh towels in the bathroom around the corner. Cereal is set out on the counter. Milk's in the fridge."

"Thanks," I said.

As Alice turned to go, Mary added, "Good night, Alice."

"Good night, Baby Sister."

She headed down the hall and a few seconds later, that light went out, and there was the click of a door closing.

"Looks like you two are going in the right direction," I said.

"It's a start."

I shifted in the recliner and adjusted my pillow.

Mary spoke again. "Thank you for what you said. You didn't have to get involved."

"Well, let's say I owed you one."

I reached out and flicked off the lamp.

A few moments later, Mary's voice reached out through the darkness. "Flex told me that you talked to Jesus."

"What?"

"Flex said you died and went to heaven and talked to Jesus."

"Well, it was twice that I died, and it was God if you believe all the hype," I said with a yawn, hoping to reduce the melodrama.

"What's Heaven like?"

"Who says that's where I was?"

"You did."

"Maybe I'm crazy and made it all up." I tried to laugh, but it came out like a hiccup instead.

"What if you're not?"

"It's a golf course, it's a poker game, it's a pedestal with an egg on it. You name it, that's what Heaven is."

"It's real." Her voice came from the darkness almost like an appeal.

"Whatever you say."

"What did you say?"

"I said, whatever you say." This time I felt like a jerk for saying it.

"No, when you were there, in heaven. What did you say to God?"

"I asked him for next week's lottery numbers." I hoped for a laugh, but she apparently didn't find that very amusing so I tried again, this time with the truth. "I promised to save the world."

"What have you done so far?"

I peered at her through the dark. "You believe me?"

"I think if you make a promise to God, you should honor it."

"I know. That's what He keeps telling me. But when He comes out in my father's robe, I start to question my sanity."

"What?"

"Nothing," I said. She didn't need to know about that part of the Price history yet.

"What an amazing responsibility," she said. "The future of our world rests in your hands. Our lives depend on what you choose to do."

"Assuming that to be true, it's not all it's cracked up to be."

"You don't believe, do you?"

I was more surprised she had bought into the idea so easily. I felt a pang of guilt over my own doubts so I lied a little with my answer. "No, I believe."

"Promise me you'll follow through."

"Well, I kind of already made that promise, you know."

"But make it to me. I'm here, right here. You can't pass me off as a delusion."

"Yep, you are here."

"Promise me." Her voice had that same hopefulness as when she wanted me to confirm that Heaven was real.

"The world is a messed up place if you haven't noticed," I said.

"I don't think the Major and people like him are going to leave it alone. They'll make things worse. I think you need to do something."

I lay there quietly. I didn't want to promise her. Part of me didn't want to feel that obligation hanging over my head; another part didn't know what the hell I'd do about it anyway. I still wasn't sure that I was sane. That part of the Price history, the part I didn't want her to know about, involved my father spending the last four years of his life living in his robe, talking to himself in the den.

The silence from her side of the room was deafening.

"Okay, Mary, I promise," I said.

She didn't say anything. I thought maybe she didn't believe me, that I had debated the point with myself too long. She'd probably heard too many people in her life make promises that weren't kept. To her, maybe I was one more person on that list.

Sheet rustled and seconds later, I felt a hand on my shoulder and a warm slender body crawled next to me.

Soon, soft lips touched mine erasing all doubt.

Chapter Twenty

The hot water felt good. I stayed there, letting it prickle my skin. I had awoken this morning in a particularly good mood. It had been a long time.

After a good ten minutes, I relented and turned off the faucet. I toweled off, putting back on the same clothes from yesterday, although I did invert the underwear, an old trick I learned from college. I kept things quiet, just in case, as I exited the bathroom. Mary still slept in the recliner, the sheet pulled up to her chin.

In the kitchen, I found that my cereal choices were Count Chocula and Fruit Loops. I opted for coffee which fortunately had been set to kick off at 5:30 and waited for me in a pot under a Mr. Coffee.

Grey entered the kitchen with the morning newspaper tucked under his arm.

"Good morning," I said as I sipped my coffee.

"You're half right." He poured a cup for himself. "Watch the news last night on TV?"

"No." *Had better things to do. Bam.* "Why?"

Grey didn't answer immediately.

Was this a lead in to an old joke? Like 'Did you see the news last night? No? Well, a toilet was stolen. I heard the police have nothing to go on.'

I love that one.

"Never told you what I do for a living last night, did I?" He sat at the table.

"I guess it never came up."

"I work for an insurance company."

I nodded. "What area?"

"It's my job to size up situations," he said.

"So you're an adjustor?"

"More like a P.I. I make sure the company isn't getting scammed. Personal injury cases. Worker's comp." He took a sip of his coffee. "You know what I'm doing right now?"

"Having breakfast?"

"Sizing up the situation."

I would have preferred a bad joke.

He continued. "Did you know you made the news last night?"

"I don't know how much you know, but there was this thing that happened yesterday." That I made the news didn't surprise me that much. I was more worried about how Grey would be taking it.

"Is that what you call it? This thing?" he said.

"Well, not to get into too much detail, but I bet my secretary had something to do with it?" I didn't plan on telling him about the explosives. That could wait until my call to the FBI later today.

"You're blaming the murder on her?"

"What?" I barely kept from dropping my cup of coffee. "No! I meant she probably called me in as a missing person? What are you talking about?"

Grey shoved the paper in front of me. My picture stared up at me and not my good side. This one had me looking like a crazed killer which the article, as I glanced through it, inconveniently reinforced. The Major must have been very busy yesterday.

"This is ridiculous."

"Says you offed some fellow in Lompoc."

I read the first few paragraphs. The article touched on Oscar's death at the quarry, but said his body had not yet been found. The murder had been reported by a Marlin Jenkins who told police how I had taken Mary hostage after killing Oscar. It also included a few words with the kids at the gas station who indicated how suspicious I acted.

"He ran off like he was trying to hide something," the boy reported.

Yeah, like the flames shooting from my rectum.

And then he told them about how I had driven off with the man I had been accused of murdering.

The article went on with interviews from people at ZTA, Hal being one.

"Doesn't surprise me in the least," they quoted him as saying. "Lately, the man's been a bit unstable. It's a high pressure game he's in. He must have snapped."

That's where I stopped reading.

"These are all lies coming from the guys at the camp Mary was at. They're trying to flush me out. They must know now I wasn't in the car. They want to pin Oscar's death on me." I sounded way too desperate.

"Yesterday," Grey looked at me over his cup, "Mary told Alice about what went on there. Of course, I heard it all as we watched TV in bed. Alice's like a tape recorder. Word for word. She could go on for hours. Well, she's talking and your picture pops up on the screen during the news. That sure put Alice in a mood. She wanted to call the police right then."

I hadn't been woken up last night by SWAT, so I let him continue although I did check the distance to the back door.

"I told her I'd call in the morning to check things out. Besides," Grey set his coffee cup down, "Mary wasn't acting much like a hostage. I said to myself, something else must be going on."

"And now that it's morning?" The door looked reachable if I caught him by surprise.

"How about if I give you a ride somewhere?" he said.

"Like to the police station?"

Grey shook his head. "Mary's a good kid. A free-spirit, no doubt, but she's got a decent head on her shoulders. I got a good read on things like that. It's my job."

"First of all, I didn't kill anyone," I said.

"Sounds like she made a mistake going into that camp. From what she told Alice, it was you who motivated her to get out."

"Second of all, I didn't kill anyone." I repeated that to make sure he hadn't missed the first time. "And *she* was the one who got *me* out."

"I don't think she would have helped you if you did what they say you did."

"They shot Oscar and drove him off a cliff. Now they're trying to pin it on me."

Grey stared at me for a few moments and shook his head. "I don't think you killed anybody." He pushed away from the table and stood. "That being said, you're going to want to be moving on." He retrieved a brown bag from the refrigerator. "I don't think Alice'll be so understanding if you're here when she gets up."

I glanced into the den where Mary still lay in the recliner.

"Best if you let her sleep," Grey said.

* * *

I felt bad about leaving Mary without a note, but I didn't want to leave anything incriminating if the police showed up later. At least, she was in a safe place now, and that's all that mattered. I could always contact her later when I straightened everything out.

"Where are we going?" I asked.

Grey maneuvered his truck over into the far right lane. "That's up to you."

A sign ahead indicated we'd be getting on I-15.

"I can catch a flight to L.A. I shouldn't have a problem getting a seat."

"That's true. Maybe they'll put you in first class since you're wanted for murder." He glanced over at me with an eyebrow cocked high.

"Crap. How about a bus?" I said.

"Same problem, you know. TSA is everywhere."

We rode silent for a few miles before Grey spoke up.

"There's this guy I know. He can put you in a car. He won't ask questions as long as you don't."

"No questions, huh?"

He flipped on the radio. "He lives on the west side of town. I'll give him a call and let him know we're coming." Grey reached for his cell in his back pocket, got distracted from driving and almost rear-ended a Cadillac slowing in front of us. He stopped short, sending his lunch and the morning newspaper flying onto the floor.

"Mind grabbing that?" he said, as he zipped around the Caddy whose driver shot him the bird.

I retrieved his lunch and noticed something when I picked up the newspaper. It was a full page ad on the back.

ARE YOU READY?
SURVIVALIST EXPO at the Cashman Center
All week long!

In the ad, it showed a color picture of a child's Big Wheel toy sitting outside a small single story home. A large mushroom cloud reached toward the heavens from over its roof. Then I caught sight of a very familiar object in the lower half of the ad – a picture of the Jeremiah Box. Copy underneath touted the esteemed Major Bartholomew King would be making a presentation on the Jeremiah Box on Monday, today, and it promised that *"Secrets Would Be Revealed"*.

I'd had my fill of signs, but this one was smacking me in the face like Sharon Stone's big moment in *Basic Instinct*.

I held the paper up so Grey could see the ad. "Do you know where this Cashman Center is?"

"Sure, we go out and watch the 51's play there all the time."

"Can you take me?"

He sighed. "I hope I'm not wrong about you."

"I'm no murderer."

He gave me a sideways glance but said nothing else. We took the next exit and rode the streets silent until we neared the Cashman Center where he pulled into the parking lot.

"Mary seems to have taken a liking to you," he said. "That's what I was told."

I thought about last night. "The feeling's mutual."

"I don't think you going on about the world ending's going to be all that great for her."

"You heard about that, huh?" I hoped for a smile and got nothing. "Yeah, well, I understand."

Grey stopped the truck next to the curb and gripped the steering wheel harder. "Maybe not. What I'm saying is that Mary's going to be better off if you don't try to get in touch again."

Apparently, I hadn't understood. I stared out the windshield, at the long lines of people waiting to get inside the convention center. Was I like them? If so, who could blame him for saying that?

"Okay, I get it." I opened my door. "Thanks for everything, Grey."

Before I could close the door, he tore off a piece from his lunch bag, scribbled something on it and handed it to me. "If you change your mind. His name's Roy."

On the scrap was a phone number.

"Hey, Buddy," he said before I could shut my door. "You're wrong about this being the end. I think we're just getting started."

I thought for a second and said, "From your mouth to God's ears."

He nodded and drove away.

I hoped he was right, but I still had to go inside.

I had made a promise.

Chapter Twenty-One

"IS THIS THE FIRST DAY OF THE LAST DAY OF YOUR LIFE?"

The banner greeted me as I entered the cavernous floor of the Las Vegas Exposition Center. Immediately to my right, a high school marching band played Iron Butterfly's *In-A-Gadda-Da-Vida* as only a high school marching band can. For those who didn't have the privilege of seeing them up close and personal, their image blazed down from a Jumbotron-style screen hanging from one of the hall's massive walls.

Booths set side by side in eight by eight foot squares displayed guns, knives, and bows and arrows of all types followed by others with equipment for metal detecting, gold prospecting and hunting. People sold canned food, dehydrated food and the water to make it edible. Men in full camo demonstrated remote control surveillance helicopters on one side of the exhibition floor while, across from them, conventioneers took tours of a large RV, armored and weaponized to allow survival inside for up to a year, or so the large sign on its side touted.

One of the longer lines snaked from a medical supply booth offering free suturing classes. A woman in a nurse's uniform handed out raffle tickets for a lifetime supply of surgical adhesive tape, the manufacturer of said tape probably betting it wouldn't be for that long anyway.

Everywhere, I saw the promotion of hopelessness. First, you create the problem and next you provide a solution. How can you sell someone medical survival training unless your potential customers believed one day they may need to use it? A bunker located in North Dakota is a hole in the ground. However, it can be sold to a survivalist as a safe haven from the approaching cataclysm. As Reverend Hedgins had told me, it was all in the marketing.

I kept to myself and tried to fit in. The people wandering the floor appeared normal enough – young and old, and, oddly enough, pretty much split evenly along gender lines. On the street, these people wouldn't stand out. However, in the context of the convention, they somehow took on an aura of freedom fighters, all struggling for the greater good or, who knows, maybe a great deal on collapsible water storage containers. They all shared a belief that the world would suffer a devastating catastrophe in the foreseeable future and an equally overwhelming need to do something about it. I guess, in a sense, they were my target demographic.

A couple of security guards strolled toward me. I ducked down an aisle, and they turned with me. I glanced over my shoulder, but couldn't tell if they were following me or simply doing their rounds. I slowed at a booth selling baseball caps and tried one on as they passed.

Maybe I should leave after all. What did I expect to happen if I saw King or, for that matter, the Jeremiah Box? Didn't I have a phone call to make to the FBI? Wouldn't that take care of my promise to do something?

A hand clamped down on my shoulder and I froze.

"Buddy Price?" a voice said.

I turned to face my accoster. He was dressed in khaki and wore a safari-style hat covering his long, flowing blond hair.

"So, it is you," he said.

"Larry!" I choked out, surprised to see a familiar face. "What are you doing here?"

"I'm working," he replied.

I almost added 'for a change', but caught myself. Larry Spangle had been a client of mine, specializing as a game show host doing gigs at no-name cable networks. Eventually, he couldn't balance his professional responsibilities with his propensity for adult beverages. On closer inspection, even now his eyes seemed a little bloodshot.

"Good for you," I said. "Glad to see you landed on your feet."

"Speaking of landing, I arrived early this morning." Larry had great stage presence, but had never mastered the art of the segue. "There's important work to be done here."

"Never took you for a survivalist."

"I'm a realist, something you," he poked my chest, "never recognized."

I took a step back. It was a strong poke. I must have made a face.

"Now, now," he said. "Don't get the wrong idea. No hard feelings here."

"Good, life's too short." I said, then caught the irony. "Anyway, looks like you're doing fine."

The hand went to my shoulder again and squeezed. "If it weren't for you, I wouldn't be here today."

Was that praise or admonishment? Safe money would bet the latter. Trying to expand his horizons, I got him a commercial hawking cereal, but, as was his penchant, he showed up blasted out of his mind. I ran interference as best I could, but the folks at Quaker Oats didn't take kindly to their spokesman repeatedly mispronouncing the product's name. Sure, I might have tried harder, but I'd had enough of old Larry. After that fiasco, I dropped him like a hot bowl of 'wedded shreat'.

Still, I tried to stay positive. "Yeah, glad I could help. Well, good seeing you."

"I've got a little secret to tell you." His arm looped tight around my shoulder and pulled me in close, almost tapping his forehead on mine. "*I know how to open your box.*"

That I wasn't expecting. King had mentioned back at the camp he had someone, but I hadn't believed him. And, honestly, Larry's greatest claim to fame to date was hosting the show *The Star Spangled Banter* whose contestants competed by answering American History trivia.

"Wanna know how?" he said, bouncing his eyebrows up and down.

"You know where it is?" I said, choking a bit on the fumes coming from his mouth. I should have said no, but a part of me, the part that makes stupid choices, thought otherwise. Maybe, just maybe, he could help me find the Box. Perhaps our chance meeting had a bigger purpose.

"Do I know where it is? I'll take you right to it."

"Okay then," I said without considering how easy that had been. That was the stupid part of me again.

I followed him to a door that led off the convention floor. The back hallway was filled with members of the high school band I had seen earlier. They and their instruments lay scattered around the cement floor. We worked our way through them until Larry angled toward a non-descript door. It opened into a room complete with big screen TV, couches and a wet bar.

Larry immediately targeted the bar and had two highball glasses on the counter as fast as you can say DT. "So, what's your poison?" he said.

"Too early for me, but knock yourself out."

"Five o'clock somewhere." He unscrewed the cap off a bottle of JW, poured a glass about halfway and held it up toward me. "To survival."

I pantomimed a toast, waited for him to take a drink and went for it. "So about the Box?"

He placed his glass down, fixing me with a stare. "You never fail to surprise me."

"Yeah?"

He tapped the side of his head. "I know what you're up to."

I swallowed the gulp of Mexico and sputtered, "Well, can't put anything past you."

"It won't be so easy. I'm a wanted man, now."

"Sorry to hear that." I didn't tell him he wasn't the only one. He wouldn't feel so special then. "But about the Box?"

"Sorry? Of course you're sorry. If you want me to come back as your client, you're going to have to fight off all the other agents. They're begging for me to sign, and although you and I go way back, I can't give you preference. So don't assume. Don't assume." He lifted his glass toward me again, his excitement as palpable as his imagined greatness.

I let out a breath. It was only Larry talking about Larry. He liked to do that.

"Me? No. But, mark my words," I pointed for effect, waggling my finger, "I will put up a fight."

"I know you will." He dropped out of sight behind the bar.

After about thirty seconds of no Larry, I edged closer, trying to see if maybe he'd passed out. "Larry?"

He popped back up, cell phone in one hand and a bottle of Chivas Regal in the other. "Look what I found." He tossed the phone onto the bar and held out the bottle. "Sure you don't want to join me?"

"I'm a little pressed for time."

He drained his first drink, refilled the glass and took a sip, his hand shaking slightly. "I bet you didn't know I have a degree in Mathematics."

"No, never knew that."

"Biology, too. Before I got into show business, I applied mathematical models against things like ecosystems. Didn't know that either, did you?"

"You never cease to amaze me, Larry."

"You should have read my bio."

"I did. I did, but it's been a while."

"I've got a unique perspective on life." He slid over a barstool already behind the bar and leaned a cheek for balance. "How about that Times article? Did you read it? You know, on Bert Bell. Last week."

I shook my head.

"Bert 'The Box' Bell."

"Oh, yeah. Sure. Sure. Ole Bert Bell." Bert was the head kook when it came to the *I-can-open-the-Jeremiah-Box* crowd.

"I was mentioned, too, you know," Larry said.

"Really? I didn't have time to read the whole thing."

"That's your problem, Buddy. You do things half-ass. That's why you and I couldn't make it work."

More likely the bottle of Stoli you drank every day.

His cell dinged.

"Need to get that?" I reached for the phone.

But Larry was faster and snatched it away. "No." I noticed a small smile creep onto his face as he read the text. "Where was I?" He shoved the phone into his pocket this time.

"You were going to show me the Jeremiah Box."

"No, I'm not finished yet. You need a little background first."

"Like I said, I'm a little pressed for time."

"I got a call Saturday night. He told me 'I have the box and need your help. Come to Vegas.'" Larry took a deep breath. "Finally, someone who believed in me."

From his time as my client, he'd come off as extremely ambitious, but the opportunities to turn that ambition into success never came along for him. It looked like Major Bartholomew King was giving him that chance. Larry must have latched on like an angry pit bull.

I glanced toward the door. The stupid part of me had taken a break and now the paranoid part took center stage, reminding me we should leave.

"All the clues were there. You simply needed to understand the relationship. The seeds of a sunflower, the family tree of a honeybee, the spirals of a shell." Larry slapped the bar. "It was so obvious."

"Well, I know how you are. Once you get an idea in your head." I tried to laugh. I looked for the time on my non-existent wristwatch. "You know, I completely forgot. There's this thing I wanted to catch, and if I don't go now–"

"From what I hear, you're the one who's caused all the trouble." Larry drifted from behind the bar.

All of a sudden, he didn't seem so drunk anymore. He partially blocked my way to the door. "Don't you want to see the Box? I can show it to you."

"Nah. Don't worry about. We'll catch up later." I edged around him. "I know you have to be pretty busy."

"Buddy?" he called after me.

I didn't look back, with the door right there. As I reached for the doorknob, it started to turn.

Chapter Twenty-Two

Major King and Flex stood in front of me, a broad smile playing on King's face. "Going somewhere, Mr. Price?"

I backed up a few steps. "Thanks a lot, Larry."

"Now, now." King entered the room while Flex played defense at the door. "He's watching after himself. That's what we survivalists do, look after Number One."

"Well, he picked the wrong…," Wait, why was I telling King this? I turned to Larry. "Larry, you picked the wrong fucking team."

"I picked the only team," he said. "The only team that ever listened to me."

"That's right," King said. "The one who appreciated your knowledge and talents." He addressed me with an arm resting over Larry's shoulder. "No one believed him when he said he could open the Box. You said you could, and we all know that was a lie. But, Spangle…" King slapped him on the back and gave him a little shake, "he's the real deal. When he opens it tonight, our devoted followers will be witness."

"You're not buying this crap, are you, Larry?" I said.

"And he will become the face of the new revolution," King sang out, then motioned me toward the sofa. "Take a seat."

"You know," I said, "I was thinking I might take off."

King nodded at Flex who took great pleasure in seeing that I didn't. I landed hard on the couch.

"And, through the wonders of the interweb, millions will know what we find inside the Jeremiah Box. And to think you could have been part of that." King picked up the remote and turned on the TV. He pushed a few buttons, switching it to an alternate feed which showed an empty stage with a lectern and table. "That's where it'll happen. After the grand opening, the world will never be the same." He tossed the remote next to me. "And tonight is only the beginning. Tomorrow and the next day and the day after that, more and more will join our revolution."

Revolution had been mentioned twice in under a minute. That couldn't be good.

King stared down at me. "Flex, see that Mr. Price sticks around."

"So you can throw me off another cliff like you did Oscar?" I tried to stand, but Flex, true to King's word, made me stick around with a strong hand pressing me back down.

"I believe you had something to do with that." King's eyes shifted momentarily toward Larry and back to me. "We'll let the criminal justice system deal with you."

"How ironic," I shouted at King's back as he headed for the door.

Too many things seemed ironic to me these days.

"Come on, Larry." King waved at Larry to follow him. "Let's see what we can do with that darned box." At the door, he turned and spoke to Flex. "Be ready. Marlin won't be long."

Flex stared at the floor, shaking his head. He muttered something that sounded a lot like "Horseshit."

"Son, didn't we talk about this already?"

"Yeah, I know."

"Come on over here." King waved him over.

Flex trudged over, shoulders slumped. "Ain't there another way?" he said.

King wrapped him in a big bear hug and whispered to him like he was comforting a small child. "It's going to be okay, son. It's going to be okay."

After a few seconds, King held Flex back at arm's length while Flex continued to hang his head.

"Look up," King said. "Look at me."

Flex slowly raised his head.

Whappp! King delivered a sharp slap to Flex's cheek leaving a dark rosy patch behind. He gripped Flex's shoulders and said in his deep, low voice. "We all gotta play our part, boy. No second thoughts. No doubts. Hear?"

"Yes, sir." Flex's other cheek now burned equally red.

King's voice softened again. "Next year, they'll be talking about what you did today."

"Yes, sir. I know that."

"Remember, a man's legacy is his greatest asset."

And with that bit of wisdom, King departed with Larry in tow.

Flex caught me staring. "What're you looking at?"

"That's got to smart."

"You wanna find out?" He snarled at me, raising his hand.

I held up my arms in surrender. "I was talking emotionally."

He deflated like a spent balloon, crumpling against the door jamb. He rubbed his cheek. "Weren't nothing."

"So I have to stick around, huh?"

"You'll get yours soon enough." He looked out into the hallway.

"So, how are you going to do it?" I said.

Flex said nothing.

"One-way walk out into the desert?" I said.

He glanced back this time. "That's up to Marlin."

"Larry, too, after he opens it?"

Again, nothing.

I worked up my most pathetic smile. "You should think about keeping me around in case he can't."

"You'll probably get a bullet in the back of the head," Flex said.

"Sorry I asked." I slumped back in the sofa and stared at the TV, at the empty stage, at the table where the Box would soon be placed, and finally opened, its secret revealed. Not that would mean anything to me lying out in the desert in a shallow grave with–

"Hey, Hollywood?" Flex said.

I snapped back to the room. "Yeah."

"I wanna know something."

"And I still have a few questions of my own," I shot back.

"I wanna know if Mary's okay." He'd somehow switched from callous to thoughtful in the blink of an eye.

"Yeah, she's fine." At least, I hoped that was the case.

"You know, she deserves better than you," he said.

"Funny. That's exactly what I'd be telling my therapist if I were home now."

"I think I could have made her happy," he said.

"Yeah?" I shook my head. "How about next time you want to love someone, try checking the hate at the door."

He stared at me, his jaw muscles tensing like he was chewing gum. Maybe he wanted to tell me something or maybe he was simply working himself up to kick my ass.

Instead, he simply nodded and looked away.

Chapter Twenty-Three

"It won't be long," Marlin said from the bar.

He'd shown up a few hours before, that walking-stick of a man who drank my Macallan. He spelled Flex from guard duty and sent him off for whatever operation he'd been unwillingly conscripted.

Joining me on the sofa, Marlin hoisted the bottle of JW Larry had started earlier toward the TV. "For some reason, the Major wanted you to see this."

"Did Larry open it?" I said. With every reality show I'd been involved with, the producers already knew the direction things were going to go. Why would this be any different?

Marlin chuckled but didn't answer.

"No? You're doing this live?" I said. "What happens if he can't?"

"You don't know, do you?" He took a long swig, watching me over the bottle.

"What?"

"The Major didn't think blondie could open that box no more than you." He shot me a yellow-toothed smiled. "Yeah, he gave him a chance to prove it, but Larry didn't come through. And, you know what? The Major don't care."

I honestly didn't see that one coming.

Marlin continued, probably enjoying it all the more with my look of disbelief and, of course, the booze. "All Major King needed was a warm body that says they *could* open it."

His believers would hear what he wanted them to hear. I should have known.

A loud pop emanated from the TV and sounds of idle chatter of an audience spilled from the speakers.

Marlin waved a veiny hand. "Okay, keep quiet now."

A few seconds later, a host strolled out on stage to polite applause. He carried himself with the practiced manner of a true salesman.

"Ladies and gentlemen, thank you for joining us this evening. For those I haven't met at previous conferences, I'm Dave Dial." He shaded his eyes as he peered past the camera into the audience. "I see a lot of old, familiar faces out there." He glanced at an index card he held in his hand. "Hey, Claude. Claude Sommers. Where are you? For those that don't know, he runs the Biofuel booth located in Space...," he glanced at the card again. "A-22. He's been coming to these conventions for centuries." Light laughter rose in the background. "...and now it's a few centuries and one. It's his birthday today. Let's give it up for Claude." Dial waited for the applause to die down. "How old does that make you?"

"Eighty-three," came a voice barely picked up on the audio.

"Well, congratulations, Claude. And here's to more to come after that."

"I'll let you know after tonight," the same voice shouted back to faint laughter.

"That's the attitude." He peered out into the audience again, scanning back and forth. "Well, I'm sure, like Claude, everyone is itching to get to the main event tonight."

I didn't feel that itch so much. I eyed Marlin who kept a firm grip on his bottle.

"But first, I want to introduce a new face to the convention. A young, inspiring singer who is sure to have a wonderful career with the voice you're about to hear, that is, if we're..." He dropped his head for a moment and then collected himself. "Well anyway, let's all welcome little Prissy Montgomery."

"Do those people know what you stand for?" I asked Marlin as Prissy walked out on stage.

"Pay attention," was all Marlin said.

A sweet girl all of seven or eight years of age gave a soulful rendition of *Somewhere Over the Rainbow* which, under any other circumstances would have been considered beautiful, but, in this venue, came off as creepily wistful. She finished to polite applause and, after giving her a hug, Dave shooed her offstage to her waiting parents who met her halfway on stage and managed a few waves of their own to the audience.

"Maybe if you went at things a little differently," I said.

Marlin ignored me.

"Fellow survivalists." Dial moved to center stage again. "The moment has come, that moment we've all been waiting for." He grinned, waiting for the murmuring to die down. "Where's that drumroll when you need one?"

A drumroll sounded. The audio guy was good.

"I am proud to introduce to you our keynote speaker this evening." He swung his arm out wide. "A man who needs no introduction other than, Major Bartholomew King of the American Federal Reservists."

Cheers and loud applause greeted his entry. Larry followed close behind, carrying the Jeremiah Box out in front of him like a sacrificial offering, but he wore a sour look on his face as if he didn't want to be there.

I felt the same way.

Marlin raised the JW to take another swig and missed his mouth. A good portion dribbled down his stubbled cheek before he found the sweet spot.

"Publicity is important. I may have some connections that could help you guys," I said.

Marlin continued to ignore me.

Larry made center stage and placed the Jeremiah Box on the table. He stepped back as King walked to the lectern and waited for the applause to die down.

"Thank you, ladies and gentlemen. I am pleased that you are here for this historic occasion. As you all know, tonight is the night that the secret will be revealed." King waved a hand at the box, and, on cue, applause exploded. Or maybe it was the audio guy again.

King held his hands up for the clapping to end.

"We all have something in common." He paused to let that sink in.

I remembered him using the same technique on me when I was with him in his office. It must be his way of mind-melding with people.

"We're all realists. We see things for what they are. That doesn't mean we're not optimistic. It means that when you show up with a glass part way filled with water, we don't argue about whether it's half empty or half full, we're only concerned with whether it's good enough to drink and how long it's going to last." A wave of laughter followed that one. "We're always looking for a better way to ready ourselves for the end. We don't want to be caught unprepared, so we remain vigilant. We build our bunkers, we store our food and we make our families safe. There is no doubt in our minds what will happen. The question is when." King scanned the audience. "After tonight, you will wonder no more. The question 'when' will no longer be of any concern, and before the night is through, the question of 'how' and 'why' will be answered." He waited for the applause to die down.

"Tonight, it's my privilege to present to you the man who has provided the answer to the opening of the Jeremiah Box. Ladies and gentlemen, I give you Lawrence Spangle."

An unlikely hero as there ever was one, Larry stood at the lectern. I could tell from the dull expression on his face, though, something was wrong. Normally, he'd be beaming brightly, soaking in the adoration. It was obvious to me that Larry understood the new reality as well as I did.

King introduced Larry and briefly described the intellectual giant that he was – how God had brought them together and together they had cracked the mystery of the Jeremiah Box. Funny how King was now part of that.

"Before I reveal the message, I have something else to show you."

He obviously knew how to draw out the moment.

"It's a short documentary by the award-winning filmmaker Joseph Drako. This film will define the journey that we all will be soon taking."

King nodded to someone off camera and the screen blinked. A rendition of Verdi's *Requiem*, which seems to be the 'go to' piece for any satanic movie sequence, blasted forth. The screen blazed in red with the title painted diagonally in a white zigzag font… *Apocalypse How?*

After a minute, I could see where Drako was headed. Images of explosions, riots and blazing buildings pointed the way toward an unremitting, bleak existence. I wondered if my part had hit the cutting-room floor. Regardless, at the end, King would be presented as the one who would lead everyone to their ultimate survival.

And that reminded me I had to keep trying to ensure my own. I turned to Marlin. "Funny, most people at the convention seem normal."

He grunted this time.

"But, I don't know, I think King has a different agenda."

"They'll learn. Now, shut up and watch."

"Maybe it's my fault. I never gave you a chance."

He grunted again.

"It's that I don't know much about survivalists."

No grunt this time, instead a low growl. "I said shut up and watch."

"I mean who's to say society can't collapse at any minute? You have to be prepared. Bottom line, that's what you're all about, right?"

Marlin had taken some prodding, but he'd had enough. He grabbed my arm. "What'd I tell you?"

He was close enough now. I lowered my head and thrust forward into the bridge of his nose.

I'd learned the art of the head butt from Sly Stallone on location for *The Expendables*. Don't bend at the neck, he said. And if you can, grab their shirt and bring them to you as well. Funny how much I'd learned over the years from hanging around movie sets.

I twisted off the sofa and onto the floor, crab-crawling a few feet back. I prepared myself for the worst in case I overestimated my abilities (something the ex-Mrs. Price constantly brought to my attention), but there was no movement. Marlin's head lay back, his mouth slightly open, blood dripping from a nasty gash above his nose.

It had worked. I had my chance. Time to get out of there, out of the conference hall and out of town.

Marlin jerked slightly and rolled prone across all the cushions, but remained unconscious. However, he must have fallen on the remote because the TV feed switched from Drako's napalm explosions and back to cable.

Flashing red and blue lights filled the screen. At the bottom, "Breaking News" scrolled across. The video feed was from a local television station shooting a portion of the Strip, the boulevard empty on this particular stretch except for a lone truck parked near Bally's. Across the street, from the camera angle, you could catch a glimpse of the Bellagio fountains dancing in the background.

"We've just arrived on the scene," the reporter explained. "The police are keeping a safe distance for now. There has been no communication yet from the occupants of the truck."

The video began a slow zoom toward the truck as the commentator continued. "We're asking everyone to stay away from the Strip at this time. We don't know if there might be others involved."

My heart sank as the shot zoomed closer. The truck was a non-descript dull brown with the word BOMB (and a smiley face inside the 'O') written haphazardly on the side in bright white letters and, in back, a light blue tarp with a familiar design. There were two occupants, a man and a woman. The camera focused on the driver. He wore a ski mask and gloves, but I knew who that would be.

As the camera panned to the passenger seat, I couldn't quite pick up on the woman's face, but the camera distinctly showed a gold cross hanging from her neck.

Chapter Twenty-Four

"The standoff continues as what appears to be an African-American male holding a young female hostage on the Las Vegas Strip."

The news guy had been fooled, but that was Flex and with what had to be shoe black around his eyes. I knew what King was trying to pull off here.

"Traffic has been closed off, and we're left to watch as police determine their next move," the in-studio anchor continued. "Let's go back to Chris Yeardley on scene. Chris, have you heard anything about their demands?"

"No, nothing yet." The on-scene reporter held his hand to his right ear as a police car arrived in the background with its siren wailing. "We don't know anything about the woman with him, but from her actions, she may be there against her will. Again, there have been no demands, but it's apparent to anyone seeing this picture, the man claims to have a bomb in his truck. The police are still trying to setup communications with the driver."

I had to tell the police that he had no intention of walking away from there. From what King had told him, he would go down in history for this. It was his legacy so, for Flex, there was no turning back. I rushed behind the bar, grabbed the phone and dialed.

"Nine one one. What's your emergency?"

"I'm calling about the bomb on the Strip," I said, trying to remain calm.

"Where are you calling from?"

"I'm calling from the Cashman Center. But this is about the bomb on the Strip."

"We already have police deployed," the dispatcher said. "They have the situation in hand."

"No, you have no idea what the situation is. The group that's responsible; I know them. They won't stop regardless what you give them. The bomb *will* go off. Do you hear me? It will go off."

"Sir. Sir–"

"They want to start a revolution."

"Sir," she said. "I'm going to need you to calm down."

"The guy behind the wheel isn't even black, for God's sake."

"You know the gentleman in the truck?"

"Yeah. His name is Flex."

"And his last name?"

"Uh… I don't know his last name."

"Flex?" Her voice dropped. "That sounds made up."

"Who cares? They want to start a race war or something, I don't know. A revolution. When the end of the world comes, they take over. Overthrow the government, create their kingdom on Earth." I struggled for a breath. "Something like that." I'd run out of air.

"Do you need us to send a medical response to your location?"

"Oh my God. Are you kidding? You have to do something."

There was a long pause on the other end. "We are, sir. Have a nice day." The line went dead.

"Have a nice day?" I banged the phone against the wall. "Have a nice day?"

There'd be no nice day as long as Mary remained in that truck. I had to get to the Strip myself. Someone needed to tell the police who they were dealing with. I fished in my pocket and pulled out the paper holding the phone number for Grey's friend, Roy. Not what I was looking for.

I found her card in my other pocket.

Chapter Twenty-Five

The minivan pulled up to the curb outside the convention center. I yanked open the door and Marcia beamed at me from the driver's seat.

"Can't live without me?" she said.

She wore a purple velour track suit with a black fanny pack. Her makeup was impeccable and I think she may have even shaved.

"But before we go anywhere, I need all the gruesome details. 'Marcia, I need you', although in most instances, I would melt over, but coming from you, I require a little more explanation."

"I need a ride to the Strip."

"Maybe some other time. Some idiot says he has a bomb, and it's going crazy over there." She drummed her fingers on the steering wheel and cocked her head. "Is there something you're not telling me?"

"Nah, it's no big deal." I jumped in and closed the door. "Going to see Mary. Can we go?" My voice may have cracked a little or maybe it was Marcia's quasi-feminine intuition.

"Where is she?" she demanded.

"Come on, it's nothing. She and her sister went to the Strip this morning and I'm worried." I needed to lie. You know how hysterical women get.

"No, something definitely is going on." Marcia shoved the van into Park and crossed her arms.

I caved faster than a sandcastle with plumbing problems. "Yeah. Yeah. She's in trouble. For God's sake, we have to go tell someone." I sucked in a quick breath and finished. "Mary's in that truck on the Strip. I saw her in the truck."

"Oh, no. Oh, no. Not my Mary." Marcia already had the van in gear.

"These guys are seriously crazy."

"The one's you were running from, right?" She pushed the minivan's engine and we skidded out onto the street from the convention parking lot.

"They're going to blow up that truck." I grabbed for the hand grip as Marcia made a hard turn.

"Did you call the police yet?"

"They don't believe me."

She blasted the horn as we blew through a red light, "Well, I'll make sure they do."

We swerved around a slower car. "Bad guys aren't going to win today. No, not today. Not on my watch."

We sped the first few miles toward the Strip without much problem, zooming down side streets, missing most of the heavier traffic. But when we neared Flamingo, which we could take directly west into the Strip, we slowed to a crawl.

"I'm getting out," I said, gripping the door handle. "I'll run the rest of the way."

"Who are you kidding? You're out of breath from the ride."

"I'm nervous."

"I have a better idea," she said.

We neared an intersection where a police officer directed traffic.

Marcia kept the van inching forward. "Growing up, I didn't have it that easy. Me wanting to play Barbie and others expecting me to fill the gap on fourth and one. Life can be cruel, but we learn how to deal with it."

The traffic cop waved at us to move through and blew his whistle, gesturing angrily when Marcia pulled to a stop.

She ignored him. "If I play by the rules..." She checked over her shoulder. "...I figured out..." The cop marched toward us, but he got no closer than ten feet when she jammed the accelerator, "...I would never win." She swung past him, zipped the rest of the way across the intersection and onto the sidewalk, dodging some ineffectual traffic cones.

The cop's shrill, piercing whistle faded.

We made the next block to Flamingo in no time, slowed by a few tourists who didn't expect to share a sidewalk with a minivan. At Flamingo, we made a hard right.

"I have to play by my own rules sometimes," she shouted, punctuated by a war whoop.

For a moment, we were Thelma and Louise racing toward the Strip, except, of course, if you've seen the movie, there was that small issue of the fast approaching canyon. Our canyon was a line of barricades and police cars blocking our path a few hundred yards ahead.

Marcia slowed the van.

"You're not giving up, are you?" I said.

Her answer was a quick left into a side road heading behind Bally's. I expected cops to converge on us from everywhere, but the hotel had been cleared of traffic and left untended. We followed the service road which curved back toward the Strip and headed for a single barrier manned by a lone police officer. Picking up speed, we blasted through the barricade, sending the policeman diving for safety and skidded out onto Las Vegas Boulevard. The minivan bounced hard over the median and came to a steamy stop on the other side.

I cleared the cobwebs, the hit having sent me into the ceiling, but I had a mission to complete. I pushed open my door. Fifty yards away, at the nearest intersection, police swarmed. The flashing reds and blues competed with the nearby casinos in the fading light. Although we definitely had their attention, no one made a move toward us.

Across the median, in the opposite lanes, Flex's truck sat against the curb, the Eiffel Tower of the Paris Casino towering above it.

Marcia already stood outside her door. "He'll know you, right?"

"Yeah," I said, "but not yet sure if that'll be a good thing."

I started toward the truck, not sure what I would say, but I had to do something for Mary.

"Do not move toward the truck," a voice from a bullhorn blared from the police line. "Turn and walk toward the intersection."

I waved my hands over my head and shouted back, "It's okay. I know them."

"Move in this direction or we will be forced to take action," the voice said.

"I tried calling, you know," I yelled.

"Should we listen to them?" Marcia said.

"Hell, they didn't listen to me. Besides, what did you say? Make your own rules, right?" About ten feet from the truck, I paralleled it until I was even with the driver side door.

"Hey, Flex, it's me." I said. "Don't shoot or, you know, blow up."

Flex stuck his head out the window. From behind the ski mask, his eyes grew wide. "Don't get no closer."

Mary leaned forward so I could see her. "Buddy, there's a bomb." Her voice sounded small and tremulous, making me want to rip open the truck door right then and there and take her away from all this.

"Easy, big fella," Marcia said, sensing my frustration.

"Don't worry. Everything's going to be okay." I said the words, hoping it would calm Mary and maybe I'd believe them, too. I edged closer to the truck. "Right, Flex? You're not going to do anything…" I almost said stupid, but caught myself. Why antagonize the poor kid? "You don't want to hurt Mary, do you?"

He shook his head, but didn't look my way. "She wasn't supposed to be here. She wasn't. She really wasn't. I didn't want this."

I could see he maintained a firm grip on Mary's wrist.

"I'm sorry, Buddy," Mary said. "I came looking for you."

"Look," I said to Flex. "I believe you. I get it. It's not your fault."

"Yeah? Sure." He banged his hand on the wheel. "Nobody's gonna believe me with all this horseshit I got myself in. Hey." His attention was diverted. "What are they doin'?"

I noticed a police officer had started moving forward hiding behind a black shield. This wasn't going to help at all. I waved my arms over my head. "Stay back. If you get any closer, he'll blow up the truck," I yelled. "Stay back."

"We only want to talk," the bullhorn guy said. "We're sending in someone."

"No way. Tell him to stop or I'll blow this thing up," Flex said to me, tension flooding his face.

I took a few steps toward the police. "I'm doing the negotiating here," I yelled back. "Pull him back or it's going to be all over."

The officer behind the shield halted his advance and peered back for direction.

"Pull him back now!" I repeated.

After a few moments of silence, new directions came over the bullhorn. "Pull back. Pull back." The officer slowly retreated back to the main police line.

I moved closer to the truck again. "They won't be a problem, Flex. I promise. Now, talk to me. Tell me your side."

"I got nothing to say."

"You mean nothing the Major wanted you to say, isn't that right? Other than go by the script. He gave you a script to follow, didn't he?"

Flex didn't answer, but I knew I was right.

"You know you're scaring a lot of people."

"That's the idea, ain't it?" Flex shouted back.

"I know there's got to be a different way to do this." I edged even closer, five feet away. "Setting off a bomb isn't going to help anything."

"He said he opened that box." Flex let go of the wheel. "He showed me what was inside."

"Yeah, Flex. Sure."

"He showed me an old scroll."

"A scroll?"

"But he wouldn't read it to me 'cept the part about the revolution. It was God's will, he said."

"Flex?"

The words kept coming like he'd sprung a leak. "The Major told me the first thing on the list was to wake up folks to the new order. A bright Light to offer to God that would open up the eyes of all to see the true Way."

I could tell he was reciting that part.

"The Way and the Light, he said. It was a direct message from God. That's what he told me." The last part came out almost pleadingly.

"And you're going to accomplish that by blowing yourself up? Is that what he told you, too?"

"He said it's my legacy."

"Funny how he's not sitting behind the wheel."

"He said it's the first step in opening people's eyes." It sounded now like he was trying to convince himself.

"It's horseshit. Isn't that what you said earlier?" I said.

Flex didn't move a muscle for a full ten seconds, and then slowly, he started to nod. "Yeah. It is horseshit."

Baby steps, I told myself. The hardest part is getting the first yes.

"And?"

"If you think about it, it don't make much sense. What's setting off a stupid bomb have to do with anything?"

"Well, how about enough of this horseshit. Let's go home. What do you say?"

"Naw." He shook his head. "I ain't going nowhere."

"Sure you can. It's not too late." Maybe I'd pushed too hard.

"The clock's already ticking," Flex said.

"What do you mean?"

"I mean the bomb's on a timer," he yelled. "I ain't the one setting it off. Marlin put a bomb in back connected to this timer." He pointed to a clock flashing red numbers on the dashboard. "Fucking Marlin and his timers. Everything's got to have a timer."

I looked and saw the timer flashing its countdown. 7:45…7:44…7:43…

I still didn't see a problem. "Well, let's go then. What are we waiting for?"

Marcia laid a firm hand on my shoulder. "Not that easy. The truck might have a trigger device inside in case anyone," she nodded toward Flex, "gets cold feet."

"Hey, Flex, is that true. Is there a trip switch?"

"Who the hell is she?" he said, now noticing I wasn't alone.

"This is Marcia. She's with me." I put myself back on track. "Listen very carefully. I'm going to tell you something I hope you can understand." I took another step. "The Major didn't really open the Jeremiah Box."

Flex wasn't looking at me again, but I pushed on.

"Marlin told me. He knows. You can ask him. Larry Spangle is only a pawn in King's scheme. Like he wanted me to be. Like you are. See, it doesn't matter to him. He needed someone to act like they could open it. So he could produce that scroll, the one he said came from inside. King wrote the message that he read to you. He wrote it."

Slowly, Flex's head lowered to the top of the steering wheel where he tapped it lightly. "Yeah, there's a trip switch. Marlin told me about it, but not where it was."

"Maybe it's on the door," Marcia said, edging closer. "Open it and boom. Or it's a spring under the seat. As soon as you take pressure off the seat–"

"I know. Boom," I said.

Flex pulled off his ski mask revealing raccoon eyes. "I'm so fuckin' stupid."

"Buddy," Mary said, leaning over, "we're running out of time."

I had no idea what to do. The timer flashed 6:40…6:39…6:38…

Marcia plucked at my elbow. "Maybe I can defuse the bomb."

"What are you talking about?"

"Listen, I had two tours in Iraq." Her voice dropped a few octaves. "I was with an Ordinance Explosive Disposal Unit. Kirkuk, Mosul. Disabled over a hundred IEDs. Will that do for a resume?"

"Yeah, okay, that'll do." Duly impressed, I took a step back to give her room.

"Okay, then," Marcia barked, now in command. "We need to find out if there's something under the seat." She pointed at me. "You go in the other side and check under the seats. I'm going in back to inspect that bomb."

"What? Inside. Yeah, sure." I said, but my feet refused to move. "Inside?"

"Remember." Marcia fixed me with a stare. "We can't let the bad guys win."

"Right." I snapped out of it. This was for Mary.

I ran to her side of the truck while Marcia hopped in back. Mary rolled down her window and grasped my hand. With my other, I wiped the tears from her eyes. "It'll be okay. We'll get out of this." I reached for the door handle.

"Not the door," Marcia shouted. She stood in the truck bed looking down on me.

I yanked back my hand as if I'd been shocked.

"Through the window," she said softly. "Through the window, please."

I did as instructed. It wasn't easy, but my adrenaline was pumping. I slid in with my legs sticking out above me. Mary pulled herself to the side as I lowered my head below the bucket seats.

"I can't see anything. Only vague shapes and outlines. I need a flashlight."

"Try the glove compartment," Flex said.

Mary pulled it open, and I heard her rummaging around while the blood slowly pooled in my head and my vision began to blur.

"Found one," she said. A flashlight appeared next to my head. "Five and a half minutes, Buddy."

I grabbed it and pointed under the seat. When I flipped the switch, no light. I tried again. "Ah, come on. Batteries are shot."

"Forget it then. Feel around," Flex said. "Feel under both seats. We ain't got much time."

"For what?" I yelled. "What am I looking for?"

"I don't know. Shit! Some wires, maybe a spring."

I stuck my hand underneath and felt around. My fingers rubbed against hard rounded metal, maybe brushed against a wire. Or was it? Everything felt like something that could be connected to a device.

I pushed myself up to let the blood drain from my head. "I can't tell. There's no way."

Flex pulled at the wheel like he might rip it off the steering column. "Oh for Christ's sake, can't you tell what a fucking bomb looks like already."

"Well, thank you for the help, young man." Marcia had returned to stand outside Flex's window. She placed a calming hand on his shoulder, "but it's not a bomb we're looking for. That one's in back." She winked and smiled.

"Can we save the moment for later?" I said.

"Try again, Buddy." Mary touched my cheek. "Try again." Her trusting eyes seared through my soul.

I dropped back, hoping this time maybe the shapes would morph into something when I felt around, but it all felt the same. As I was about to pull myself up, a light blinked on and everything under the seats became visible. The shapes, which I could only feel before, became seat coils and padding. I could clearly see that the space under Mary's seat was clear.

"Who turned on the light?" I said.

A familiar voice responded. "Looked like you needed a little help." It was God.

I tried to pull myself up, to see where he was, but couldn't move.

"I'd stick to the task at hand," He said.

"What are you doing here?"

"Don't you have a bomb to find?"

"What? Is this all a big game to you?"

"Time's running out, Buddy."

"No freaking kidding. How about a little help," I yelled.

"No need to shout. I didn't do this to you."

"Maybe you could have stopped them. Did you think about that?"

"I don't involve myself in the details." His voice was calm and soothing, which pissed me off that much more.

"We're not details. I'm not a detail. Mary's not a detail."

"Every life is precious, but not everyone can live forever. It doesn't mean I don't care, but sacrifices must be made to drive a point home."

"I can't believe you're saying that."

"It's all in how you see things. Tell me, Buddy. What do *you* see right now?"

I looked again. Under Flex's seat, I spotted the plate, the spring, and the wire as Marcia had said I might find. The light blinked off.

"It's there. I see it. I mean I saw it. I mean, the seat's wired under Flex's seat." I waited for God to respond, but instead it was Flex.

"Ah, damn it! Wouldn't it figure."

Mary helped me up, briefly holding my face in her hands. "I knew you could do it."

Squirming back out the window, I planted my feet on the pavement. Peering in at Mary and Flex, I could see that they hadn't heard my discussion with God. If only they had.

I held my hands out for her. "Okay, you're clear. I can get you out."

"Now, very carefully," Marcia said, "without touching Flex's seat…"

When Flex grabbed Mary's arm, it was clear he had different ideas. "It's a two-person deal. She ain't going unless I'm going."

"The hell she's staying with you," I said, leaning through the window trying to break his grip.

"Wait." Marcia's sharp voice stopped our struggle. "Flex, if you keep moving in your seat, you're going to set off the bomb. Now, listen to me. Let Mary go. I'll get you out. Do you understand? I will get you out."

Flex maintained his grip as the digits on the clock blinked down. Four minutes to go. 3:59…3:58…

"Flex," I said. "Let her go."

He stared at me but didn't loosen his grip.

"Is this what you want to be remembered for?"

Flex slowly shook his head.

"You talked about opening up eyes. Well, open up *your* eyes. Do you want to be remembered for killing innocent people? Is that your legacy?"

He stared at Mary and then blinked. "I'm sorry. It's not what I want at all." He released her arm. "Go on. Get somewhere safe."

I checked the timer. A little more than three minutes to go. "Come on." Mary grabbed around my neck and I pulled her out. A smattering of applause echoed from the intersection.

"What now?" I said to Marcia.

"You need to go," she said, pointing down the street.

"What about you?"

"No time to argue." She reached behind and pulled around her fanny pack. She unzipped it and extracted a miniature Swiss army knife. "You'd be amazed what you can do with this." She put on a brave smile.

Flex cleared his throat and handed her the inoperable flashlight. "Maybe it'll work if you bang it some."

She took it. "Thanks, dear, I'll give that a try." She looked back to me. "Go," she said, the creases in her forehead deepening. "Now!"

We took off toward the barricades. Officers met us half way and led us back to a protective position behind a SWAT van, the man with the bullhorn quickly joining us.

"You're in a helluva lot of trouble, you know that?" he said.

"No time for the tough guy act now. My friend's still out there."

"We're doing what we can," he replied.

"How about using that thing to convince my friend to save herself? There's not much time left. Here, give it to me."

"Settle down." He pulled the bullhorn out of reach. "You've lucky to be alive."

I'd heard that before, but I still didn't feel so lucky. The bomb was going to go off and Marcia was still with the truck.

"She dies and this is your fault," I yelled. "Do something."

"Tell me what you know."

"The bomb's in back; it's on a timer. Got to be less than two minutes now."

He quickly fired off some instructions in his radio and pulled an officer next to him.

"Officer Broward will wait here with you." He backed away and brought the bullhorn to his mouth. "Everybody, take cover. Everybody, take cover," he announced as he walked away.

"That's it? They aren't going to do anything?" I blurted to Mary.

"Buddy?"

"It isn't fair. The bad guys are still going to win." I took a deep breath and pulled Mary closer "I go by three simple rules in life. Don't put your genitals on the internet, don't own a dog that can kill you, and try not to be too annoying." I kissed her and then let her go. "There's one more I'll add to the list as soon as I get back." I spun toward our guard, plucking the regulation flashlight from his utility belt grip.

"Hey!" was all I heard him say as I ran for the truck.

Don't be the hero. That would be the fourth one, if I survived.

Marcia poked her head up as I reached the truck and banged on the side. "What are you... Go back. Go back. There's nothing you–"

"Here. Take it." I held out the flashlight for her.

She stretched over the side and grabbed it. "You're insane, you know that?"

"No time to argue," I said, panting. "Anyway, I kind of agree."

The timer flashed through the back window. Fifty-five seconds to go.

"You're cutting it close," she said. "Now get out of here." She refocused on the bomb with the added benefit of directed light.

Was that all she had to say? I was kind of hoping for a little more gratitude.

"Hey, Hollywood. If I were you, I'd do what she says," Flex said.

"How much time?"

"Forty...thirty-nine...thirty-eight...," he counted down.

What the hell was I doing standing here? Didn't I remember my newly added rule? What more did I expect to prove?

Instead of bolting, I leaned into the truck bed. "Marcia, it's not going to happen. Come with me."

She looked up, the beam of light projecting an eerie shadow on her face. "No! You go!"

She fumbled the flashlight and it rolled out of her hand. I grabbed it and shone the light back on the bomb and its exposed wires. Marcia shot me a grim look, but quickly returned to the task at hand.

"Twenty-four...twenty-three...twenty-two...", Flex counted down from the cab.

I glanced over my shoulder and saw Mary standing next to the SWAT van with good Officer Broward holding her back. Inside the truck, Flex stared straight ahead. I wondered if maybe he could have turned things around given enough time. I wondered about myself as well. What would I have done given more time?

I felt the flashlight being snatched from my hand. Marcia pushed me back.

"Run!" she yelled.

"Ten…" Flex intoned.

Yes, I wanted to survive, but, for some reason, I couldn't get my feet to move.

"Nine…"

Yes, I wanted to get back to Mary.

"Eight…"

I'd known Mary all of three days, but somehow my heart had opened up and let her in.

"Seven…"

What was I doing about to throw it all away? What was I more afraid of?

"Six…"

Dying in a ball of fire or maybe having someone love me?

"Five…"

I stumbled forward.

"Four…"

I took another step.

"Three…"

Run!

I'd covered only a few dozen feet when I heard Flex yell out 'One'.

Too late for regrets now.

A rush of sound and light enveloped me. I closed my eyes and waited for the force of the explosion to hit. This must be time dilation. I'd read about it somewhere, no doubt compiled within my treasure trove of useless information.

The explosion surrounded me. I dove to the street, covering my head with my arms, waiting for the flames to eat at me.

Music played somewhere in the background; it wasn't so bad. I had felt no pain after all. And here I was, already in Heaven?

It was a beautiful symphony and somewhere a whoosh, whoosh of the… I don't know, what was that?

I opened my eyes and looked behind me. The truck was intact on the boulevard. There was no fire, no destruction; nothing except the bright flashing neon of the Strip and, across the street, water spouting toward the sky in a well-timed choreography.

The bomb hadn't gone off after all, but the fountains at the Bellagio had.

I slowly rose to my feet.

Marcia stood in the truck bed, waving her arms to the police. "It's safe now. It's safe."

Before I could turn around, Mary was in my arms, smothering my lips with her soft kisses, holding me tight to her as if she would never let me go. She stared deep into my eyes. "I wouldn't have been able to live with myself if you hadn't made it."

I kissed her back, wanting that to last forever. Where's the time dilation when you need it?

"Hey, guess what?" Marcia now stood outside the truck with Flex who held her tight around the waist, a relieved goofy smile on his face. "The good guys won after all," she said.

And as if to underline his new lease on life, Flex planted a big wet kiss on her right before a trio of police officers gang tackled him.

Mary buried her head into my chest as I suppressed a laugh. "Think I should tell him?" I said.

She looked up at me, her eyes dancing. "No, let him enjoy the moment."

Chapter Twenty-Six

I rolled over, turned off the alarm and stretched. The thousand thread count sheets brushed lightly over my skin and the always-on air conditioner sighed from above. I hung my legs over the side of the bed and let my arms reach for the ceiling which was a lot higher than my bedroom back at the condo.

Soft arms encircled my waist and pulled me back. I fell into Mary's arms. She kissed my forehead and brushed her hand over my hair.

"Stay," she said.

"I can't."

"We'll have breakfast in bed." She kissed me again.

"I have to meet with the detectives."

She frowned. "And what will I do?"

"You can stay here and wait for me." I tugged at the sheet.

She tucked it close to her chin and pouted. "But I'll be bored without you."

"Why don't you get out? See some sights."

"I've seen them already, but I'll show you some," she said with a sly smile and flashed me some side boob.

"How about when I get back?"

"Maybe I won't wait." She rolled away, but still kept an eye on me.

"You're not mad, are you?"

"I guess you'll have to take that chance." She turned toward the wall.

"It shouldn't be too long." I patted her exposed rump and got up.

The strong granite walls of the shower surrounded me as I let the hot water dance off my back. The tiny pricks felt like miniature acupuncture, a salve for my soul tortured by the longest weekend of my life. I watched my troubles roll off and circle the drain. Life was good once again.

After only a few hours at the station last night, I had been released. Flex was kind enough to come clean on Oscar's death, and they decided not to press any interference charges against me or Marcia.

I lathered and rinsed, enjoying the silky smoothness of the serious state-of-the-art water softening system the Galaxium Resort and Casino had installed for its guests in the Presidential Suite. I turned off the water and opened the shower door. When I reached for the towel, I saw that I wasn't alone.

"Mind?" I said.

"Nothing I haven't seen before." God held out a towel.

"All the same." I took it and wrapped it around my waist. "What are you—" I caught myself and lowered my voice. "What are you doing here?"

He peered out the bathroom window overlooking the Strip. "We're not done yet."

"I thought I'd handled my end well enough." I leaned my butt against the sink and crossed my arms. "I've spread the word. This box is headline news and with me connected right along with it." I let my arms fall by my side. "For better or worse."

"No, you did great." He sucked at his cheek. "You did great."

My face grew warm.

"I'm not judging you," God said, holding up his hand. "It's just that there's more to do."

I'd hoped these visions, these experiences, whatever they were, might be over, but this was one problem I hadn't rinsed away. I'd try now. "No, I think I'm done."

"That's not how things work." His smile remained patient.

"I know you gave me another chance and I'm obligated. I get it, but what you've asked me to do is impossible. I could spend eternity trying to change people's lives. One, maybe two, but the whole world? All I can do is give them notice. It's up to everyone else to do the right thing."

"I know what I'm doing." His deep voice echoed in the bathroom.

"Geez, keep it down, will ya'?"

"She can't hear me, Buddy."

I lowered my voice on the off chance she could hear me. "Level with me, God. What's inside the Jeremiah Box?"

He stared me down. "It's not for me to say."

"Well, I think you should. It almost got me killed." He still hadn't blinked. "Why should I listen to you anymore?"

"Maybe because I'm *God*." His voice boomed.

"Or a tumor in my head."

"It won't be the first time I've had to deal with that attitude." He sighed. "Come over here. Look out the window. Tell me what you see."

Out the window, the Las Vegas Strip beckoned – from the pyramid-shaped Luxor on one end of the Strip to the Stratosphere at the other. Then, in a flash, that scene winked out replaced by a brutal landscape of torched rubble, shattered buildings and a sky churning with dark swirling, blood red clouds.

"Think of this as a gentle reminder." The blue sky quickly returned as he eyed me. "You don't seem very impressed."

I picked up a bottle of complimentary Galaxium cologne and splashed some on. "Give me a dozen good CGI programmers, and I can do the same thing."

"Time's running out, Buddy." God shifted his feet, his smile fading. "Three days and counting."

"Yeah, yeah, you keep saying that. Almost as if you're anxious." I tilted my head to get a better look in his eyes. "Not very God-like if you ask me." I didn't like the idea of questioning God, but I'd dealt with some in the industry who thought they were, so nothing new for me.

My elbow must have hit the cologne because it clattered into the sink. The sound grabbed my attention and when I looked back, He was gone.

Maybe I'd pushed things too far. Who knew? If it was a nasty tumor creating these images in my head, or something hereditary…

Well, all bets were off either way. I planted my hands on the sink and stared into eyes that stared back equally confused. Finally, we both blinked and decided to do the thing we were so good at. I opened the door to that little closet in the nether regions of my brain, shoved everything inside, nice and tidy, and shut it tight.

I wouldn't think about it anymore.

After donning the plush white robe provided for Presidential Suite guests, I exited the bathroom. While I was in the shower, room service must have come and offloaded a full complement of assorted breakfast items. Along with the cinnamon rolls, we had omelettes, bacon with coffee, milk, OJ and a bottle of Dom. I ducked my head in the bedroom to look for Mary.

"Hey, are you–"

She was on the phone, but when I entered, she spoke a few more quick words and hung up. "They brought in breakfast," she said and shot me a big smile.

Maybe a little too big. "Yeah, I saw."

"I'm famished." She pointed toward a fresh pile of neatly folded clothes sitting on the end of the bed. "Compliments of the house."

The clothes were a pair of Calvin Klein slacks and a shirt whose brand I didn't recognize. "Free suite. Free clothes." I nodded a few times and couldn't resist. "Was that him?"

Her smile disappeared. "I told you. It's not an issue anymore."

An "old friend" had put us up in the suite last night. Since I was mostly happy to be alive, I wasn't going to pursue it. I opened that closet door, and shoved those insecurities inside along with the rest of my baggage.

"Okay, let's eat," I said.

Chapter Twenty-Seven

In the early 1990's, Las Vegas went through a tectonic shift in its presentation. New establishments began appearing up and down the Strip, pulling customers away from the old standbys with casino wonderlands like Treasure Island and Excalibur that were designed for adults and kids alike. The Galaxium went up during that Renaissance. With a theme based loosely on the universe, the hotel décor followed mostly along the lines of science fiction, with a predictable Star Wars bar and a Restaurant at the End of the Universe. Countless alien-related objects were displayed in glass cases all around the interior, but the biggest attraction hung in the lobby, a giant replica of the Enterprise – but not the space shuttle. Rather the one commanded by Captain Kirk. I guess they figured it would be a bigger draw.

I gazed down at it from the fourth floor balcony which overlooked the atrium. The lobby itself was packed with news crews, photographers and journalists. I'd had enough experience in the business to guess what I'd be facing after yesterday. They were waiting down there for yours truly. I found a house phone.

"Front Desk," a cheery female voice answered. "May I help you?"

I could see her behind the desk from my vantage point above. "Hi, this is Buddy Price."

"Oh, Mr. Price. How wonderful that you called."

"Shhh. Not so loud."

She lowered her voice and partially covered the receiver with her hand. "I need to inform you that there is a situation down in the lobby at the moment. You may want to—"

"Yeah, I already know. Fourth floor. Look up." She lowered the phone and peered up, first right, then left and caught sight of me on the far edge at the railing.

She raised the phone back up to her mouth and continued, whispering. "I can arrange a discrete pickup at the north service exit. You can reach that using the stairwell at the end of the hall to your left."

"Perfect. Not looking for any attention right now."

"Of course. And one more thing. There's a woman that has been at the Front Desk since early this morning wanting to contact you. Of course, since you asked not to be disturbed..."

"Forget it. No one knows I'm here."

"But, Mr. Price, everyone knows you're here."

Of course she was right, but no one I would know.

"She says she works for you. A Stacey Dennison? Would you like—"

"Yeah. Look, I do know her. Send her with the cab." I hung up and headed for the stairs. I guessed she'd forgiven me after all. It would be good to have her around in case the press found me.

The north service exit emptied onto an alley used for making deliveries. I hung near the door until I spotted a cab headed my way.

As it pulled up, Stacey pushed open the door. "Well hello, Mr. Hero." She scooted over to the middle to make room.

She had another passenger with her. "Who's he?"

"Maybe a 'Hi, Stacey' first?" she said.

"Okay. Okay. Hi, Stace." I got in. "Who's he?"

"Where to?" the driver asked as the cab pulled away from the curb.

"Metro on MLK," I said.

I glanced back to Stacey still waiting for my answer. Instead, her travelling companion shot out a hand accompanied by a bright smile that reminded me of someone I had met not too long ago.

"Oral Hedgins, at your service," he said.

Resemblance confirmed.

"Junior, of course. Daddy is currently incarcerated as you know."

"He's the one who came Friday," Stacey said. "The one you got so mad at me about."

"Yeah, water under the bridge, right?" I said.

She pursed her lips and nodded.

I could see the Senior in Junior, with his megawatt smile, sparkling eyes full of something that, well, made them sparkle, down to the dark, simmering tan that I bet he applied only this morning.

"You're wondering why we're here," he said.

"I'm wondering why *you're* here."

Stacey answered for him. "We're starting a new religion."

"Praise be to God, I am." He clapped his hands together as if in prayer, and his eyes shot toward the ceiling of the cab.

"I'm happy for you, Junior, but what does this have to do with me?" I said. W*ait. Had she said, we?*

"Well." He rubbed his hands together fast like a fly on a fresh pile. "You'll be playing an important role."

"Now, hear him out." Stacey must have seen my expression, which was somewhere along the lines of I *don't give a...*

"Do me a favor," I said, tapping the driver on the shoulder. "Pull over."

"Wait," Stacey said. "Let him at least explain."

The cabbie glanced back. "Can't until the end of the block."

"Okay, you have until then to pitch me the idea," I said to Oral. "And that's more time than I usually allow." He could talk all he wanted, but I knew what my response would be in the end. No more religion, no more boxes, no more nothing for me. After surviving last night, I knew that I'd gone as far as I could go. I'd turned in my resignation.

"You'll be our messenger," Junior said. "We'll spread the word and save the world. So many believe in you already. After what happened last night, there will be countless more."

"Yeah, for all the wrong reasons, wouldn't you say?"

"It doesn't matter. As long as they're listening now, that's the important thing. And they *are* listening to you."

"Who's listening to me?"

The taxi slowed and the driver asked, "Still want to stop?"

"No. No. Keep going." I focused back on Stacey. "Who's listening to me? Because I haven't been talking to anyone."

"Oral's taken the liberty of enlightening others," she replied.

"There are people in my business that are very interested." Oral chimed in. "You've grabbed a lot of people's attention. What you have to say goes a long way."

"But I'm not saying anything," I yelled. I was somehow being sucked back into this mess.

"What about all your talk about the new Buddy? How you're going to change your life? You talked to God and found a new lease on life. Here's your chance to do that."

"You did this." I poked a finger toward Oral. "You turned her against me."

"I have a mind of my own, you know." She swatted my finger away from him. "I'm tired of you treating me this way. Like I don't matter. Like I can't think for myself. Well, that's changed." She crossed her arms and melted back into the seat. "At least I can, even if you can't."

"Stace?"

Her eyes moistened. "Have you checked your email lately?"

"I've been a little busy."

Oral leveled his gaze. "She's working for the Lord now... and me."

"What? Slick here talked you into coming to work for him? Come on, Stace. Don't do this to me."

"It's not about you." She wiped her eyes, apparently reenergized by Oral's words. "It's about me. This is *my* sign."

"It will be called the Jeremiah Truth Church of God," Oral said.

"I don't care what you call it." I shot back.

"We're going to Texas and reinvigorate my father's flock. We will have the Jeremiah Box, and its secret will be revealed."

"Haven't you heard? It's been opened," I said.

He dismissed that with a wave of his hand. "It was the ranting of a madman. And if you look at the video of their conference," he eyed me with a lifted eyebrow, "it never showed him actually opening it."

"It's true. He didn't open it. Did you watch?" Stacey said excitedly, fully recovered from her misting jag.

"No, I was a little busy." I threw my hands up in the air. "Even if he did pull off the fake, this is still crazy."

"As crazy as you've been for the past few weeks?" she snapped back.

Not exactly what I wanted to hear. I took a deep breath and tried to calm myself. "Look, I'm sorry. I shouldn't have yelled."

"It doesn't matter. I've made up my mind," she said.

The tension still roiled inside the cab like clouds of a thunderstorm. We rode in silence the rest of the way until the cab slowed at our destination.

"Metro," the driver said, pulling over to the curb.

I stepped out. "He'll pay," I said, pointing back inside at Oral, Junior.

"Buddy?" She moved over to the open door and looked up at me. "Will you come with us?"

Her eyes shone bright and wide with that unbridled enthusiasm she had brought to work every single day at ZTA. No matter how much of a pain she could be, I still looked forward to that excitement, that innocence which proclaimed each day would be a wonderful adventure. Now she was going to leave me.

And it was all my fault.

Chapter Twenty-Eight

I didn't give her a straight answer. I couldn't. I didn't have one.

"I'll let you know" is what I said. That's my go to line when I want to leave my options open. I use it mostly for saying no, without having to say the actual word. It comes in handy in my line of work, but in this case, I simply didn't have an answer.

I left them in the cab. Fortunately, my interview with the detective inside the station finished quickly. I filled him in on a few more details about King, and he let me know what progress they'd made. FBI agents had already raided the compound but found no one there. That was it, no further leads as to his whereabouts. The detective suggested that Mary and I keep a low profile for the next few days in case of any further trouble.

I grabbed another cab which took me back to the Galaxium. He dropped me off in the alley at the service entrance, and I made my way back to the fourth floor elevators. As I waited, I noticed a large amount of activity down below, but it wasn't paparazzi this time. They were all gone, probably on to more lucrative photo ops of crotch shots from drunken starlets. Instead, they were replaced by laborers struggling with dismantling the current lobby centerpiece. A three-story high sign hung on the wall behind it promoting the attraction soon to come, *Stanley Kubrick's 2001: A Space Odyssey*.

My elevator dinged its arrival, but I stood frozen. While scanning the new exhibit, I had caught a glimpse of a familiar face in the crowd below.

Nah, no way.

I rode down to the lobby and ran to where I'd last seen him heading into the Star Wars Bar. I hesitated for a moment, unsure if I wanted go further, but decided to enter. It didn't take me long to find him sitting across the dimly lit bar. My heart pounded hard in my chest. Maybe I didn't need to know. I didn't get a chance to change my mind when he saw me and waved me over.

"You look like you just saw a ghost," Oscar said, pushing out the chair next to him. "I thought you'd take it better."

"You're alive?" I wanted to reach out and touch him, but couldn't bring myself to complete the act. "What? How? Why?"

"I'm here, Chief. It's me."

"You flew off…" The words trailed off, jumbled amongst the countless others working their way into questions.

"You're right about that."

"And…and…what the hell?"

"I'm here to see how you're doing."

I touched his hand. "You're real?"

"Well, reality is relative," he said, his smile disappearing.

"Try me," I said and sat.

"I guess there's no easy way to tell you this, but just to say it. I wasn't kidding earlier. I'm your guardian angel." He paused for the big moment and let me have it. "Your *real* guardian angel."

I laughed, probably not what he was expecting, but it was the best I could manage other than maybe crying, or running screaming from the bar. I laughed for almost half a minute with a slow downgrade to chuckling and a little whimper near the end. "No. No. You're what I would call a big problem." I waved at a cocktail waitress who hovered near the bar talking with the bartender.

"We do exist."

"I bet you do." The waitress arrived. "Scotch," I said.

I nodded toward Oscar.

"I'm good," he said to me.

"Did you hear that?" I said when she turned to leave.

"Do you want something else?"

"That someone didn't want a drink?"

"You said you wanted a Scotch, right?" she said, her brow wrinkling.

"No, someone else." I ticked my head ever so slightly toward the chair where Oscar should be.

"Do you want to change your order?"

"And?"

"And what?"

I gave up. "Make it a double."

She left, shaking her head.

"You sure know how to impress the ladies," Oscar said.

I was fairly confident I was alone at the table as far as anyone else was concerned. "So this whole time you were my guardian angel?"

"It was my job to make sure you stayed healthy."

"Starting with the alley?"

"You sure know how to piss people off."

"Yeah, it's what I do," I said.

"Including the Big Boss." He pointed a finger toward the ceiling.

I waited to respond because the waitress returned with my drink. "Would you like anything else?" she said.

"Keep an eye on me," I said. She nodded, but didn't seem ready to leave. "Do you want me to pay now? You can bill my room."

"You know you look like that guy on the Strip from last night."

"Yeah, I get that a lot."

She sat next to me, across from Oscar…if he was there. "So what are you going to do for an encore?"

"I have a feeling I'm going to find out pretty soon." I couldn't help but glance over at Oscar…if he was there.

"It's not only about saving the world. It's a battle for your soul, Chief," Oscar said.

"I heard they wanted you on *Survivor*," she said.

"That's a bunch of crap." My reply could go both ways, but it was mostly meant for Oscar.

"The Devil will reveal himself soon, and you have to be ready," he said.

She answered without realizing she was involved in a three-way conversation. "I know. I know. Okay, what about that preacher from Texas who wants you to join his new religion? What about that?"

"What? I've got to save the world and now Beelzebub's showing up?" I said, responding to Oscar's last comment.

"Who's Beelzebug? she said.

"Bub. Beelze*bub*," I said to her.

"He doesn't like being called that," Oscar said.

"Oh, sorry. Don't want to hurt any feelings."

"Oh, you didn't hurt my feelings," the waitress said. "I get things wrong like that all the time. I'm not mad." She gave me a coy smile.

"You've got your hands full," Oscar said. "Might as well not piss him off, too."

"Why not? It's what I do," I said.

"Well, you seem like a nice enough guy," she said.

"He's not all sugar and spice, honey," Oscar said to the waitress, but, of course, she didn't hear him.

"I get off at six tonight." She snaked a hand out to touch my arm. "Maybe we can have a drink or something."

"This is all my imagination so it doesn't matter." That was for Oscar and, well, for her, too. I don't usually get hit on by cocktail waitresses.

"Have you seen a therapist about that?" Oscar said.

"No, I mean it. I think you're cute," she said.

"I wouldn't be the first to hear voices in my head," I said.

Oscar answered. "You could do a lot worse than mine."

Her smile faded a little. "I'm not a voice in... I'm right here. Are you okay?"

Two drunken couples with yard-long cocktail glasses staggered into the bar, shouting something about winning a large jackpot.

"It gets harder from here," Oscar said.

"Duty beckons." The waitress rose. "I'll check back on you in a minute. You can let me know what you want."

"I don't need any more visits from you. It's causing me nothing but problems." That was actually meant for Oscar, but...

"I thought that–" she said, a frown appearing.

I was too focused on Oscar to worry about her. "And right now, I've got a beautiful woman waiting for me upstairs. You aren't going to ruin this for me."

Oscar said. "It won't be me that ruins things."

"You know what. You're an asshole." She searched her pocket for my bill and slapped it down on the table. "A simple no would have been good enough." And she stalked off.

"You're going to need my help," Oscar said.

Truer words had never been spoken.

I answered him the best way I knew how. "I'll let you know."

Chapter Twenty-Nine

On my way back to the suite, I met the first goon at the head of the hallway. He eyed me and said something into his cuff as I passed. Another mountain of a man stood guard at the door to the suite, blocking my entry.

"Don't worry. This is my room." I whipped out my keycard.

He snatched it from my hand, checked both sides and slid it through the slot in the door's lock. When the light flashed green, I took a step forward, but he held a hand to my chest. "Wait here."

He pushed open the door, knocking lightly, and I could have sworn shrinking a few inches in the process. "Mr. Davino?"

A man rose from the sofa. "Yeah, Mike. What is it?"

Mary was with him on the sofa, and she stood as well.

"It's okay," the man said, who I assumed was Davino. "He belongs."

As Mike handed me back my card, the man approached, hand extended. "Sonny Davino, glad to meet you. I run this joint." He was compact with a curly perm and the distinct odor of Old Spice. I couldn't help notice his shoes, an unnatural shiny black and white with pointy toes and what appeared to be an extra two inches in the heels.

I shook his hand. "Buddy Price."

Mary's face seemed flushed, and she kept flattening out her pants that seemed straight enough already.

"I want you to know we appreciate all you've done for us," I said.

"Sure, Price. Any time." His smile was too bright, and not in an Oral way. "Anyway, can't stay. Got this new exhibit to deal with."

He patted my shoulder and walked past me toward the door where he stopped and turned. "Mary and I go way back." His smile seemed to fade. "I'd do anything for her."

Mike opened the door.

"Take care of yourself, Buddy." Sonny scanned me up and down. "Hope the clothes fit."

As soon as the door closed, Mary peeled away toward the bar. "Want anything?" she said, in my opinion, trying way too hard to be casual.

"That's the old friend, right?" I tried just as hard.

"Soda?"

"How old?"

She returned with a Coke in hand. "We need to talk."

My stomach did a flip. She slid down on the sofa, tucking a knee up toward her chin and offered a sad smile.

"I just changed my mind about that drink." I hopped up and headed to the bar where I found a bottle of Jack. It would do for what I wanted.

"He's more than an old friend, isn't he?" I said while pouring.

"Sonny told me…" She paused. "You're on the news. A lot of people are saying you're a hero."

"You can't believe everything you see on TV." I downed the glass and started pouring the next. *For me, it's more like you can't believe everything you see, period.* "I'm thinking about going back to L.A as soon as I can get a flight." I kicked back the second one.

She let her knee slide down. "Going back?"

"It's gotten a little unreal here, if you know what I mean. Wanna come?" I threw it out like an afterthought although it had been on my mind all day. Her eyes lowered and searched the seams of the sofa. I knew what was coming. I poured another glass and tossed it back.

She looked up and tried to brighten. "They said you're going to start a new religion."

"Did they?" I'd already heard that from the waitress. I wondered how far the news had really spread.

"You'll be able to save the world now." She forced a smile.

"Screw the world." I downed another which hit the spot because the room shifted a little.

"But it's your chance to tell people your message."

"Forget it. The tumor changed its mind." I poured again, this time almost to the rim. "So, did you change your mind, too?"

"I'm sorry?" she said.

I kicked it back. "I thought we had somethin'." I used massively heavy air quotes when I said it which caused a lil' spill, "But what do I know? Don't think too much thought about what I think because…I…what I think." I lost track of where I was going. "I see dead people, you know."

"You need some rest, that's all."

"Guess what? Oscar is officially my guardian angel. He told me so just an hour ago at the bar downstairs. Had a few drinks with him. At least, I think I did. Not sure if the waitress would agree though. Know what he told me? I'd be needing his help."

"For what?"

"Beats me," I said with an exaggerated shrug which required me to refill my glass. "Oh, no. Wait. That's right." I poured again to the rim. "He said something about the Devil and fighting for my soul." I took a drink to help me think more clearly. I held up a finger and tapped my forehead. "Sonny. Maybe it's Sonny he's trying to warn me about."

She looked down again. "Don't make this harder than it already is."

"I mean, who has hair like that these days?" I rubbed my hand along my own hair, or what little had grown back, and in the process, sloshed my liquor. I watched it run down the sides of the glass, and then I refocused on Mary. "I thought you had better taste than that. Oh, no. Wait." I poured a little more so the rim wouldn't be lonely. "You came here with me. Can't be that good."

Liquid pooled around my glass so I stopped pouring. When I looked up, Mary was in front of me and pushed my glass to the side. "What are you doing?" she said.

"What are *you* doing?" I pulled the glass back. "I poured that. Why shouldn't I drink it?" I showed her I meant business by picking it up which took several seconds of effort. "So, answer my question. Not the one I asked now…the other…the other one." I tried to keep the questions straight in my head, but it was getting difficult. I hiccupped.

"It's not what you think," Mary said.

"Don't rely on what I think." I tapped my head again. "Remember? I have a tumor."

"I was going to tell you…" She let the words drift away.

"Tell me what?" The bar top cracked with the sound of my glass as I put it down. I could hear my words coming out a little weird, but that was because my tongue wasn't working for some reason. "You still haven't said anything."

She wrung her hands and started to speak.

"Naaahhh, don't bother. I saw that show you put on for King." I tried to point at her, but my finger slanted off to one side. I followed it toward the right, but I knew she got the idea. "I'm onto you, sister."

"You're an asshole," she said and I felt a burning sensation on my cheek.

"Whoa, whoa, whoa. What's with the ass…" I burped. "…hole? Everybody's piling on all of a sudden. First the waitress…" When I blinked, Mary had magically teleported to the sofa. "…now you."

"Sonny and I hit a rough patch. It's why I left in the first place. I didn't know those old feelings would still be there," she said.

"So you came back to find out?"

"He would always take me out. He's kind and caring and generous."

"…and brought poor ole me in case, huh?" My glass phased in and out of focus. It looked so sad being half full. I took a sip. It didn't taste as good now, maybe because so much was on my chin. I wiped it off with the back of my hand.

I blinked again and Mary wavered in front of me now. *How does she do that?* Her eyes glistened with tears.

The moment was there. All I had to do was take her hand. Hold it in mine and tell her everything would be all right. Tell her I loved her. We'd take off and head back to Los Angeles together and live happily ever after.

Isn't that the way it should end?

Who was I trying to fool? I'm Buddy Price and I don't know when to shut up.

"I sure could use a burrito," I said with another burp.

Her cheeks got fiery red, and I felt a sting on my cheek again. This time I thought I caught her slapping me.

"You can go to hell," she said.

A door slammed somewhere in the room. Mary was gone. *Teleporting again, I suppose.* The bar leaned heavily against my shoulder.

Phew, dodged a bullet there. I straightened up and took another sip but found myself looking at the ceiling through the bottom of an empty glass.

Where was that bottle? Who took it?

I was better off alone.

And she without me.

I mean I talk to God.

I wondered where He was. Shouldn't He be here? Giving me some kind of advice? Or Oscar, my guardian angel, helping me to figure things out?

Where'd she tell me to go?

Damn! Where's that bottle?

* * *

I woke up to two men in earnest conversation, their voices coming from the main room of the suite. It took a few more moments to drag myself from my dream state, but those were definitely voices out there. I was back in the bedroom, lying in bed, fully clothed and on top of the spread. I lifted my head and checked the time. Two fifteen. In the morning or afternoon? I checked the window and confirmed it was still dark. Or mostly. This was Vegas after all.

My head pounded with each beat of my heart and my throat felt like I'd swallowed sandpaper.

I rolled out of bed. An otherworldly flicker came through the open doorway, and I realized that one of the voices sounded suspiciously like Christopher Walken. Edging toward the door, I saw that the TV was on. I must have turned it on at some point before I passed out last night.

Still, I smelled the undeniable odor of cigar-smoke wafting through the room, the smell which made me want to hurl right there on the carpet.

Walken stopped talking and I noticed the television screen now displayed the word MUTE in the lower left corner.

"Over here, kid," a voice said from the other side of the room.

In a chair against the far wall, a small, bald man in a burgundy smoking jacket blew out a cloud of smoke from a short stub of cigar.

"Whoever you are, I just called security," I lied.

The red coal glowed in the semi-darkness of the room as he let the cigar hang precariously between his thumb and forefinger. "Sit down. We need to talk."

"Who the hell are you?"

"That's not important. Take a seat."

"I'm fine where I am." I placed my hand on the door frame as a statement as well as to keep from falling over. I felt like shit.

The man snuffed out his cigar in a nearby ashtray. "Suit yourself."

When he stood, I edged back a few steps.

"I ain't here to hurt you, kid. If I wanted to, you wouldn't have woken up."

"That supposed to make me feel better?" I took a deep breath. "Okay, how about this? You stay over there where you are and I'll stay over here, and you can tell me whatever it is you want to tell me, and then you leave. How's that sound?"

"Always negotiating something, huh, Buddy?"

"How… how do you know me?"

"I don't like going around sneaking into people's rooms in the middle of the night so I–"

"How do I know that?"

"What?"

"Maybe you do this all the time," I said.

The man laughed and settled back in his chair. "Smart ass, no matter what the situation."

"So what *is* the situation? Why are you here?"

"I gotta keep a low profile. People would get the wrong idea if they saw me." He reached his hand into his inside breast pocket.

I backed toward the bedroom a little more.

"Take it easy." Instead of a gun, he pulled out a fresh cigar. "I'm here to make you an offer." He lit it and exhaled a cloud of smoke.

As the cloud dissipated, it hit me who my visitor was. Oscar had warned me, and here he was, sitting in my hotel room. "I was wondering when you'd come." I had to show no fear.

"So you know about me?" he said.

"I was warned."

"Good to know my reputation still precedes me. You never know these days."

"Say what you have to say. I have a headache."

"You should go easy on the liquor, kid."

"You here for an intervention?"

He shook his head. "Okay, this is it. I came here to warn you that you're making a mess of things."

"Tell me something I don't already know," I said.

"Let's talk reality because you don't seem to have a firm grip on that."

"Yeah, it's a tricky subject for me these days."

"Leave all this end of the world shit behind. If you do, maybe you'll have a chance at a normal life. I can help with that. I have a lot of pull in your part of town. Lots of people owe me favors."

I nodded slowly. *Now that I could believe.*

"And I'll see to it that you get the girl, too."

"No, I already blew that."

"You wanna wake up one morning old and alone?" He tapped his cigar in the ashtray. "Do what it takes and be happy."

"Is this where you whip out the contract?" I remembered breakfast with God.

"How about this? I'll do you this favor for free."

"I don't want you talking to Mary," I said.

"Give me some credit. I do things more subtle-like. She'll never know."

I shook my head. "Not a good idea."

"Okay, I've said what needs to be said. The choice is up to you." He stood and headed for the door. When he reached it, he turned back to me. "I'm always around when you make up your mind."

And with that, he left in a puff of smoke.

Actually, he walked out the door. Not as dramatic as it could have been, but who's to say you need drama when you're the Devil.

Chapter Thirty

Stacey stood in the hallway. "Oh my god, Buddy, you look awful."

I stepped back to let them in and ran a tired hand through my aching bed head. Nothing like starting the morning with a hangover and some déjà vu. The clock behind the bar showed it was close to eleven now.

"What do you want?" I mumbled.

Behind her was Oral, carrying a Bible in hand along with a concerned look on his face.

"We called, and you wouldn't answer. We were worried," she said.

They followed me in as I stumbled to the sofa and collapsed. "Can you come back later?"

Oral appeared in front of me and sat on the coffee table. "Abuse of drink is from Satan; wine is from God."

"What do they say about whiskey?" *Maybe I should have asked him myself last night.*

"I'll call room service for you," Stacey said. "You need protein. How does a cheeseburger sound?"

"How 'bout I york right now and save us all the trouble?"

"Brother Buddy," Oral said, "there is so much to talk about."

"Is that what you're going with? Brother?" I struggled to sit up. "Stacey, can you get me some aspirin?"

"Sure," she said and left for the bathroom.

Oral pressed on. "The Devil wants to take you down the wrong path, but you must resist."

"My only concern is resisting this hangover."

"All right, Brother Buddy. I'll order that burger if it's what you need." He headed for the phone.

"Will you stop with the Brother thing?" I yelled after him and immediately regretted it. The jackhammer inside my skull went to work again.

Stacey returned and handed me two aspirin and a bottle of water. I popped them and took a long swig. The water helped a little with the bale of cotton in my mouth. She took the glass, sat next to me and rubbed my slumped shoulders.

"What's wrong?" she said.

"Nothing's wrong."

"I didn't spend all this time working for you and not know when something's wrong."

"Headache, Stace. Only a headache."

"No, it's more than that. I can tell."

I glanced over at her. "You're not going to stop until I cave, right?"

She smiled and shook her head.

"She left me." I thought getting it off my chest might make me feel better, but saying it only made me feel worse.

"Who?"

"The girl… at the truck."

"Oh. I didn't know. Well, it doesn't surprise me." She sputtered. "What did you do?"

"Nothing," I said, but she wasn't buying it. "Okay, I may have said things."

"Did Bad Buddy come out to play last night?"

"I think she would have been good for me."

"Really? She doesn't seem your type."

I wasn't sure where that came from. "No, she's perfect." I shot back. "Understanding and patient. She gets me."

"Too tall I think."

"Too tall? What?" I shook my head. "Look, don't try to help." She'd made excuses for me in the past when I'd been dumped.

"I don't know how to say it…" She bit her lip. "…other than just to go ahead and say it. She's coming to Texas with us. Maybe I can talk to her." Stacey stood, fumbling with my empty glass. "I never knew you were interested in… I mean, you're all open-minded and all, but the women I've seen you with. It's that… I mean she was being all heroic with disabling the bomb and all, but I…"

"Aw, Stace." It was Stacey being Stacey. "That's Marcia. Geez, I'm talking about Mary, the one *in* the truck."

"Oh." She let out a long breath. "Good. I thought you might not have known."

"I prefer my women with original parts."

"Well, Mary seemed cute from what I could see on TV."

I did a delayed double-take. "Wait? Marcia's going to Texas with you?"

Oral had finished his phone call to room service and rejoined the conversation. "Yes," he said. "She and her friends have agreed to be our goodwill ambassadors. We must spread the word. Time is running out?"

How does he know that?

"She is seen as quite the hero as well," he said.

"Does he know?" I said to Stacey

"Yes, he knows, Buddy," she said, levelling her gaze. "And it doesn't matter. Our church will accept everyone."

"So you're definitely going?" I said.

She nodded.

I lowered my head. Everybody was leaving. Stacey. And Mary. Even Marcia.

"Go then. I don't care. Nothing matters."

"You can still come with us," she said.

"And be your prophet for the end of the world. No, I quit that business. I made it official yesterday."

"We need to pray." Oral took Stacey's hand and mine for a little impromptu prayer circle.

I shook off his grip. "How long did they say–?"

"Shhh!" Stacey stared me down.

"Lord, please hear my words," Oral prayed. "Brother Buddy is in pain and searching for an answer. He's lost in darkness and he needs your help to find his way. God, help him in the face of Temptation for he will surely be tested. Help him be strong in the face of the Devil for he will try to deceive him. Help him find the way." Oral opened his eyes. "You must not give up your quest."

"Can I get an Amen?" I said.

"The Devil wants you to give up, but you must be strong." He grabbed my arm. "If you come with us, we can protect you."

"Nice try, Junior. I'm not buying it." I pried him off. "Way too many people have been telling me what I should do lately. I think it's about time I took over steering the old HMS Buddy myself."

"Once you sit with him, your life will never be the same."

"The only person I'll be sitting with is Bernie Kopelbaum at Trident Talent. Next week, we've got this deal which will—" I saw I wasn't impressing him. "Okay, time for you to go." I herded Oral toward the door.

"Buddy, it's the end of the world starting now. You must be the one who will warn people. You are the face of the Rapture."

"If you want to take over being Mr. Apocalypse, be my guest. I'm going home and try to disappear for a while. If you know what's good, so should you."

"I'm sorry you feel that way," Oral said.

"Yeah, well, I'm going to be just fine."

"Buddy?" Stacey said.

She threw her arms around me. "I'm going to miss you." She held on tight and stepped back, a sniffle escaping.

"So you're still going?" It was hard looking her in the eyes.

"If you change your mind, you know where we'll be."

"Be strong, Brother Buddy. You must be strong," Oral said.

"Go. Leave." I opened the door. "Go save the world for me."

When they were gone, I headed straight for the sofa. I had a helluva hangover, and I needed to relax, maybe watch a little ESPN SportsCenter. And I had some food coming. I rubbed my forehead. A little protein would help. And maybe I'd take a nap. Then I'd give Hal a call and have him set up a return ticket to L.A.

Time to start over. Put it all behind me like it never happened. I needed to focus on myself again. Let Oral save the world.

There was a knock at the door. I headed over, but when I opened it, instead of room service, it was one of Davino's bodyguards.

"Good morning, Mr. Price," Big Mike said with an unwelcoming smile. "It's checkout time."

Chapter Thirty-One

It was mid-afternoon, the worst part of a very hot Vegas day, when I neared my destination. I trudged down an empty, hot-baked road, having left civilization behind; well, mostly the suburbs. My sweat had laid waste to the pants and shirt I wore; the same ones I wore from Friday – Big Mike had been instructed to make sure I didn't leave with my new threads.

It was just as well. I'd found that shred of brown paper in my pocket and made a call.

After Big Mike escorted me out of the Galaxium, I wandered around a little with no particular place to go until calling ZTA, collect, to coordinate an evac back to L.A. That's when I found out from Hal's secretary about the media coverage I'd received, not from any heroic actions I'd performed on the Strip, but headlines regarding my possible involvement with the Jeremiah Truth Church of God, along with a few outliers who claimed I was the Second Coming. Then Hal got on the phone and let me know I was also the star of a porno, recently released by Walter Turpin Productions to sterling reviews. Who knew how efficient Walter could be? And also funny how I had top billing.

I thought Jake was the one being screwed that day, but really it was me all along.

Hal told me that my services would no longer be needed.

I topped a rise and saw a double-wide trailer positioned back from the road in the middle of a large dirt lot. Beyond the lot, essentially its backyard, skeletal remains of junked cars littered the scene. Row after row of cars and trucks reached toward the red-tinged mountains on the horizon, a junkyard ripe for harvest.

"Looks like a bumper crop." I laughed.

When no one laughed along, and I was disappointed, I knew heat stroke was imminent.

Roy's U Pick It displayed on the side of the trailer. As I approached, I made out a small "Closed" sign hanging on the door. No one appeared to be inside.

I knocked anyway. Nothing. I knocked again, louder, and a woman, arms and neck covered in assorted snake tattoos, appeared in the back, eying me suspiciously.

"We're closed," she said, her voice barely audible.

"I called earlier," I yelled through the door, but her eyes showed no recognition. "Grey sent me."

She hesitated for a moment and then approached. She cranked open the louvers of the door's window and spread dirty lace curtains. "What's your name?"

"Buddy. Buddy Price."

She extracted a cell phone from her pocket and made a call. A few seconds later, she looked up. "Go outside, around the corner." She pointed to my left.

"Got any water?"

But she already had her back to me. Customer service was closed once again.

When I turned the corner, two doghouses faced me, with large metal spikes driven into the ground, chains leading to empty dog collars. Despite what she had said, I decided to wait on the other side.

I found shade from an old El Camino parked next to the trailer. I slumped to the ground, leaned against the tire and must have dozed off.

Next thing I knew, the angry growl of an engine woke me. I jumped to my feet and waved at an old pickup that had shot through a gate in the chain-link fence. It turned hard, spewing dust in its wake and skidded to a stop next to me.

A thin, red-haired girl sat behind the wheel. She leaned over and shoved open the passenger door.

"I got stuff to do, you know," she said.

Two telephone books duct-taped together served as a makeshift highchair to give her visibility over the dashboard. Two blocks of wood extended from her shoes, providing her the distance to reach the brake and accelerator. The sight didn't instill much confidence.

"You know, I've been driving since I was five. Get in."

I got in. She jammed the pickup into gear and spun the truck so that we headed back toward the gate.

"Take it easy, Maria Andretti," I said as I peeled myself off the door.

"Who?" she said over the roar of the engine.

I didn't feel like explaining.

We sped through the gate and headed out into a land of junked cars. Up close, it was no longer a jumble of junk, but rows neatly organized by similar makes and models.

"You the new transporter?" she said without looking over.

"New?" I said.

"You ever done this before?"

"How hard can it be?" I shook my head and ducked as a bump threw me off the seat. "How old are you anyway?"

She slammed her left block of wood down on the brake pedal and spun the wheel sharply to the right. We ground to a stop and dust flooded the cabin. Two mongrel dogs scampered across the road, tails tucked.

"Stupid dogs. They do this all the time. Like they want to die or something. Go home," she shouted out the window.

They didn't listen, instead heading off deeper into the junkyard. She restarted the engine which had died from our sudden stop. "Ten." She glanced over at me. "Quit looking so scared. I've only wrecked once."

Second thoughts crowded my brain like the lingering dust in the truck cabin. "Yeah, well, we all do stupid things."

We ran down a row of Camaros and turned at the end heading for a pile of scrap metal in the narrow valley below. As we neared, the pile took on shape and substance, and became a warehouse. She drove the truck around back and pulled inside through a large open roll-up door. Inside was an exotic car aficionado's wet dream with at least a dozen cars parked in neat rows – Bentley, Porsche, Lamborghini, Jaguar, and a vintage Shelby Cobra.

We pulled to a stop. The little redhead stripped off her extensions, connected a strap and flipped them over her shoulder. She dragged out the phonebooks and held them under her arm like school books. She leaned back in and gave a quick honk of the truck's horn. "Don't just sit there."

I got out and saw a man waiting at the entrance to an office. He wiped a handkerchief across his bald pate, removed his sunglasses and repeated the process for his entire face.

"Hey, Kitten," he said. "Can you look at the Ferrari? She wouldn't start this morning."

"Yeah, okay," she said, scampering off into the recesses of the warehouse.

"Roy Jones." He extended his hand out, but not directly toward me.

I stepped over and shook his hand. "Buddy. Buddy Price." I noticed his eyes were mostly a milky white.

An engine roared to life, the sound echoing off the warehouse's metal interior.

"That's my girl." He replaced his sunglasses and felt for the door frame. "Let's go talk."

A tower fan in the corner churned up the hot air in Roy's office. He made his way behind his desk and sat, doing the handkerchief thing again on his head. "A/C is out. You'll have to suffer with the rest of us." He waved his hand in the general area in front of the desk where a hardback chair was positioned. "So Grey sent you, huh?"

I took his advice and sat. "Yeah, he gave me your number, said you might be able to help."

"That was yesterday, right?" He pressed a button on a desk clock.

"The time is four thirty," it announced.

"I still need to get out of town," I said.

"Don't we all."

Kitten returned from her work on the Ferrari, dumped her big girl accoutrements in the corner and slumped into a chair against the wall.

"How is she?" Roy asked her.

"The sense wire to the alternator was loose is all. We're okay now."

His chest puffed with pride. "Taught her everything I know. She'll take you back to the road."

"What do you mean?"

"I run a tight schedule. Deliveries have to be made on time."

"Okay, I can do that," I said.

"Don't need you now."

"Wait." I jumped to my feet. "Grey said you could help." My tongue felt heavy and my head spun. I collapsed back in the chair. "Got any water?"

"Kitten?"

"Sure, Daddy."

She retrieved a bottle of Arrowhead from a mini-fridge in the corner. As I took a long swig, she stayed next to me. "Can you give me a minute?" I said. She retreated back to her chair.

"So where's home?" Roy said.

"Los Angeles." Boy, I needed that water.

"Want to get back, huh?"

"Something like that." I drained the bottle. "Thanks."

"Thanks for what?"

I tipped the empty bottle toward him and then remembered. "For the water."

"Don't you have someone you can call?" Roy said.

"Not really."

"Parents?"

I shook my head. Why get into family issues?

"He's shaking his head, Daddy," Kitten piped up from the back of the room.

"Brother? Sister?"

"Only child."

"Wife?"

"Ex. And not in a good way."

"Anyone at all?"

I shook my head.

"He's shaking his head again," his ever-vigilant daughter said.

"Sucks to be you," Roy said, wiping his head again.

Kitten walked back over to the desk. "Want me to take him now?"

"Yeah, we got work to do," Roy said, nodding.

He stood and Kitten touched his arm, leading him the rest of the way to the door and out into the warehouse. I followed.

A candy apple red Ferrari was now parked next to the truck.

"Oh, I forgot my things," she said, letting go of her father's hand.

As she headed back to the office, the phone rang inside. "Get that, will you?" Roy said over his shoulder.

I guided him the rest of the way to the vehicle. The door of the Ferrari lay open, a soft ding, ding, ding sounding from inside.

"Couldn't do this without her," he said to me.

"Yeah, I see," I said, instantly recognizing my faux pas. "Uh, sorry about the 'I see' thing."

"Forget about it," Roy said. "Comes with the territory."

Sure, a small part of me might have regretted my choice of words, but the other part, the Bad Buddy part, had already focused on the Ferrari and the keys sitting in the ignition.

Chapter Thirty-Two

With the wind in my bristly hair, the last of the sun fell on my face.

I nudged the accelerator and felt the g-forces working on me, pressing me back into my seat. With a flick of my hand, I snapped into the left lane and passed a slower car. In fact, all the cars were slower. I was heading home; albeit in a car taken from a blind man, but let's not quibble with the details. I felt free.

The light turned red and I braked at the intersection. Three kids in a minivan stared down at me, noses pressed up against their window. I glanced over and gave them a smart salute. In return, one kid flipped me off. The light turned green, and I accelerated to forty in about two seconds, putting them quickly in my rearview mirror.

If life were only so easy.

Up ahead, a sign pointed to the entrance to I-215. Take that to I-15, then to the 10 and I'd be home in four and half hours. I turned on my blinker and checked over my left shoulder for traffic. When I turned back, Oscar sat in the passenger seat.

I jerked the wheel to stay in my lane. "Come on."

"What?" he said.

"You scared the crap out of me."

"I'd be nervous, too." He winked. "Didn't know you had it in you."

"Yeah, well, I do." I frowned. "What the hell do you want?"

"Where are you going?"

"Home."

"Need some company?"

"No, I'm fine." I checked my rearview mirror. "Go haunt someone else."

"I'm not a ghost. I'm a guardian angel."

"Or a figment of my steaming pile of imagination."

"I'm here for a reason, Buddy."

"Yeah. Yeah. End of the world. Still trying to recruit me. Well, if you've been paying attention, I already said–"

Oscar held up his hand. "No, there's something you need to know. I've been reassigned."

"Oh?"

"This might be the last time you see me."

"Good then." I passed the entrance to the freeway and kept driving. "So, how's it work? Someone new get assigned to me?"

"Don't worry. You should be fine on your own."

"Yeah. About time." Funny, but I didn't feel so free anymore. "Anybody I know? You need references or anything?" I said with a short laugh.

"As a matter of fact, it *is* someone you know."

"Who?" I glanced over. "Hope you didn't get Zimmerman. If you thought I was a pain…" I gave that stupid laugh again.

"No, someone closer."

There could only be one. "Mary?"

"She needs extra attention these days. No one seems to be on her side."

"Hold on a minute." I slowed the car. "I'm on her side."

"Which side is that? The one running out of town in a stolen Ferrari?"

"I'm sure it was already stolen." I merged into the right lane. "And no one's running. I think she made it clear what she wanted."

"People say things. You should know that better than anyone."

"You know something I don't?" I asked.

"Of course I do."

"And?"

He straightened in his seat. "How about I let you in on a little secret?"

Chapter Thirty-Three

A party girl stumbled across the Galaxium drive, drink in one hand, high-heeled shoes in the other. "Babe, wait. Wait for me."

She chased after an equally inebriated fellow stumbling toward the hotel entrance. She crumpled to the ground in front of me. Cars lined either lane so I couldn't go around her. Slowly, her head appeared over the hood, a crooked smile on her face. A strap had fallen off her shoulder, and the rest of her party dress seemed ready to follow. She balanced hand over hand, making her way to my side of the car.

"I think your friend is waiting for you," I said.

In fact, he'd slumped against one of the columns, head down against his chin.

"I don't care. He's an ass…hole." She eyed my car. "I bet you're much nicer though." She leaned hard on one hand, tottering dangerously toward falling into the car.

"Sweetheart, you're not a very good judge of character." I pried her hand off the door and held on until she seemed moderately under her own power.

I let go of the brake with the intent of simply sliding on by, but even though sloshed out of her gourd, she reacted fast and, probably because she was sloshed out of her gourd, she jumped onto the hood of the car. She began screaming holy hell, and I instinctively braked which rolled her off like a sack of stewed potatoes, stewed being the operative word. From any bystander's point of view, the stuck up prick in the Ferrari had hit a poor, innocent woman trying to walk across the street. Not the attention I needed.

Several people immediately ran over to help, including the girl's newly conscious and pissed off boyfriend. I jumped out of the car, but the boyfriend turned on me. He advanced in long strides, a hand cocked back ready to strike. Like I've said, I'm a lover, not a fighter, (I've said that, haven't I?) so I backed up a step with each one he advanced. Fortunately for me, he had the same problem with balance as his girlfriend, and no doubt, blood alcohol content as well, and promptly tangled his feet, face-planting hard into the pavement at my feet.

So I had two apparent victims on my hands, and the growing crowd seemed to be turning on me. *What? No one watches the news these days? I was the hero from the other night, remember?*

The first security guard on the scene reacted to the finger pointing from the crowd and detained me with my arms behind my back. Another soon arrived, but stopped short of helping his comrade in arms; instead his attention was grabbed by the victim/party girl who had regained her feet and was proceeding with a slow, seductive strip tease for her new, adoring fans.

"See, she's okay. She's just drunk," I said to him and his associate.

The guards had picked up on that, but mostly the clothes coming off part. The crowd crept closer and two guys, with money to burn, pushed from the crowd, greenbacks in hand. One knocked into the guard restraining me and because his attention was mostly elsewhere, I found myself momentarily free. I spun from him and melted into the crowd like the *Howard the Duck* franchise. I dodged people pressing in to get a better view and made my way out the other side.

I fast walked it into the Galaxium, keeping my head down in case of eyes in the ceiling and tagged along with a group of Asian tourists heading into the main lobby. Unfortunately, they stopped at the newly installed Kubrick exhibit to grab a few photos of the giant fetus now starring as the main attraction, and I was on my own again.

Two of Davino's goons jogged toward the entrance where my shiny red and stolen Ferrari was still the center of attention. I kept my back to them, and in doing so, saw what I was looking for. I spotted Mary exiting from one of the shops down the Galaxium's own miniature Rodeo Drive. She had a new, shorter haircut, but otherwise, still my Mary. She kept her eyes trained toward the ground. Sonny was at her side, one hand guiding her with a grip on her upper arm, Big Mike following behind, his hands full carrying shopping bags.

They walked to a nearby bank of elevators and disappeared inside.

I knew where I had to go next.

I got off on the thirty-second floor, one floor below the top floor and the Presidential Suite. I knew Big Mike would be waiting there, out in the hallway like before. I had one shot at this, and I had to do it right. Unfortunately, I had no idea what that was. I ran up the flight of stairs and cracked the door on the penthouse floor. No muscle near the elevator so I edged out into the hall. Big Mike sat, as expected, outside the suite.

I glanced at the fire alarm on the wall across from me but quickly discarded that idea. Davino would take her with him.

And then I got it. "Presidential Suite, please," I said into the house phone positioned next to the fire alarm.

"One moment, sir. I'll put you through."

Sonny picked up on the third ring. "Davino."

Several years ago, I helped a producer on a Dreamworks project. At his bachelor party, the strippers were giving out freebies. I was one of the few who didn't partake, can't remember why, but it maybe had something to do with my laryngitis. By the end of the evening, I could only communicate in intermittent screeches, mostly defending myself against the groom, who seemed to have taken offense that I had not joined in. Ten months later, a similar sounding voice came from a neurotic jellyfish complaining about the lack of a spine in a new Pixar movie called *Sponges*. I can put two and two together.

I copped the same high-pitched, tremulous voice. "Mr. Davino, there's a situation occurring in front of the Galaxium. Two people were hit by a car, and there's a problem with the crowd."

"Why the hell are you calling me? Send Jimmy. That's his job."

"We can't find him."

"Then tell Joey."

"Can't find either of them. You know how they are." Probably the two I'd seen running for the entrance earlier. "It's getting nasty." I covered the phone. "Sir, put that vase back right now."

"Son of a bitch. I'll be right down," Davino barked back.

Hanging up, I retreated back into the stairwell. I kept the door cracked and watched until Sonny and Big Mike disappeared into the elevator.

As soon as the doors closed, I ran down the hall. I had maybe three minutes before they'd reach the hotel entrance, and another five for them to return when they realized it had been a ruse. Regardless, I still couldn't bring myself to knock.

In the car, Oscar had told me Mary was telling me those hurtful things so I'd leave. He told me that she knew if I stuck around, Sonny would find a way to make me disappear. He wanted Mary all to himself.

What if that's what I wanted to hear? That Mary still cared. What if that was only what I hoped to be true? What if I'd inherited from my father more than just a tendency to eat too many sweets? What if? What if?

My hand hovered.

Then I remembered something Donald Trump told me at a charity event about hope. He said, "Hope is a hotel. You furnish each room from the bottom up with life's experiences. It's up to you which floor you eventually live on."

I wanted that top floor so I knocked.

There wasn't much time. I knocked again and the door finally opened.

Mary stared back at me. Beautiful, sweet, and very upset Mary. "What the hell are you doing here?" she said.

Crap! So much for the top floor.

"God, you smell like a sewer," she said and turned with a flourish.

I followed her in. "I shouldn't have left," I said, getting right to the heart of it. "I know you were telling me those things to protect me, but it should have been the other way around. I should be protecting you."

She turned on me. "You have no idea what you're getting yourself into." She shook her head and turned away again.

"Let's go. I've got a…" I was about to say car. "…cab outside waiting to take us away from all this."

"Don't be a fool. This is where I'm supposed to be. I have to be."

"I know what's going on." I pulled her to me, but she turned her head away. "Oscar told me everything. It's going to be okay."

"Oscar told you," she said, ripping my hand away. "Ha. Now that's a good one. Your dead friend is still telling you what to do? Did he tell you that you needed a shower?"

"Uh, yeah..." When she put it that way, it didn't sound so good. "And no."

She grabbed a pack of cigarettes from a side table. "When are you going to stop this ridiculous idea of yours," and she extracted one, "that you're supposed to save the world?" She lit it and exhaled a plume of smoke. "Or me. And don't be stupid thinking that somehow you and I will be together and live happily ever after. I'm not your responsibility. I don't want you here. So go!" She waved at the door.

Her words stung worse than I could have imagined. I'd been so sure, or maybe at least hoped really hard, that it would have gone differently.

I would have written it differently.

The door should have opened to Mary, her mouth quivering at the sight of me. Tears would well in her eyes, and she should have fallen into my arms.

"Baby, I'm so sorry," I would have said.

"It's okay, Buddy. It's okay. It's my fault," she would have answered.

"No, it's not. It's mine. I should never have said those things. I've got issues. My ex-wife dumped me for my best friend, and they're living in Barbados right now and–" Okay, maybe I wouldn't have gone that far.

Too wordy. I snapped back into the room.

"You deserve better than this," I said.

She swung her arms around the suite. "No, I think I'm doing fine."

"We can go to L.A. Start fresh. You and me."

Tears welled. Maybe I'd changed her mind. *Here comes the hugging.* Instead, she walked past me and picked up the phone.

"Do I need to call security?"

"Mary?"

Her hands shook as she started to dial.

"Okay. Okay. Put the phone down. I'll go."

I headed for the door where I turned for one last look, but her back was to me. Just as well. It would be easier to leave, to forget, if I didn't see her face.

I promised myself this would be the last time I would feel anything.

Behind me, I heard the door open and I turned.

Actually, I was wrong.

My face definitely felt Big Mike's fist.

Chapter Thirty-Four

I came to in a small, dimly lit room, sitting in a folding chair in front of a wooden table, another chair opposite me. The walls were battleship gray with dried water streaks angling toward the floor. I tried scooting the chair back, but one leg was stuck in a drain. A bucket and mop rested ominously in a corner of the room.

Handcuffs locked my hands to the chair, my ankles secured to the legs of the chair by nylon rope. "Oscar? Hey, Oscar? Now would be a good time," I said.

No answer, not that I expected one.

"I need your help." I dropped my chin to my chest. This was how it would end. Bits and pieces of me collected in a bucket, the rest swept down a drain. "Will you please answer?"

"Hey, Chief."

I jerked my head up.

"All you had to do was ask," he said.

"Son of a—" I cut myself off. "I thought I told you not to do that." Oscar sat across the table from me.

"I can go." He started to stand.

"No. No. Forget I said that. I need you to get me out of this." I rattled the handcuffs in case he hadn't noticed.

Oscar did stand this time and moved behind me, one hand under his chin. "Now that might be a problem. I've never picked one."

"Can't you like shoot a lightning bolt or something?"

"I'm not the one who does lightning."

"But you're my guardian angel."

He shook his head. "No Chief, remember. Not anymore."

"Come on, get me out of this," I yelled, but with little effect.

"Nope. Sorry. Can't."

"Okay, fine. You're all about Mary. I get it." I decided to try a different tactic. My voice rose. "Well, let me tell you about Mary. She's not this little Miss Innocent we thought she was. She's all in with this Sonny Davino. I went to her suite and she shot me down big time. Not anything like you said. Totally…shot…me…down."

Oscar shook his head again. "Buddy. Buddy. Buddy. And I thought you were such a scholar of human nature."

"What the hell are you talking about?"

"She's still trying to protect you. If she shows any interest, you're toast with Davino."

"I'm toast if you don't get me out of these." I wrenched at the handcuffs.

"Sorry, Buddy," he said and headed for the door.

"Okay. Okay. Wait. Let's say that's true, then she's still in trouble. Get me out of these, and I can help her. I'll get her away from him."

"Come on. You've given up on her. I can tell."

"No, I haven't. I believe you. Really. I do."

To tell the truth, I didn't know what I believed at the moment. I might be talking to thin air for all I knew. But, I didn't get a chance to find out. The door opened and Big Mike entered, followed closely by Sonny Davino.

"Good to see you again, Buddy."

"Yeah? See me?" I was on my own. Oscar had gone. "Then how about getting me out of these handcuffs."

"That's no way to start a conversation." Sonny pulled out the other chair and sat.

"How about why am I here?" I said.

He leaned forward as if to tell me a secret. "Yeah, why *are* you here?"

"Why don't you ask Big Mike?"

"No, not here in this room here. Why'd you come back to my hotel?"

"I got some bad advice."

Sonny nodded. "Will you get a load of this guy?" His smile faded. "You know, there are people out there who still think they can cheat the system. A couple of guys tried Bluetooth and Wi-Fi to hit one of my Blackjack tables. We played it up like we were real proud of them; they were stars for winning so much. We brought them downstairs promising food, booze, the red carpet treatment, you know. Well, let's say the carpet ended up red for a different reason."

The Joe Pesci impersonation was getting old.

"Look, I get it. You're trying to scare me."

He pushed out his chair, the legs groaning against the cement floor. "This is one big game to you, huh?" He stood, moved next to me, placing one hand on the edge of the table, the other pushing against the back of my chair.

Maybe I'd underestimated the brutality of this guy. So what that he wore two-tone wingtip shoes and a bad perm, he could still be a psychopath.

"This is the thing," he said. "I'm worried about Mary."

"Yeah, that makes two of us."

"She hasn't been the same since she came back."

"You try spending the summer in Lompoc without air conditioning," I said.

Sonny stepped back and looked at Mike. "He's popping jokes like he's some kind of comedian."

Big Mike shook his head.

"What I'm saying is I thought she..." I couldn't say what I wanted to say — I thought she loved me. That would set him off so I lied my ass off. "...I realize she wants you."

"Yeah, I know that, you fuck." He leaned in closer. "I bought her this hot red dress. We're going to dinner tonight, the two of us. A little candlelight. A little Sinatra playing in the background. Who knows what'll happen?" He started pacing in front of me. "See, that's the way I want it from now on. Her and me doing what we do. But I'm worried because I don't trust you."

"Trust me? Of course, you can trust me. Back in Hollywood, I'm known for my—"

He held his head. "Ah shut up, will ya? You're giving me a headache."

I decided to shut it for once and waited for his lead.

"I think you're one of those guys who keeps coming back and coming back," he said. "I can't trust you to be smart and stay away."

"No, I get it," I said. Big Mike seemed to have inched a little closer for some reason. "I'm done. Writings on the wall. I'll go. I'll leave town."

Sonny nodded at Big Mike who stepped behind me. I felt my right hand being released from the handcuff. He brought it around, pushed it on the table, and held my wrist.

"What are you doing? I told you I'd go."

Sonny nodded again and Big Mike wrapped his hand around my middle finger. "Pain is a great motivator, but somehow we still forget. Fortunately, you have ten good fingers to help you remember." He banged the table with his fist. "No one ever steals from Sonny Davino."

"Hold on. Hold on now," I said. It was about to get very real.

Sonny grimaced and partially turned his head. "This might hurt a little."

As Big Mike applied pressure on my finger, there was a muffled ring of a cell phone. Sonny extracted his phone and looked at the caller ID.

The pain coursed up my arm, my finger about to reach its snapping point. "Noooooo."

"Wait. Wait," Sonny said, holding up his hand. "I can't have him screaming. I gotta take this."

The cell rang again and Big Mike released my finger.

"OK? A little quiet, please?" Sonny answered. "Yeah. Yeah. Okay. Bring her down." He paused. "In the Break Room. Yeah." He signed off and repocketed it. "Okay, here's your chance. Mary is coming down. She wanted to make sure you understood once and for all."

"She said that?"

"You sound surprised?" he said with a raised eyebrow.

Yeah and a little hurt. No matter how much I wanted to convince myself otherwise, this was real. She didn't want me around. "No. No. I'm glad. Maybe you can dispense with the finger-breaking thing."

"Mike, do me a favor. Get rid of that bucket. It don't look so good."

Big Mike nodded and proceeded to gather up the bucket and mop.

"And how about the handcuffs? She'll never believe me if I'm handcuffed," I said.

"Believe what?"

"Let's make this a two-way street. I'll tell her I'm done with her, too. That way, you're free and clear on both ends. Isn't that what you want?"

Sonny gave it a moment to process. "Yeah. Okay. We'll see how it goes. Mike, unlock him." Big Mike put down the bucket and released my other hand.

I rubbed my wrist. I was out, but I wasn't all the way out, of the room, that is. And then, of course, there was Mary.

As Big Mike picked up the bucket and mop to take outside, the door opened and someone I did not expect entered. It seemed to be the same for Sonny.

"What are you doing here?" he said.

Standing in the doorway was my visitor from the other night. He no longer sported his burgundy smoking jacket. Tonight, he wore an all-white tuxedo, complete with tails. *False advertising, I'd say.*

He entered, pushing Big Mike back into the room and shut the door behind him.

"I thought we had an agreement," Sonny said.

Instead of answering him, the Devil addressed me. "You should have gone when you had the chance, kid."

"I'm not a very good listener. Ask any woman."

He focused back on Sonny. "You know you're screwing everything up."

"This has nothing to do with you," Sonny said.

"The deal was you take over the Galaxium. The rest, I still have a say."

"Not anymore. I'm changing the deal," Sonny said. "Mike, see him out."

That didn't make sense. How did Sonny think he could tell the Devil what to do? But Big Mike didn't move a muscle.

"Mike, did you hear me?"

Big Mike nodded. "Yeah, I heard you."

The Devil stepped forward and clapped him on the back. "Mike and I've worked together for a long time. He still knows who's boss." He whispered in Mike's ear who then nodded and exited the room.

For the first time, Sonny showed fear. He laughed and kicked lightly at the chair with his foot. "I know, too. It's that I got business with this guy," he said, nodding toward me.

"This business has nothing to do with our business," the Devil said. "It takes your eye off the target. It causes problems, and we don't need no problems."

"Yeah. Yeah. I know, but…"

"But what?"

"It's about my girl," Sonny said almost with a whine. "He's getting in the way."

"Forget her, Sonny," he said. "She's with me now."

As if on cue, the door swung open. Big Mike walked in and right behind him followed Mary. She wore the sexy red number Sonny had mentioned which definitely accentuated all the right curves. As an added accessory, Oscar's cross hung around her neck.

The Devil broke out in a big smile and hugged her with one arm around her waist. "Isn't she beautiful?"

Mary gave him a kiss on the cheek, ignoring me entirely.

"You're with him?" I said.

She cast me a withering look. "He's helped me before. Why wouldn't I go back?"

There was so much I hadn't known about Mary. So much. This was an entirely different persona I hadn't yet met. I was such an idiot to think…

"And, believe it or not, he's going to help you now," she said.

"I don't want his help."

"What do you mean? He's saving you."

"There's always a price to pay," I said, "and I'm not willing to pay it."

Her cheeks rose a few shades of red. "You are so maddening, Buddy Price. I think you really are crazy."

On the contrary, it was proof I wasn't crazy. Sonny and Mary, each talking to the Devil like he was standing right here in the room. I saw him, she saw him. I wasn't crazy. I was pretty happy about that at least.

"I'm willing to help you, Buddy," the Devil said, "but only if you give me something in return."

"I don't make deals with the likes of you."

"Damn it, Buddy!" Mary said. "Will you just listen to him?"

"No. No. It's okay," the Devil said, holding Mary back who appeared ready to physically assault me. He addressed me again. "Sure you make deals, kid. You've done it before, and you'll do it again especially if it saves your ass."

"I'd rather be dead," I said. Not really sure I meant it, but it sounded good.

Mary pushed the Devil's arm away and got in my face. "You're impossible. I thought I knew you."

"I thought I knew you, too. I thought you were this good, kind and caring person who I…" The words wouldn't come, I didn't want to admit it, but I forced them out anyway. "…I fell in love with."

"Buddy?" Her mouth fell open.

"And I hoped you might feel the same, but I was wrong."

"You love me?" she said, her voice softer.

And as I have a tendency to do, I didn't know when to shut up. "And now you've gone and sold your soul to the Devil."

"What's wrong with this guy?" the Devil said, a quizzical look crossing his face.

"Ignore him, Jack," Mary said. "He tends to exaggerate."

"I'm not exaggerating this time. I mean every word. Wait. What?" I said. "What did you say?"

"I said you exaggerate," Mary repeated.

"No, who's Jack?"

"I'm Jack," the Devil said. "What the hell are you on, kid?" He looked at Mary. "He on something?"

"Jack?" I said. Satan, Lucifer, Mephistopheles. I've heard all those before, but not Jack.

"It's his name, dummy." Her cheeks had turned full beet. "I have half a mind to turn right around and leave you here. Damn it, you're so frustrating."

"You're Jack? Just Jack," I said.

"Yeah. Jack Davino. I run this joint."

"Come on, Dad," Sonny said. "You said that was my job now."

And for once, something made sense.

Chapter Thirty-Five

I opened my eyes.

Knock. Knock. Knock.

There it was again. I rolled over and pulled Mary into my arms. "Wake up. Food's here."

"Good, I'm starving," she said, blinking away sleep and yawned.

"Stay here. I'll get it." I got up and loped over to the door of the Presidential Suite.

I opened it to a small woman dressed in room service garb, pushing a rollaway cart covered in ornate, silver plate covers. "Your dinner, Mr. Price."

"You can put it over there."

She placed it in the corner of the room and quickly departed. Mary appeared at the doorway, dressed in one of those white Galaxium bathrobes.

I lifted a plate cover and the smell of basil wafted up. "You're going to have to tell Jack again how much I appreciate what he's doing for us."

"He gets it, Buddy. He gets it." She pulled up a chair to the table. "Let's eat."

I'd spent the first hour after the Break Room incident apologizing profusely to Jack Davino, offering different ways to repay his kindness and getting him to forget that I thought he had been the Devil. But he made it easy. The favor he wanted in return for helping me was to get his cousin's daughter into pictures. As a starting point, she needed an agent. It was the least I could do. I now had a new client, Candy Foxx. Of course, unless she wanted to work with Jake "The Snake", we'd have to work on that name.

After that was all squared away, Mary and I returned to the Presidential Suite and spent a few more hours getting reacquainted.

All was right with the world. We were together.

Jack told us we could stay as long as we wanted; he offered his plane to go anywhere, but best of all, he promised that his son wouldn't bother Mary or I ever again. To clarify things, and because I didn't want to carry around the guilt, I made sure he didn't mean Sonny would be whacked. Mary gave me a good shot in the arm for that one.

The dinner consisted of poached salmon on a bed of egg noodles and a side of braised asparagus. It was when we were working on our cheesecakes that I noticed Oscar standing behind the bar.

"How about a little Crème DeMenthe to pour on top?" I said, trying to keep it together.

"That's perfect."

I made my way behind the bar and searched for a bottle. "What are you doing here?" I said in a low voice.

He didn't acknowledge me.

"If you came for your cross, it's in the other room."

Still no response.

"Hey," I said a little louder.

Mary looked over. "What?"

I dropped back below the bar. "Umm, how about instead…," I popped back up, "…some Godiva Chocolate Liqueur?"

"Sounds absolutely sinful," she said.

I grabbed that bottle and headed back, doing my best to ignore Oscar. He had no problem returning the favor, remaining grim and silent where he stood.

"Where do you want to go?" Mary said.

"You tell me." I tilted the bottle toward her. We'd been talking about getting away on a little vacation. I didn't want to deal with all the hysterics I'd face back in L.A.

I poured thin strips along the top of the cheesecake. "How about the

Caribbean? Sit out on the beach. Catch a few rays. Have a few drinks with those umbrellas in them." I concentrated on the cheesecake so I wouldn't glance back toward the bar.

"Definitely." As she took a bite, she giggled. "Let's do this right."

She hopped in my lap, scooped up a little piece and guided it toward my mouth. "Open up."

I had to look toward the bar. I'd had my fair share of adventures, but letting someone watch wasn't one of them.

"What's the matter?"

"Nothing." I opened my mouth.

Oscar had gone.

She fed me a few more bites, taking one herself while I chewed. She tapped her finger on the tip of my nose. "What if we share the rest in there?"

She extended a hand and then pulled me into the bedroom.

"What's this?" I said, stopping next to a chair.

"It must have come today," she said, crawling into bed.

"Who from?"

"I don't know." She opened her arms toward me. "Come here. I'm still hungry."

Instead, I picked it up to check. No return address.

"Lots of women were sending you things." She let her arms fall slowly down.

"Groupies already? Jealous?" I said with a smile as I tore through the brown parcel paper. "Whatever it is, it's heavy." I turned the box to get a better angle on it. "Let's see how creative my fans can be." I ripped open the lid.

"Buddy?" Mary said.

I stared down at the open carton.

"Buddy? Are you all right?"

Maybe not. Sitting atop a pile of Styrofoam was the Jeremiah Box.

"What is it?" she said.

I touched its lid, felt along the raised numbers, traced along the curly-cue spirals of the familiar floral pattern. "It's the Box," I said.

"What?"

"The Jeremiah Box." I carried the shipping carton over to the bed and set it down in front of her.

"But why?"

"I don't know."

It was clear who had sent it which had me worried.

"I'd almost forgotten about it," she said.

"Me, too."

Not exactly forgotten, but I had moved it to very low on my list of priorities. Sure, it had gotten me where I was today, but I'd come to my own conclusion about it. Hitchcock liked to call it the MacGuffin. It was that mysterious object that set the whole chain of events in motion. It was always nothing, simply a load of nonsense, but it got the story rolling. The Jeremiah Box was my MacGuffin. I'd come to terms with the idea, but now, it had reappeared. Not very MacGuffin-like, if you ask me.

Then Mary made a terrible mistake. She lifted it out of the carton.

Two things happened simultaneously. First, I saw Oscar. He blinked back into existence, standing next to Mary at the bed and reached out for her. The second thing, registering in my peripheral vision, was a bright red number five coming on inside the carton, displaying from a timer nestled in amongst all the little packing peanuts. As if in slow motion, the lines making up the digital five faded and new lines formed to show a four. My eyes traced wires which snaked from the timer and wound their way to a coil linked up with a white block of something or other.

Lifting the Box out had triggered a timer.

My hands already clutched both sides of the parcel. I may have shouted something at Mary, but to my ears, it was incomprehensible like a tape recorder played slowly, words low and deep. Her eyes blazed wide, her mouth open, moving, but I heard nothing.

The number flashed to three. With the carton in hand, I clipped the edge of the dresser and Styrofoam flew. The force spun me around, and I snatched the bomb as it floated up. I took another step and found myself right outside the bathroom. I had no reason to go there, but that's where I was headed.

The timer flicked to a red pulsing two.

Each step seemed to take an eternity.

Fucking Marlin and his timers.

I was inside the bathroom when two became one. And then I knew. The safe, strong granite walls of the shower appeared in front of me. Those walls offered the only chance.

One second to oblivion.

I had known what to do after all.

One second to save Mary.

I dove for the shower and felt heat against my face like sunshine on a warm spring day.

Chapter Thirty-Six

The warmth enveloped me as I floated toward a familiar bright light guided by little specks that whirled about me as if they were in some kind of wild dance. One by one, they left as I drifted closer.

I felt no fear, no pain, no need to struggle. There was only a deep feeling of love and peace.

Suddenly, I found myself in a white-walled room with music playing softly from speakers I couldn't see.

Was that Marvin Gaye?

I blinked and God stood before me.

He reached out, placed a hand on my shoulder and smiled that beautiful God smile I'd seen the first time we met. "Good to see you, Buddy. Glad to see you made it in one piece."

The love faded ever so slightly. "Not exactly funny under the circumstances," I said.

"Don't worry. Mary's okay. You saved her." He patted me on the back and turned. "Come with me."

It was good to know Mary was safe. Although, for some reason, it hadn't been something I was overly concerned with. It seemed almost as if I already knew.

"We've got a lot to talk about." God strode along, wearing his long robe and on his feet, like before, were those stylish sandals.

I followed him into a long hallway with the same stark, white walls. I could judge no discernible end in either direction. "I'm really dead this time, aren't I?"

"I'm afraid to say, but bombs do tend to have that effect."

"I can't believe it," I said, shaking my head. "It wasn't supposed to happen this way. I had to save everyone."

"Don't worry. The world's going to be fine," He said casually.

Too casually.

"Wait," I said. "You can't be serious. No big deal is all you have to say."

He stopped and turned to me, his expression now bordering on pained. "Listen, Buddy, it's about time I leveled with you."

"I don't like the sound of that." I had used the phrase too many times myself, and it never ended well for the person on the receiving end.

"It was always more about you, not the world. It was about how you needed to make a change." He nodded, apparently satisfied with coming clean. "And you did. You stopped thinking only about Buddy Price. You made a choice and saved someone else at your expense. I'd say you passed with flying colors." He started walking again.

His confession fused me to the floor. "This was all a test?"

"No. No. No," He said over this shoulder. "I learned my lesson on that one."

I willed my feet to work again and caught up.

"Don't get Abraham started about his kid," God said. "He'll never let me forget." He shook his head. "That's the downside of eternity." He waved his hand and a door appeared in one of the walls of the hallway. "No. This was more of a bet."

"A bet?" I tried hard to keep my voice from rising.

"Yeah, I do that sometimes." He opened the door and motioned me to go in.

"About what?" I waited for his answer.

"About you."

"What's so special about me?" I said.

"I didn't say that, although you did make it easy, thinking you're the center of the universe."

"Yeah, I get that sometimes, but…"

He draped his arm over my shoulder and led me through the door into another room, this one with the same intense whiteness as the room before but bigger, more ballroom-sized.

"What was the bet?"

"One day, Lucifer and I were talking–"

"Wait. You two talk?"

"Sure."

"Aren't you like mortal enemies?"

"Yes, but we still talk." God directed me deeper into the room. "He's the one that made the big mistake. He had it good here, but he's what you would call 'slumming it' now. But I'm not one to rub it in his face. He's got self-esteem issues. Can I tell my story now?"

"Sorry," I said.

We reached the other end of the room and with another God wave, a door appeared in the wall. God opened it and we exited into a lush green field; above, the sky, cobalt blue, and all around, bright yellow flowers reaching out to the horizon.

"Any allergies?" God said.

"No." I noticed a little tremble in the corner of His mouth. "Joking, right?"

"Of course. I do that, too. Have you ever seen a platypus?" He waited for a laugh that didn't come. "I get it. Still a little disoriented." He started across the field and I followed. "Anyway, Lucifer and I were talking, and we got on the subject of human nature. It's not the first time we had the good versus evil debate. He said, let's find someone and see which force, good or evil, will win in the end." God slowed, searching the ground. "You were picked because of who you were."

"Well, all right," I said. "At least that's something. You must have picked me for a reason."

"Yeah, there's that. See, I didn't pick you." He bent down and picked up a long, thick stick. "Lucifer did," He said, straightening up.

"Oh." *Crap!*

"It gets better," He said.

"I can only hope."

God started off again, using the stick as a walking cane, and I followed.

"The Devil started bragging about this guy, you…" He dipped his head toward me. "…who was self-absorbed and selfish, and had made an adequate life for himself."

Adequate? I thought I'd done better than that.

"I mean he wouldn't shut up about you. Buddy Price did this. Buddy Price did that. It was too much. So I had enough and threw out a bet." He may have blushed a little. "I said you could change, that you could become a decent, caring person, be motivated to do good things for others. Learn compassion, empathy. Those positive qualities we all should strive for. Well, Lucifer must have thought he had it in the bag and agreed."

"What was the bet for?"

"Bragging rights mostly."

I questioned my reality once again. Maybe I was still back in the suite. Maybe the bomb had not gone off and I was lying on the floor of the bathroom, having slipped and knocked myself out. Maybe that reality was better than what I was about to hear.

"Bragging rights?" I said.

"I know. I know. I told you something else."

"Damned right you did. It was about saving the world."

He gave a sheepish smile. "I threw that in for motivation."

"I mean, what the hell?"

"Watch the language." His voice rose. "Remember where you are."

But it didn't slow my rant. "I went to all that trouble with the Box and it didn't mean a thing?"

"It's the journey, not the destination," God said with his deep, melodic voice.

"And what's that supposed to mean?"

"It means you'll get over it." He took a deep, calming breath. "Besides, you proved him wrong."

"And look where it got me."

"If this isn't satisfactory, we can always do streets of gold, although I'd advise going with something else. Gold wears thin quickly."

I didn't feel like asking him much more. We walked in silence until we reached a bench underneath a large oak tree.

"You and I both know you never wanted to save the world," He said. "It was more of an inconvenience, right?"

"I did at the beginning…with that stupid box. You really had me going. And now I feel like such an idiot for believing."

"Faith comes in all flavors."

"That sounds like a tagline for a *Ben and Jerry's* commercial."

God sat and motioned for me to join him.

"No one knows where their life is headed," He said. "There's no magical book that tells your story. It unfolds as your life unfolds. Every day there are forks in the road, and you make your choice about which direction you want to go. A few years ago, you stopped making important choices. The box, saving the world – those were motivators for you. They were things you could make choices about, things to get you out of your rut. If you were going to have a shot at proving the Devil wrong, you had to start somewhere. And, well, I think you did that. In that hotel room, you made the biggest choice of them all. To give your life for someone else. And for that, I'm so proud of you."

With those five words, 'I'm so proud of you', all the anger and frustration I'd stored to unleash on God about stringing me along simply drained from my body.

My eyes welled up, and I choked back a sob. "Yeah, thanks…I guess." Out of habit, I stuck out my hand. "That means a lot."

"A handshake?" God laughed. "Now, that's refreshing. You don't know how tired I get of all the worshiping. Sometimes, people just need to relax."

I couldn't help but laugh now as well. "Amen to that."

"And don't get me started on predestination," God said. "You won't be going back for a long time if you do."

I laughed again, but then it struck me what God had said. "What was that you said?"

"I said don't get me started on– "

"No, the other thing. About me going back."

"Oh, I didn't mention that yet?" God stood. "Lucifer said if he lost, you would… it would require you… well…"

"Require what?" I said, standing now.

"… to go back."

"What? And you make it sound like a bad thing?" I asked.

He smiled, the brilliance of which didn't stop my next question.

"Hold on," I said. "It sounds like if he lost, which would mean I won, that you both were expecting me to be dead either way. Because otherwise, why would I have to go back?"

"No, that wasn't very fair, was it?"

"What if I'd lost?"

"Let's not sweat the details," God said, quickly waving his hand.

"No, let's," I said.

"The good news is you're going back."

Sure, I could have hammered Him a few more times for bad judgment, but who was I to scold God? I let it go.

"So, shall we?" He pointed in the direction of the mammoth white building we'd exited from earlier.

As we walked back and the cool air brushed against my face, I relaxed again. Sure, I knew I could get used to this, but I quickly pushed the thought out. I wanted to see Mary again.

"I assume you're going to take care of the mess back in the bathroom," I said, focusing on more practical matters.

"Come on," God said. "I created the Universe. A few billion billion billion or so mixed up atoms scattered in a hotel suite in Las Vegas? I think I can handle that."

"Yeah, I guess that's what miracles are for."

"If you want to stay, I can pull some strings. I'm God after all. But keep in mind, if you do go back, you don't necessarily have a free pass back here. That's going to be up to you."

The temptation was definitely there, but I had already started thinking of Mary which made my choice infinitely easier. "No, I'm going back."

"This time you earned it."

We neared the building and stopped at the sole visible door.

"What happens next?" I said.

"Not much. One second you'll be here, the next you'll be there."

"That easy?"

"Any last words?"

"What?" I said, suddenly scared that maybe I'd misinterpreted something earlier.

"No, don't worry." He chuckled. "That phrase has an entirely different meaning here."

I tried to think. What should I say? I used to pray, but let's be realistic, I was never a hundred percent sure He was listening. Now, with him standing right here in front of me, I knew I couldn't waste the opportunity.

Maybe I should ask Him to teach me that smile. I could really use that.

Then it came to me.

"I want to know the secret of the universe."

"Secret of the universe, huh?" God pondered this for a moment and said. "How about – 'we're all in this together.'"

I eyed him. "Is that really the secret?"

"Can't hurt."

"Okay, I get it. It's a secret. Well, then how about tossing me something like a catchy tag line?"

"How about – 'can't we all just get along?'"

"That's already been done."

"Look, Buddy, you'll figure something out. Besides, there's more to any 'secret of the universe' than just words. Look deep inside yourself. Find the meaning there."

"Okay, God. I'll give that a chance." I hadn't really expected to get a straight answer, but I figured it was worth a shot. But, maybe he was right. I'd see what I could do this time around.

"You have another question?" He said, gazing into my eyes.

This guy was good. "I have to ask. Why does the Devil want me to go back?"

While God gnawed on the inside of his cheek, I felt the old stomach acid churning to a slow boil. Maybe I shouldn't have asked after all. It's sometimes the things you know that are the hardest to swallow. Maybe the secret of the universe is – 'ignorance is bliss'.

"Well, Buddy, he thinks he can tempt you to change back."

I let out a long breath and laughed. *Was that all?* "Hey, God. I work in show business." I spread my arms out. "It's all about temptation."

"Well, I never thought about it like that." He winked and opened the door for me. "I guess it shouldn't be a problem then."

As I started through, I looked back at the peaceful field. It wasn't going to be as easy as I thought. "You know, I *could* see myself staying." The heat rose in my cheeks. "I've never felt like this in my life. Full of hope. Full of possibilities."

"Yes, we do have that here. But, you know, this time, you're taking some back with you."

I took one last look around. "This is real, right? It would be a shame if I was making all this up."

He smiled. "Life is what you make it."

I smiled back. "Now that I can use."

God stepped back and raised his hand. "Ready?"

And, this time, I think I was.

A WORD FROM BUDDY

Thanks for reading my story. If you're interested in learning more about me and my new agency… that's right, I'm no longer with Zimmerman… I've started my own agency, the Buddy Price Talent Agency… To learn more, you have the following options:

Website: www.buddyprice-agent.com
Email: buddy@buddyprice-agent.com
Twitter: @AgentBuddyPrice

To get on my client list, you can sign up on the website. I'm always looking for new talent. And by doing so, I can keep you up to date on the sequel to *My Life as a Sperm*.

You can also learn more about the author, William Darrah Whitaker, or contact him at:

Website: www.wdarrahwhitaker.com
Email: darrah@wdarrahwhitaker.com
Facebook:.   www.facebook.com/wdarrahwhitaker
Twitter: @WDarrahWhitaker.

Tell your friends. Spread the word. Like I always say–

> "Talent can take you places, but it's
> who you know that keeps you there."

> \- Buddy Price

www.ingramcontent.com/pod-product-compliance
Lightning Source LLC
Chambersburg PA
CBHW050024180626
46810CB00002B/561